THE
ACCIDENTAL
SOLDIER

A NOVEL OF WORLD WAR II
BEN BAILEY

Barringer Publishing, Naples, Florida
www.barringerpublishing.com
Cover, graphics, layout design by Lisa Camp
Editing by James Barrow

ISBN: 978-0-9831963-0-1

Library of Congress Cataloging-in-Publication Data
The Accidental Soldier / Ben Bailey

Printed in U.S.A.

DEDICATION

This book is dedicated to my wife Sherry
with love, affection and appreciation.

ACKNOWLEDGMENTS

The inspiration for writing this book partially came from two gentlemen who have since passed away. Professor Bill Hoffman of Hampden Sydney College served during World War II and later became a fine teacher and celebrated novelist. Dr. Gordon Prange of the University of Maryland also served in the war, was a stimulating teacher, and a highly praised writer of World War II history.

Several persons have read all or parts of the novel including James Robison, Jean Harrington, Joyce Wells, Lloyd Gill and Sherry Bailey. I benefitted greatly from their insights into my work and the suggestions they made.

The protagonist of my story suffered through several medical crises which Dr. Clarence Hart, Barbara Voelker and Alice Schwalbe helped me to clarify and understand.

T. C. Johnson helped me to navigate my way through the computer age answering questions and solving problems that I encountered along the road to publication. His keen knowledge of the mysteries of the strange machine saved me many hours of frustration and greatly enhanced the finished publication. Jim Bollinger also helped with his computer knowledge.

My father, Dr. and Professor Lt. Colonel John W. Bailey, served in the war, although he was in his late forties, he brought this period to life for his pre-teen son by sending foot lockers full of memorabilia home from Europe. The post cards, stamps, magazines, photos, uniforms and military equipment that he sent stimulated the imagination of his son. His stories of the war sparked an interest in me which I have shared with those who read this novel.

Three people have been of enormous help to me. Jean Harrington taught me the difference between the process of writing non-fiction and fiction. Joyce Wells improved the quality of the work with her editing skills. Sherry, my wife, helped me through all the stages of the growth of the manuscript. Her encouragement to write, her plot suggestions and writing skills helped me move along the path to completion. She suggested the title of the book.

This book is a work of fiction, and of course, the ideas expressed in the book are mine and mine alone.

Ben Bailey
December 2010

CHAPTER I
ATLANTIC CROSSING, 1939

"When you get to Germany, you might consider not dancing with Jews," Karl said.

Stunned, I resisted the urge to throw my drink in his handsome, arrogant face and looked about, relieved that the Greenbaums were nowhere in sight and then commented, "I pick my own dance partners." Although annoyed, I explained, "I was seated at a table with several women and danced with all of them."

"I understand your situation, Mitchell," Karl said with a

frown, "but I suggest you follow my advice."

The ship lurched a bit and my beer sloshed onto the bar. Karl quickly caught my arm to steady me. I pulled away from his grasp, emptied my glass in one gulp and banged it on the bar top.

"What's the old expression?" asked Rolf, the other German standing at the bar. "When in Rome, do as the Romans do."

I didn't need this. "So you spend a few months clerking in the German Embassy in D.C., and now you tell the rest of the world how to act?" I replied.

"Since you are an American going to Germany, I thought you might benefit from our advice," Rolf said.

"Thanks, but no thanks."

I sat in silence until the red-faced Irish piano player returned from his break. He carefully sat his Guinness pint on the piano top. "Come on folks," he urged, "sing with me: "Roll out the barrel. We'll have a barrel of fun." The man's voice was a clear tenor.

Most of the bar patrons joined in the fun. When we finished singing, we cheered and applauded. The Irishman chatted with the people seated near the piano.

He turned to me. "What's your name, mate?"

"Mitch."

"Mitch," he said with a big smile on his face. "What's the difference between an Irish wedding and an Irish funeral?"

I had no idea.

He looked to the crowd around the piano. No one knew. "It's simple, mates. One less drunk."

The crowd roared with laughter. The jokester seemed proud of the party reputation of the Irish.

His up-beat personality failed to lift the gloom that hovered over me. I couldn't let Karl and Rolf's ugliness towards the Jews pass. I addressed Rolf, "So what's your problem? You don't like Jewish girls?"

"We like German girls," Rolf said, "not Jews."

In a disgusted voice, I said, "Look, suppose a blue-eyed, blond German baby falls into a swimming pool, and no one sees it but a Jewish girl? She jumps into the water in her street clothes and saves the life of the child. Would you dislike her then?"

"This is a very difficult question that you propose," said Rolf.

"Yes. To you it is difficult, but what would you do?"

Rolf thought for a moment and then replied, "Well, first of all, it is not likely to happen. It is not realistic."

"Maybe not. But what if it did happen?" For some reason, I wasn't able to let go and kept probing him with my needle.

"One must consider the deep philosophical question involved, before one can answer."

"What would you do, Karl?" I asked again, resisting the urge to smile. I had him and he knew it.

Rolf slowly sipped his beer. "We Germans watch our children very carefully. This would never happen."

"Oh really?" He had sidestepped the question, the creep. "It's smoky in here, I need some fresh air."

I pushed away from the bar, yanked the door open and went out on the deck. Outside in the cool night air, I walked and walked, trying to calm down. The brine of sea air filled my lungs and beneath my feet the power of the ship's engines throbbed. I was furious and frustrated.

"Arrogant bastards," I said out loud. "Nazi jerks give me their specious arguments and expect me to be convinced."

Eventually, I found my favorite deck chair along the port rail and flung myself on it, staring at the stars and studying the sky and the golden crescent of a half moon. My thoughts drifted from the Aryan-Jewish question to the American treatment of the colored in the States, particularly in the segregated South where I grew up. I had no Negroes in my school and very seldom saw any in my neighborhood. We did have a colored maid at one time named Grace, and we loved her dearly. What her attitude toward her segregated life had been, I didn't have a clue and before tonight had never given the racial question much thought. Like most Americans, I simply took it for granted. It was the way things were. Coming from my sheltered life in North Carolina, I knew very little about the racial question in the United States and none at all about what it was like in Germany. But if Karl and Rolf were any indication, I was about to come face to face with hate-mongering such as I had never known.

■ ■ ■

It was my third day on board the U.S.S. Simmons. As one of about three hundred passengers in tourist class, I had a small cabin to myself. Thanks to my parent's generosity, and at a considerable sacrifice, I was en route to Bad Aibling to learn German in preparation for earning a Ph.D. in European history. Dressed in my usual attire of a light blue shirt, tan pants, a navy blue blazer and rep tie, I entered the dining room and took my place at the appointed table. The formally dressed waiter greeted me and brought me iced tea.

"Good evening, Mr. Morgan," he said with a big smile, placing a napkin on my lap and handing me a menu.

I was the first of our group to arrive and sat back to enjoy the ocean view. The weather was nearly perfect with blue skies and an occasional white puff of cloud. The Atlantic was choppy but not so rough as to cause problems for the passengers. The wind seemed brisk on deck, but that was not unusual. My serenity was interrupted when the Greenbaums arrived accompanied by the ship's head steward.

"Mrs. Greenbaum, I am so sorry this happened," the steward explained. "We'll patrol your hallway as much as possible."

"We didn't pay to travel on your ship and be insulted," Mr. Greenbaum said.

"What happened?" I asked Jacob, their ten-year-old son, who slipped into the seat next to me.

"Somebody put a sign on our cabin door."

Leah, their fourteen-year-old daughter, sat on the other side of me, and said, "It read: No Jews Allowed!"

"My gosh, what a stupid thing to do," I mumbled.

The steward made his departure. "I'll report this to the captain," he promised.

The last member of our table group, Sarah Goodman, a middle-aged librarian from Atlanta, joined us. She was horrified at learning what had happened.

Mr. Greenbaum stared at his empty plate, his red face full of anger, perspiration rolling down his cheeks. "We have no peace and quiet," he said, "even on a ship in the middle of the ocean."

Mrs. Greenbaum was pale, her hands clasped tightly together on the tabletop. "Why can't they leave us alone?" She asked no one in particular. I tried to get her to talk about their visit with relatives in New York. She went through the motions, answering my questions in one or two word responses. Finally, she looked at me with a frightened expression. "When we get back to Hamburg, I'm afraid we'll experience more of this anti-Semitic behavior. Most of the time I am too frightened to leave the house."

"I'm a lawyer," Mr. Greenbaum said. "These days no one wants a Jew to represent them in court, not even other Jews."

"Could you have stayed in New York?" I asked.

"Yes, we could have," he answered in an agitated voice, "but our home, our friends and my business are in Hamburg. We have lived in northern Germany all of our lives. Why should we have to leave?"

A cloud of concern hung over our table. I had no answer for him.

∎ ∎ ∎

It was my last full day at sea, and I was anxious to get to Europe. I strolled through the ship and passed the front desk. To the side was a large map of the Atlantic Ocean bristling with colorful pins the staff had used to chart our course. I stopped to examine it. Tomorrow morning we would dock in Holland and the first leg of my adventure would be complete.

After dinner that night, I went up to the ballroom to join my dining group. The large room had a stage, bar, and intimate round tables where the passengers could enjoy after-dinner drinks. The band was playing "In the Mood." The music made me nostalgic for my college days. Many people danced, but our group sat back and enjoyed the party atmosphere.

Timing my invitation with some slow music, I asked Sarah, the librarian, to dance. We held each other at arm's length and chatted while we danced.

"Have you read Margaret Mitchell's *Gone with the Wind?*" she asked.

"No. Do you recommend it?"

"Highly. It's a vivid portrayal of the South during the Civil War, with several characters in the book you won't soon forget."

"I'll give it a try, when I get back to America."

"What novelist do you like to read?" Sarah asked.

"My favorite is Ernest Hemingway. I've read *A Farewell to Arms* several times. I really related to his story of the young American going to Italy to serve in the ambulance corps during the Great War, his tender love affair with Katherine, the English nurse, and his terrible disillusionment with the war at the end of the novel."

"Well, we are even. I haven't read it, but with an endorsement like that, I certainly will."

The music stopped and we returned to our table, where I thanked her for the dance. I sat next to Mr. Greenbaum, and we talked of world politics for awhile. He mentioned the law profession, and I shared that I had considered going to law school at one time. At this point, I asked if he would mind if I invited Mrs. Greenbaum to dance. He thought it was a splendid idea. She was agreeable, and we moved to the floor.

After we circled the floor a few times, she looked up at me and smiled. "I think my daughter has a great big crush on you."

Embarrassed, I must have turned red. "I had no idea."

"I can tell by the way she acts around you."

"Well," I stammered, "I'm honored. With our age difference, perhaps she sees me as the sophisticated college guy, while she still has high school to experience."

"No doubt that's part of it."

I continued, "She's a beautiful girl who would make a wonderful mate."

"I agree with you," Mrs. Greenbaum said. "You two would be an excellent match in five or ten years."

"I'm flattered you would even consider me for your daughter." As we danced, I smelled a sweet fragrance of perfume in the air. I wondered if it was French.

"It would be nice if you danced with her," she added with a mischievous laugh.

I nodded. I held her chair for her, before I sat back in my place. There was more conversation. Then a woman carrying a small child came over to our table and stood by Leah. She introduced herself and spoke in German.

"I want to thank you for saving my child." Tears began to run down her cheeks. "We took our eyes off of him for a moment, and he must have fallen." She paused. "You saved him from a nasty accident."

Leah smiled. "It all happened so quickly. I saw him reach

down for a toy near the edge of the steps. He fell down one stair and was about to go to the bottom. I'm glad I was there to block his fall."

The lady reached down and grasped Leah's hand, smiled and walked away.

Silent for a moment, I was stunned by the coincidence of how I'd challenged Rolf and Karl with a similar incident. It was true, life was full of unexplained connections. I watched the woman return to her table, sit down and hug her child.

"Wow! What you did is very special. You endangered your own well-being to keep the child out of harm's way. You're my hero!" I leaned over and kissed her on the cheek. "Why don't we celebrate with a dance?"

Leah was a graceful dancer, and I complemented her. She was light as a feather. After our dance, we returned to the table. I held the chair for her and then excused myself from the group to escape the smoke-filled room. As I reached the door, I saw Kurt and Rolf seated at a table drinking their beer. They held out their glasses as if to toast me, but I just nodded and kept going, glad they had seen me dancing with Leah again. "To hell with them." Their scare tactics didn't work on me.

■ ■ ■

During our last dinner together our group talked non-stop. All of us seemed truly sorry that our time together was over. I exchanged addresses and promised to visit the Greenbaums, if I ever got to Hamburg and to exchange Christmas cards with Sarah. I wished each one good luck and a safe journey.

Not ready to turn in, I made my way to my favorite deck

chair to reflect on all the excitement that lay ahead in the next few months.

I broke out of my dream world, when Karl and Rolf staggered by in a drunken stupor. They were laughing and saying in English over and over, "How do you do? How do you do?" I doubted that they recognized me sitting on the starlit deck as they continued weaving along the rail. I was glad to see them lurch out of sight.

■ ■ ■

It was the summer of 1939, and I had embarked on the greatest adventure of my life. I had graduated from college and had spent the last two semesters studying history in graduate school at the University of North Carolina. Now I was off to become fluent in German and French, two of the requirements for a Ph.D. I dreamed of becoming a history professor, sharing with my students the love and enthusiasm I had for learning. I could have stayed at the university and taken classes in the two foreign languages, but I believed it would be a better use of my time to go to Germany and France to read their newspapers and talk with the people in their native languages. That was my master plan, but after talking with Karl and Rolf, I hoped the plan wouldn't blow up in my face.

CHAPTER 2
MY NEW HOME IN GERMANY

The train ride from the west coast of Holland to the southern highlands of Germany served as a fine introduction to Europe. The June sunlight shown on the busy cities of France, the rural villages and landscapes of the wine country. The majestic Alps and the peaceful valleys of France, Switzerland and Germany were breathtaking. Smiling children waved at the train, and sweaty farmers toiled in the warm sun of the day. It was the summer of 1939 and I was filled with excitement and determination to learn from the people of Germany and France.

At the small town of Bad Aibling, some forty kilometers southeast of Munich, I emerged from the train, glad to be at the end of my long journey from America. The town was near the mountain foothills on the banks of a clear, narrow stream that wound through the verdant countryside amid rocks, green grass and abundant wild flowers. I was impressed with the cleanliness of the small town. The streets were swept and flowers adorned many of the buildings.

People were busily going from one task to the other and paid little attention to me, even though I must have stood out as a stranger with a large suitcase at my side. I searched for a tourist information building but found none. I wondered whom I might ask for directions. I finally decided to start with the storage of my suitcase. At the baggage room in the train station, I greeted the clerk in my broken German and asked him to hold my bag, until I could pick it up later. He told me the section of the town where my host family lived was only eight blocks north of the rail station.

I moved along my appointed route. The blocks were long, and I gradually left the small business district and entered a residential area on the outskirts of town. In my correspondence with the family with whom I would stay, I learned that the population of Bad Aibling was around ten thousand people. Large and prosperous looking farms surrounded the town. A mining company and a large construction firm provided most of the employment opportunities for the residents. On the edge of town was a substantial Luftwaffe training base for fighter pilots, called the *Flughorst Kaseme.*

Eventually, I matched the address I had with a very solid but plain looking house in the middle of the block. An ample yard with large maple trees protected the building from the midday sun. It looked like a well-kept house and no doubt was comfortable inside. I knocked on the door in some anticipation, and shortly a woman of about fifty answered the door.

"You must be Herr Morgan," she said and smiled while extending a warm greeting.

I returned her smile. "And you must be Herren Muller."

"Ah, it is so good to meet you, but just call me Inge," she exclaimed in an excited voice. "Please come in, and meet my husband."

Fritz was a large man with graying hair and rough hands. His work clothes indicated he had recently returned from his construction job. We chatted for a while, and I learned their daughter, Greta, had moved to Munich, where she worked in a law firm office. Their son, Hans, had recently enlisted in the Luftwaffe and was stationed in town, where he attended the cadet pilot training school. Fritz and I drove in his truck to the train station, and I retrieved my bag. Upon our return, he showed me to my room, where Inge had left some cookies and milk.

The bedroom consisted of a dresser and a double bed. I hung my clothes in the closet and put my toiletry items in the attached bathroom. There was also a reading chair, a lamp and a small shelf full of history books and novels. I sat in the chair and surveyed the room. I would spend a lot of time here reading these books as well as the few books in English that I had brought along. My main task for the next six months was to learn to read German and speak it fluently. My four years of studying German in college would serve me well. But there was no substitute for being in the country and speaking with as many people as possible in their native tongue.

I was restless and decided to take a walk around the neighborhood, so that I might get my bearings. I located a café, bakery and park in my wanderings before I returned home. The fresh air and the long walk had exhausted me. After dinner I went to my room and read for awhile. To fight off sleep, I wrote an entry into my daily diary. I could hardly wait for the new day.

■ ■ ■

The next morning, I enjoyed a breakfast of hard rolls, jam, cheese and fruit juice. I got further acquainted with the Mullers. They kindly offered me the use of their son's bicycle. I planned to settle into a routine of jogging and biking during the day with time out to talk with anyone who was gracious enough to listen to my awkward German. I would take lunch in a local eatery or buy fruit and bread from a grocery store and bakery. I wanted to sharpen my language skills and also get in the best physical condition that I could.

Wearing blue shorts and a gray T-shirt that had the words "Virginia Beach" on the front and relatively new gym shoes, I emerged into the sun-drenched morning. I jogged through the neighborhood. The yards were neat and filled with flowers. Some had piles of fireplace wood stacked on the porch, each piece exactly the same length. I waved to a few people in their yards or walking down the street, but none seemed ready to engage me in conversation. I got a friendly smile, but they hurried on their way. I must have had tourist written all over me. It was not long before I was out of town and into the rural setting of farmlands and forest. I ran for about a mile, and then settled on a fast-walking pace. The trees were beautiful with some in bloom. I located a stream of fresh water gurgling over small rocks. My shirt was wet with perspiration. I sat for a while and enjoyed the quietness of my surroundings. I wiped the moisture from my forehead and neck and stretched my muscles. After twenty-five push-ups, I began my return to town.

About two miles later, I came upon a wonderful park on the outskirts of Bad Aibling. As I walked through the park, I noticed a group of men playing backgammon. I leaned against a tree and asked one older gentleman if it was alright if I watched. He was in deep concentration, but he managed an affirmative nod. They really enjoyed each other and seemed quite happy. I played backgammon in college and was once fraternity champ. It was a good game, and I enjoyed their method of winning. The game was intriguing to watch.

I eventually moved to another part of the park where bocce ball was the sport of choice. I had never played this game, but soon the men included me. They explained the rules of how to throw the ball and the skill of scoring points. They were one person short of the four persons needed to play, so I was chosen. There was much kidding and laughing, and I enjoyed the experience immensely. However, I was definitely a hindrance to my team which lost badly. I either rolled the ball short, or I failed to knock one of my opponent's balls out of the way. It was all in good fun, and at least I talked with the men and learned of the verbal abuse they handed out during the game.

For lunch I decided on the Café Arnold in town. It was a three-story building with large windows on the first floor where indoor seating was available. The second story of the white building had additional seating with smaller windows and flower boxes below each window. The flowers were bright red and yellow. There was also an open deck with tables and chairs, where I chose to sit. A waitress approached my table.

"What would you recommend to eat?" I asked.

She smiled and said, "Everything is good. You cannot go wrong." She stood with pencil ready to write down my order. My clumsy effort to strike up a conversation was pathetic. I settled for a ham and cheese sandwich and a glass of beer. She nodded and quickly walked to the next table. She was a rather young girl, maybe in her late teens, who seemed serious. I tried to flirt with her when she returned with my food, but her interests were elsewhere. Clearly, I was more charming to the older crowd than to those in my age bracket. The beer was refreshing, and I demolished the sandwich in short order. I had worked up an appetite with my morning exercise.

After lunch I borrowed the Muller's bicycle and rode into the countryside and to the foothills of the Alps. I enjoyed the breeze in my face and rode for miles. I found a stream and relaxed beside it in the sunlight. After some push-ups and sit-ups, I rode until I was exhausted.

That night I read part of a book that I found in my room entitled *The Germany I Love.* It was a history of Germany during the post war period and seemed rather negative of the Weimar Republic period. It was good background for the Germany I lived in now.

■ ■ ■

The next day, I again walked and rode the bike, trying to strike up a conversation with anyone who might be available. Returning to the park, I watched the backgammon players. One of the older men sitting on a park bench alone had played the day before, but now he watched the players as I did. I wheeled the bike up to him and said, "Why aren't you playing today?"

He smiled and offered me a place beside him on the bench. "My friend had an accident," he said, "and so I do not play today."

"I'm sorry your friend can't play. By the way, my name is Mitchell Morgan from North Carolina in the U.S.A."

"Glad to meet you," he said. "I know of your state as I am an American Civil War buff and have read a great deal about that time in U.S. History. My name is Helmuth Von Schwartz. Besides being a teacher, I was fortunate enough to have served in the Great War."

A twinkle came to his eyes, as he expressed his pride in serving in that capacity.

"I imagine that you have many interesting stories of your service in the war."

"Yes, I do," said Helmuth, "but I am more interested to learn if you know how to play backgammon."

"As a matter of fact, I do."

With that, he pulled out the playing board, found a table to play on and we began throwing the dice. We played many games and at the end, it was clear that he was a polished player. We shook hands and I stood to leave.

"I would be happy to escort you through the park and into town, if you like," he offered.

"That would be great," I said.

"Your German is not bad," he said, "for an American. What brings you to Bad Aibling?"

"I've recently graduated from college and plan to continue my study of history in graduate school. Since I'll be tested in German and French languages, I will live in those two countries, use their languages and learn more of their cultures."

He nodded and smiled. "I am a retired professor of literature from the University of Munich. In my college days, I learned English and French, but I wasn't able to travel to the United States."

"Eric Remarque's *All Quiet On The Western Front* is one of my favorite novels," I said. "It's a devastating account of Germany's fate in the Great War. That scene where the German soldier was in the battlefield and spots a beautiful flower was memorable."

"Yes, it was a powerful anti-war statement. I only hope our statesmen of today haven't forgotten the lessons of Remarque's wonderful book."

The two of us talked for a while, and I enjoyed our conversation. We passed a large group of young boys and girls.

Helmuth explained that they were members of the Hitler Youth, who gathered often to exercise and socialize. The teenagers were a fine looking group of young people and seemed to be in splendid physical condition. They sang songs and appeared to be very disciplined.

We came to a smaller gathering of young people in another part of the park. Helmuth explained that they were a church group. Several women seemed to be in charge. One of them led the teenagers in singing "Ave Maria." A blond girl in a long skirt, who looked to be about fifteen, stood and sang a solo. She had fair skin and blue eyes. The boys and girls were intent on her singing. Helmuth and I stopped under a tree and listened. It was a moving moment for me. The lady in charge followed the song with a prayer. I looked at Helmuth, and thought I detected a moistening around his eyes. We walked on in silence.

Helmuth and I saw several families enjoying picnics and a rough and tumble soccer game before we arrived in the town center, where we shook hands and agreed to meet the following day for more backgammon.

■ ■ ■

Time flew. I loved what I was doing, and I was convinced the Germans were the best people in the world. They enjoyed the outdoors, good food and drink. They worked hard and enjoyed life. I felt right at home. My German was improving daily, and my vocabulary had doubled in the short time I had been in Bad Aiblling.

My host family was wonderful. Inge was like a mother to me.

She had a warm smile and made me feel right at home. I learned she appreciated the praise that I heaped on her for her gourmet productions of wiener schnitzel, lamb shank, sauerbraten and homemade spaetzle and dumplings. More important, there was plenty of it. Fritz was no match for the happy, outgoing Inge. He was more introverted and many times just plain tired, when he returned home from a hard day's work. He enjoyed telling stories of the hard times of the Depression.

"Have you maintained a job all during the 1930s?" I asked.

"Oh yes, I had steady work all during this time, while other Germans suffered."

"Has Hitler been good to the workers?" I asked.

"Initially, I had negative feelings for the Fuhrer. He broke the strength of the Labor Unions in the early 1930's, but now we have full employment, impressive new highways and a building program that provides work for many of the former unemployed laborers. I do have some misgivings about Hitler's foreign policies, but on the whole, he has made good progress in Germany since the Great War.

■ ■ ■

I began to write in my journal and I thought of my parents and how appreciative I was for their generous financial support and for the faith they had in me to make intelligent, mature decisions during this exciting time in my life. I would never forget their love and encouragement they showed me. Much of this I expressed in my nightly journal entries. I would cherish this adventure now, but particularly in the future, as I looked back on these precious days.

Helmuth, my backgammon friend, had become an integral part of my new life in Germany. In many ways, he was a mentor to me. The teacher in him spilled out, as he explained much about the German people and their culture. He told me of the Great War in which he participated and his feelings about the German defeat. One day between backgammon games in the park, he paused and explained.

"There were two wars, you know. In the first one we beat the Russians in 1917. It was a significant and deserving victory. In the second war, which ended in 1918, we lost to the French, British, and your people. Some Germans felt it was a stab in the back by the people on the home front, who just quit fighting. The German Army was not defeated; we just stopped fighting. I am glad though," he said softly. "We would have lost in the long run, and many thousands more people from both sides would have died. It was a bad time, and the unfair peace settlement at Versailles only made it worst. To force the Germans to take the full guilt of starting the war was ludicrous," he said with obvious emotion. "We were no more to blame than the French, Russians, British, Austrians and the Serbians. I get very angry when I think about this."

I admitted to him that in my college history classes, my professor had shared similar feelings with the class. But it was not a popular notion that many Americans embraced.

A few days later, after more backgammon, he made an announcement. "I have a rare treat for you, my young friend." With that, he pulled out of his knapsack a Coca Cola. "I got this just for you to remind you of your own homeland."

I was moved and wished I had better words to express my appreciation. I took the bottle and expressed how much it meant to me, not so much for the drink, although I enjoyed it, but for how special it was that he had taken the time to give me such a gift. I shook his hand and held on for a time, while I looked him in the eyes and said, "Thank you."

He had some beer for himself, and again he talked of the war. Later, he invited me to his house for dinner to meet his family, to prove to them that I really existed, and that I was not a figment of his imagination.

CHAPTER 3
THE DINNER PARTY

In preparation for the dinner party, I focused on what to wear to the dinner at Helmuth's. It wasn't very difficult, as I had a limited wardrobe. I selected a pair of dark gray pants and a blue shirt to go with my navy blue sport coat and red with blue stripped tie. My cordovan loafers with navy blue socks filled out the picture.

As I did not want to be early, I walked slowly towards my destination. I waved at a couple of kids playing soccer and retrieved an errant kick. I approached a neighbor, Frau Grismacher, who was about eight months pregnant and inquired about her health. She looked healthy and was enjoying the late afternoon sunshine. I slowly drifted from my neighborhood and approached Helmuth's home. I checked the address he had given me. It was situated on a corner, a stone home of generous proportions. The yard was well-groomed and trimmed to perfection. A wood pile of perfectly cut logs was stacked neatly. I climbed the stairs to the front porch and knocked on the door. Helmuth greeted me with a warm handshake and invited me into a spacious living room.

"Welcome to my home, Mitchell," he said.

A trim lady of roughly his same age smiled and said, "I am Helmuth's wife, Ingrid. It is so nice to meet you. He has told me what a fine backgammon player you are."

I smiled. "I learned it all from Helmuth."

Ingrid excused herself to continue the meal preparations. Helmuth showed me into the living room, and I gazed admiringly at his fine collection of books, which lined one of the walls. As I did this, their dog, Colonel, charged from the adjacent room and jumped on my leg seeking affection. I scratched behind his ears, and he curled up at my feet for more attention. Helmuth excused himself to get a book from the second floor. I moved into the back corner of the room scratching the dog and tussling with him good naturedly.

Soon, there was a knock at the door. This time an attractive young lady about my age dashed from the kitchen and greeted what appeared to be a young German Army officer. His silhouette in the doorway seemed overwhelmingly large from my vantage point in the corner. The couple hugged and came into the room.

The dog rushed to greet the new arrival, as I approached them.

The girl saw me first and offered her hand in welcome. "My name is Gretchen, and you must be Mitchell, the American backgammon player. I am Helmuth's granddaughter."

Then she turned to her friend. "This is Lieutenant Hans Gustav, a former schoolmate of mine."

He extended his hand, and we greeted each other enthusiastically. "Welcome to Germany, Mitchell. It is good to meet an American. I would like to hear all about your country."

"Thank you," I said. "I am a student here trying to learn your language and customs. It is a pleasure to meet you."

At this time, I turned to see the final member of the dinner party arrive. It was Herr Winkle who was Helmuth's age and trying to master the art of walking on crutches. He had been Helmuth's backgammon partner before his bad fall and broken leg. He was introduced to all, and we adjourned to the dining room for drinks and conversation. Ingrid had a maid, and so she was free to join in the camaraderie around the large dining table. Candles and flowers graced the center of the table. Sparkling silverware and expensive china hinted at the extravagant meal of which we would partake.

I sat on one side of the table with Herr Winkle. Gretchen and her soldier friend, Hans, sat on the other side, with Ingrid at one end and Helmuth at the other. I questioned Herr Winkle about his injury. He kidded me as to whether I was adequately taking his place in the backgammon games.

Helmuth chimed in with, "He's holding his own. I can't wait for Winkle to return so that I might win a few more games."

The friends laughed because it was widely recognized that Winkle and Helmuth were two of the best players in Bad Aibling.

Our attention turned next to Hans and his military activity. "I have trained in various camps throughout Germany, and we are ready for anything. At one point, Herr Hitler came to review our corps and to give us a little talk. He was a striking figure, so militaristic. But the most impressive thing about him was his ability to speak to the troops. His message was clear, and he delivered it in a way that aroused the men almost to a fever pitch. He was exciting and charismatic. We are all proud to be a part of what is happening in Germany."

Herr Winkle added that Hitler had achieved a great deal for Germany since he took control in 1933. "I remember how hard it was to feed our families just a few years ago. Times were very difficult. Today we have full employment and many are prosperous. The nation has a focus. Now we can hold our heads high since the awful days after the war. We don't hide under the shadow of Versailles anymore."

"Yes," added Helmuth. "We have reclaimed the Rhineland and completed the *Anchlus* with Austria. We gained the Sudatenland from Czechoslavakia. Today, most German people live under the banner of the Fatherland. We have accomplished this without the loss of blood. The rest of Europe is in decline, while Germany is on the rise. We are powerful and mighty, while France and England have fallen behind. And it has been the statesmanship of the Fuhrer that has accomplished this. We are very thankful and proud of our accomplishments."

"What is your reaction to all this, Mitchell?" Hans asked.

"Are Americans impressed with our accomplishments?"

I was afraid it would come around to me, but I could truthfully say, "I am, indeed, impressed with Germany's progress. The economy seems strong, and the people are full of patriotism and purpose." I paused because I hesitated to add my next point. "Has it been too costly in terms of the freedoms that people have lost? I hear there is turmoil in the streets with the Brown Shirts and the Communist thugs battling it out. What about the large camps for political dissidents? I wonder if this is healthy." I remembered the treatment of the Jewish family on the ship, but realized it would be impolite to voice my objection, so I fell silent.

After a brief time, all three men tried to speak at once. Helmuth took the floor. "In my mind, the Communists are not an option. I would rather die than live under Communist rule. If Hitler is the only other viable choice, then I support him."

"Yes," the other two chimed in. Hans was more vehement. "I am willing to give up my life to stop the Russians. Life would not be worth living under Stalin. He is a butcher. He would kill us all."

I had to agree with them concerning life under the Reds. It would be intolerable. "Yes," I said. "I would fight the Communists, also."

My gaze drifted around the table, as I listened to the others elaborate on the anti-Communist theme. Hans was a nice looking young man in his early twenties. He was the prototype German with blond, thin hair and blue eyes. He was about 5' 10" with a solid build. His training must have been vigorous, and it seemed he would make a fine soldier. He was, however, rather rough in his manners and rigid in his thinking.

I glanced at Gretchen. She was also blond haired and blue eyed. She had beautiful facial features and her smile was infectious. I enjoyed looking at her as she ate and exchanged her views with the others.

After a filling dinner of pork shank and apple strudel for dessert, I could honestly proclaim this the best meal that I had eaten in Germany. We adjourned to the back yard, and the flowers that were so plentiful. Gretchen took me from one garden plot to the next, naming the flowers and beaming with pleasure, as I said the gardens were the best I had ever seen. Some of the men smoked pipes, and the women chatted. It was a thoroughly delightful evening. We seemed to enjoy each other's company, although it was clear to me that Gretchen and Hans were very close friends. I was there because of my friendship with Helmuth.

We returned to the house for coffee in the living room. I didn't like coffee, but I took a cup and sipped it occasionally. My hosts had many questions about America, and I tried to answer them as best I could. I explained how difficult the Depression had been for many of my countrymen. In reality, we agreed that Hitler and Roosevelt had come up with many similar programs in their respective nations. The public works programs and government financial help for farmers and industrialists were solutions that both leaders had implemented. Roosevelt had supported labor union development, while Hitler had crushed the unions but saw to it that German workers had a decent life without unions. While the backgrounds of the two leaders were quite different, their methods in reaching the people and the similarities in their government programs were striking.

When the conversation lagged, Gretchen moved to the piano and played some of their old favorites. She was musically talented and encouraged us to sing along with her. She ended with "Lili Marlene," a song that Hans enjoyed. Helmuth had a far-away look in his eyes, perhaps thinking back to the days of the Great War when this music was so popular. It seemed a fitting end to a perfect evening, and I expressed my joy in sharing this fine time with such delightful people. We all shook hands, and I made my way to the road and my hike home.

■ ■ ■

The summer days passed quickly. I biked in the country and stopped by my favorite stream of bubbling water with my makeshift lunches. After placing a bottle of beer in the cold stream, I sat back to enjoy nature.

It was a good life, and I wished the time in Germany would never end. Thoughts of eventually moving on to France and learning about their culture and language entered my mind. I wondered if there would be war. In a very selfish way, I hoped that my plans would not be interrupted by a European conflict.

Helmuth had enlarged our backgammon group to four with himself, Herr Winkle, myself and another friend named Peter. We had our own tournaments and wonderful afternoons filled with laughter and companionship. I was lucky to have fallen in with these fine men.

One morning, I decided to explore the section of town where

the Flughorst Kaseme, or the Luftwaffe training base for fighter pilots, was located. I rode my bike down the main road, Adolph Hitler Street. The facility was totally fenced in. Soldiers guarded all the entrances to the base. I rode through the neighborhood nearby and noticed that the streets were all named after famous pilots from the Great War. Richthofen Strasse was named after the famous German ace, the Red Baron. I got as close to the air base as possible. One large building, served as the barracks. It had two large entrances which opened onto a terrace, where the cadets could sit and read or enjoy the view of the snow-capped Alps to the south.

As I could get no closer to the sprawling airport, I returned to town and my favorite tavern, the Café Arnold. Luck was with me. My favorite bar maid was on duty. She took my order of a beer and smiled at my feeble effort to strike up a conversation with her. She was cordial but not enthusiastic. Then her face lit up into a bright smile. Several Luftwaffe cadets boisterously entered the café, and she rushed to take their drink orders. I finished my beer in silence.

I realized that I was homesick. The Germans were nice, but it wasn't home. I was restless, and my thoughts turned to the question of war or peace. The military presence was all around me. There were banners hanging from the buildings. The large swastika and the red, white, and black colors were as bright as the colorful flowers of mid-Summer, which graced the gardens and window sills of many buildings. I wondered if I would see Gretchen and Hans again. They seemed to symbolize the beauty and militarism of Germany.

CHAPTER 4
WAGNER'S OPERA

I returned home one day from a bike ride, and to my surprise there was mail. There was a nice long letter from my parents telling me of the improving economy in America. It was good to hear from them. There was also an invitation from Helmuth and Ingrid inviting me to join them with others to attend the opera in Munich. Wagner's *"Gotterdammerung"* was playing, and it would be a wonderful opportunity to see and hear this great German masterpiece. I accepted at once and began to read everything available to learn about Wagner and his works.

As the time approached, I was truly excited. My blue sport coat, khakis, and loafers would have to do, as they were the extent of my formal wardrobe. I joined the Von Schwartz's at their home. It was nice to see that Gretchen was going, but so was Hans Gustav, attired in his impressive military uniform. I had purchased a box of chocolates for Ingrid, to show my appreciation for being included in the party. We had extra time, so Ingrid opened the candy, and we sat for a while and enjoyed the sweets. Hans had brought a cold bottle of champagne, and we sipped some of that, also.

Helmuth stood and held his glass high. "I would like to propose a toast to Lieutenant Hans Gustav," he said. Helmuth continued, "To great success for you and your unit in the army maneuvers along the Polish border."

We clicked our glasses and, with a beaming face, Hans told his audience, "My men are well-trained and ready for the operation. We have a fine unit, one of the best in our division," he said with obvious pride.

Gretchen said, "Hans' unit will be leaving in about a week for eastern Germany for extensive training and maneuvers."

The conversation drifted from the injustice of the Versailles Treaty and the Polish Corridor, which Hans and Helmuth felt was justly the property of Germany, and the many ethnic Aryans who lived there. Next, the conversation changed to Goethe's impressive literary works and finally, to Richard Wagner and his great romantic operas. My attempt to interject my views on Wagner's works was met with polite nods, but now it was time for us to motor to the train station for our trip to Munich.

The Bad Aibling Station was crowded with Luftwaffe cadets, businessmen and country-folk traveling to the big city. We climbed the steps and into the coach car. It was about three quarters full. The two couples with me took seats, and I sat three benches behind them. I was alone on my bench and contemplated the opera I would see. This would be one of the highlights of my adventure in Europe, and I was excited. With Wagner, Munich, the opera and good friends, it would be special time.

The short trip to Munich was right on time. We walked from the station toward a nearby restaurant. The streets were busy with people doing their chores. Nazi banners hung from many of the buildings and indeed, the dominant colors on the landscape were red, white and black. It was difficult to talk, as we hurried along the walkway to the restaurant.

Soon we came upon a crowd that had gathered on a street corner. As we approached, I heard shouting and turmoil. The people were all focused on a street tram. A woman in a white dress was being removed from the vehicle by a number of large, gruff men dressed in brown uniforms. The young woman had white powder smeared all over her face. Her head was shaved and her blond braids pinned to a sign hung around her neck. In bold letters were the words, "I have offered myself to a Jew." I watched in horror as she was pushed and shoved through nearby hotel lobbies and cabarets among cries of "whore and slut." A rather excited young man came to my side doing his part to persecute the woman. He had tried to spit on her. He was perspiring profusely and actually had a sewer smell to him. The crowd came my way and passed close to where our group was standing. I could see the horrified look on the woman's face. Her head was bleeding in places. I wanted to stop this nightmare, but in a moment she was gone.

I asked the man next to me, "What was her crime?"

He excitedly explained. "She was discovered in the arms of her Jewish fiancé."

I stood in a daze, as the mob moved past us and farther down the street. Hans took Gretchen's arm and they moved on. Helmuth and Ingrid started to follow before they realized that I was frozen in place. Ingrid took my arm, and the three of us hurried to catch up with the young couple ahead. We walked in silence to the restaurant. Fortunately, it was early enough to get a table. We studied the menu in silence until the waiter arrived to take our drink requests.

We ordered wine and sat in silence. Finally, I looked at my good friend, Helmuth, and said in a halting voice, "Is this what Germany has come to?"

Helmuth looked puzzled and confused.

Hans was quick to answer. "My friend, Mitchell, you must not be upset."

I stared at the soldier dressed in his splendid uniform. He continued, "These were just street ruffians. Probably a love triangle. Nothing to concern you."

"But no one tried to stop the thugs."

"It's a religious question," Hans said. "We know nothing of the background of the incident. They were probably 'beef stock'

Nazis, brown on the outside—red on the inside. We must not let it spoil our evening."

I looked at Gretchen for support. "It looked to be more of a racial situation," I said.

She, too, seemed upset, but she forced a weak smile. "Some low-life Germans were caught up in the power struggle that the homeland was experiencing. Hopefully this is just an isolated incident."

I returned to my menu, as the waiter approached our table. We ordered our meals and continued in an awkward manner to talk of the opera we would attend. After a second wine, I relaxed somewhat and enjoyed my meal.

I left the restaurant with my group and we made our way toward the Munich Opera House. On my way we passed the *Marienplatz*, where I saw the famous tower above the huge square and the Glockenspiel that clanged out the hour, as figures of knights and ladies danced in front of it. Men in military uniforms were everywhere. Downtown Munich seemed like an armed military encampment. Polka bands blared in the distance. Swastika flags flapped in the breeze and signs read: "One Reich!" "One Fuhrer!" and "Thousand Year Reich."

The Opera House was massive with white stone columns at the entrance and a grand marble staircase. Inside, the high ceilings and crystal chandeliers were breathtaking. With the others, I made my way to our seats in the middle section, three-fourths of the way to the rear. I settled into my aisle seat next to Helmuth. The velvet seats and large stage were impressive. I sat watching the attractive audience walking by, with women made up in the finest clothing and jewelry.

After a short time of watching people, my focus turned to reading the program. Richard Wagner was born in 1813 and his accomplishments during his seventy year life span included "Tristan," his greatest work and his monumental "Ring Cycle." "Gotterdammering," the opera that we would see and hear, centered around such characters as Siegfried and Brunnhilde. As I tried to sort out the plot, Helmuth leaned over to me.

"Mitchell," he whispered, "you know that Hitler is addicted to Wagner's music. He has seen almost all of his operas to the point where he is obsessed with them. Some reporters have written that Hitler is Wagner's heir, that he believes in Wagner's ideas on race, in German cultural superiority, and that the Aryans will dominate the world just as Wagner portrayed in his operas."

With Helmuth's introduction and information from books I read about Wagner in preparation for today's outing, I settled back to enjoy the performance and gain another perspective into German culture. The Prelude was moving and the three acts that followed were based upon Medieval legends of folklore and pagan Nordic mythology. Wagner wove some of the basic questions of life such as love, goodness, evil, heroism and faith throughout his opera. The romantic story-line moved from Siegfried to Brunnhilde, to the Rhine maidens, and from the Funeral March to the dramatic scene of the beloved Valhalla going up in flames consuming the two main characters into redemption and eternity.

The opera was emotionally draining, but I had little time to reflect on it. The audience rose as if one and stood at attention with arms raised and sang the national anthem. I stood with the rest of the audience, but did not sing.

As we left the Opera House, Gretchen pulled on my sleeve and leaned over to speak to me. "We're planning to get a bite to eat and a drink at a nearby restaurant. A friend of mind whom I knew at school will join us. She plays violin in the Opera Orchestra. I hope you will like her."

It was a surprise as no one had said anything to me about this. "I'm sure I will."

We walked several blocks to an attractive building and were seated in a large room, with many tables, a dance floor and a small orchestra. We ordered drinks, and soon a petite and attractive young lady joined us. She sat next to me and across from Hans and Gretchen. She had a pleasant smile and black hair. We shook hands, and she smiled at me. I was thrilled to think that I might have been set up with a date. Her name was Heidi. I asked her about the orchestra and her musical training. She was easy to talk with and also asked about my life. Hans listened and tried to lead the conversation in another direction.

The musicians began to return to their seats from intermission and tuned their instruments. I wondered if I should ask Heidi to dance, or if that would be too forward. When the music started, Hans sprung to his feet and to my amazement, he asked Heidi to dance. I noticed that Gretchen was ready to stand anticipating his request to dance, and seemed disappointed when Hans and her friend glided to the dance floor. I was embarrassed for her. She quickly covered up her feelings, and we continued our conversation as if nothing had happened. I concluded that Hans just wanted to put Heidi at ease by taking the first dance.

Gretchen smiled at me, and I beamed back at her. Her fluffy blond hair fell on her rather broad shoulders. The short, red-velvet dress was accented by a pearl necklace and displayed her long shapely legs. We both watched Hans in his stiff but impressive military attire and Heidi, with her magical smile and doll-like features, as they floated across the crowded floor. They were agile dancers in the flower of their youth. They laughed gaily, as they returned to our table at the end of the dance. I stood to greet them and prepared to ask Heidi for the next dance. It was not to be. The music started and off she went with Hans in a whirl back to the dance floor. The band played "Lili Marlene," while I stood awkwardly, wondering what to do next. Gretchen was at my side, and she put her hand on my shoulder as if to dance. It was difficult to know how Hans would react to my dancing with his girl, but there was little time to worry about it.

Gretchen and I danced to the slow rhythm of the music. She smiled at me, and then we danced cheek-to-cheek. Was she trying to make Hans jealous? It didn't matter. She spoke softly into my ear. "Thanks for dancing with me."

"Thank you," I said. "This makes a wonderful night even better."

With that I drew her closer. Her body felt better than one would have imagined.

I finally did dance with Heidi and also had several dances with Helmuth's wife, Ingrid, but most of the time was spent in the delightful company of Gretchen. I was confused, but enjoyed the evening immensely. By midnight, we were all at the train station with the exception of Heidi who had returned to her Munich apartment. I was tired and ready to go home. Hans and Gretchen sat together, as did Helmuth and Ingrid, leaving me to sit alone.

■ ■ ■

I dozed and wondered how Gretchen and Hans were doing. I was seated so that I could see them, but they mostly slept during the trip. Back in Bad Aibling we took a taxi to Helmuth's house.

On the front porch, I hugged Ingrid and shook Helmuth's hand vigorously, and thanked them profusely for a wonderful time. I said good night to Hans and Gretchen. My farewell to them was cut short as Hans stepped up to me and walked me down the sidewalk a short distance. I was surprised. He looked at me in a stern manner. "Why did you dance so much with Gretchen?" he asked in an unpleasant voice.

I didn't know if he was serious or not. "Why did you dance so much with Heidi?" I said in return.

He moved closer to me. "That's none of your business."

I now realized that he was serious. "Well," I replied. "My other option was to sit with Gretchen, while you and Heidi danced the night away. Besides, Gretchen is a very fine dancer."

Hans got even closer to me, his face inches from mine. "This is none of your business."

I could feel the blood rising in me. I faced him squarely. "If you feel so strongly about Gretchen, why didn't you dance with her?"

His hand came to my chest and he gently pushed me away. His face was getting red. "This is none of your business," he repeated.

My muscles flexed and I shoved him back. "If you acted like a gentleman, there would be no problem."

Now he was really mad. "I can do whatever I want," he hissed. "You stay out of it." With this he shoved me harder.

I stepped up to him and put my hand on his chest. My face was so close to his, I could smell his cigarette breath. He was breathing deeply.

My pulse pounded in my temple. "I'll interfere with your actions if you misbehave. I will make it my business." I shoved him harder.

"Stay out of my business," he shouted.

"No, I won't stay out of your business!" I replied.

As we advanced towards each other, Helmuth, who must have heard us from the porch, quickly stepped between us. "Gentlemen, gentlemen," he said in a calming voice. "Please don't insult my wife and me by acting in this manner."

He looked at Hans and then to me. I stepped back. What should I do? Thoughts of plummeting Hans raced through my head. I saw the shock on Ingrid's face. There was a trace of a smile on Gretchen's face. I put my hand on Helmuth's shoulder.

"Please forgive me, sir," I said quietly. "I meant no disrespect to you or the ladies." As I turned to leave, I murmured, "Good night."

That night, sleep came with difficulty. Many thoughts zoomed in and out of my mind as I lay restlessly in bed. Had I acted as an American roughneck and displayed very little sensitivity to my good friend, Helmuth? I hoped he would forgive me. I wondered if Hans was right. Should I have turned my back on his bad behavior? Maybe I had been too friendly toward Gretchen. Her charming smile reappeared in my mind. I had wanted to be even closer to her, but she was practically engaged to Hans. It was getting time to leave Germany and to continue my studies in France. I hated for things to end on such a sour note. On the other hand, when Hans had pushed me, I was close to taking a swing at him. What an arrogant bastard! I was in great physical shape, and I could have taken him down a peg or two. But, being a soldier, he was in good shape, also, and probably had been taught self-defense. Who knew? I would have to talk with Helmuth in the next several days to see how he felt.

Eventually, my mind switched to visions of Wagner's great opera. It is understandable that Hitler could be moved by this excellent music. I thought of Brunhilda and Siegfried and the inferno of Valhalla. The majestic mountains, beautiful landscapes of Germany and the wonderful people of the land were memorable. But there was a dark side too. The image of the shaven head of the German woman, who had dared to love a Jewish man, and the Nazi banners blowing in the wind kept coming to mind.

CHAPTER 5
MOUNTAIN HIDEAWAY

For the next few days after the opera, I returned to my routine of reading, jogging, lunchtime picnics and biking into the nearby foothills of the Alps. Although I enjoyed the mountain vistas and rushing streams, I realized my time in Germany was about to end. Having become relatively fluent in the German language and culture, it was time to move on to new adventures in France. The August nights gave a hint of the change in seasons.

The next day I returned to the park and hoped to find

Helmuth and his backgammon playing friends. They were at the gaming table. For a moment, I watched the men enjoy the companionship and the competition. As Helmuth completed his game, I approached his table. I didn't know if he would be upset with me because of my confrontation with Hans, or if he would be glad to see me.

When he spotted me, he stood, smiled as if glad to see me and extended his hand, "How nice to see you, my friend." He beamed.

We shook hands enthusiastically. I greeted his companion, and we all exchanged pleasantries. Eventually, his friend excused himself to run some errands, and Helmuth and I settled down to some serious backgammon. Today was his day. He seemed to throw doubles almost every try. He quickly had an impressive winning streak.

As casually as possible, I asked, "How is the family?"

"Ingrid is fine," he replied.

"How is Gretchen?" I asked.

"Gretchen is fine also," he said with a grin. "Hans and his unit have been ordered into northeastern Germany for maneuvers along the Polish border."

"It is odd that they would move to that area," I said.

"What do you mean?"

"Well," I hesitated. "Haven't there been problems between German and Polish citizens along the border?"

"No, no," he said confidently. "It is not unusual to set up field camps in Pomerania and Brandenburg. You are too suspicious," he added, as he boxed the backgammon board. "We had a fine day," he said. "Let's meet tomorrow afternoon."

■ ■ ■

The next day when I arrived in the park, Gretchen was there instead of her grandfather.

"Helmuth will be a half hour late today," she said.

"Do you play backgammon?" I asked.

"No," she replied, "but I would love to stroll through the park with you."

"Have you heard from Hans?" I asked, as we started our walk.

"No. He is not a good letter writer."

In awkward silence, we passed by a daisy garden.

She looked at me and smiled. "I am planning to go mountain climbing next week and wondered if you would care to go with me?"

I was caught off guard by her question. I stammered, "I, ah, would love to. Would I need special equipment?"

"No, it would be more uphill walking than anything else. We would carry backpacks and water canteens."

"It sounds like fun." I still found it hard to understand why she invited me.

"We have a family cabin in the mountains, that we sometimes use," she continued.

As I mulled this over, I realized we had returned to the place where I was to meet Helmuth, who was not there yet. We stopped walking and she looked at me, but the sun was shining in her eyes. She squinted and tried to shield her eyes with her hand.

"It will be fun," she said. "I will give you more details in a few days."

"Swell." I could think of nothing else to say but "swell."

She waved and walked away. I stared at her confused, but excited.

I tried to piece it all together, but it made no sense. Was she interested in me? I didn't think so. She already had a serious boyfriend. Was she trying to thank me for standing up for her on the opera night? I doubted it. Was she bored and trying to pass time while Hans was on maneuvers—probably.

■ ■ ■

The next morning I woke hearing a strange, excited voice. It was the radio. The Mullers must be listening to the news, I thought. I dressed and came out of my bedroom to find the glum faces of the Mullers.

"We have attacked Poland," Fritz said hesitantly.

I looked on in disbelief.

"Germany crossed the border at 4:50 this morning," he added.

"Why?" I asked. "It doesn't make sense."

"The air force flew over the frontier to surprise the Polish Air Force on the ground. We have immobilized many of their planes. The navy has shelled the port of Danzig causing significant damage."

"Where are the Polish forces?" I asked sharply.

"They seem to be non-existent," Ingrid replied.

"This means war," I said. "The British and French will join the Polish to fight against Germany."

"Maybe they can reach an understanding or a compromise," she said hesitantly. "Hitler has managed this before. He could promise no more aggression."

"He already did that with the Sudatenland, and yet, he went right on into Czechoslavakia," I argued. "The French and British have already promised to support the Poles."

"Fritz was in the Great War in 1914, and it was awful," Ingrid said with emotion. "What will the United States do?"

"I have no idea, but generally Americans have to be attacked first, before they go to war."

"Germany will not attack America," Fritz said confidently.

"Probably not," I agreed.

We sat glumly listening to the radio. German forces were advancing rapidly and with little or no opposition. It must have been noticeable that I was hoping the Poles would put up a strong defense. It wasn't happening. I excused myself and went to my room. Now that Germany was at war, I pondered my stay in Bad Aibling. I wrote a letter to the U.S. Ambassador's office to start the paper flow for my leaving the Third Reich.

Eventually, I went for a bike ride into the countryside. The weather was cool and sunny. I peddled hard and arrived at a favorite stream, where I had spent long hours reading and thinking. Later, I returned to the house and read a little of Hitler's *Mein Kampf*, played some of Fritz's recordings of Wagner's operas, and listened to the radio about the war. The Poles were fighting back, but Hitler's "blitzkrieg" moved quickly towards Warsaw. I also thought about Gretchen and our hike that she had planned. Her actions were confusing. I was attracted to her, but I could see little future for us. I was planning to leave Germany and she was all but engaged to marry Hans. I should learn her intentions on the hike.

■ ■ ■

On the following Sunday, Gretchen biked to my place. Earlier she had lent me a backpack, and she checked to see if I had packed the things she had suggested. I had a change of clothes, a warm jacket, sweater and long pants. The day was not cold. I wore my hiking boots, shorts and a sweatshirt. Also, I had packed lots of food as well as six bottles of beer. She looked great: well-tanned and healthy. She greeted the Mullers, and we were soon on our way. It took a few minutes to adjust to the awkward backpack while riding my bike, but soon we were into the country getting close to the foothills of the Alps. It was a glorious day, and it felt good to be alive. After an hour of peddling, we came to a small settlement, and a place to store our bikes. Here our hiking trail began. I was glad to be rid of the bikes. Off we trudged along the trail. We talked of the opera and her grandparents.

"Have you heard anything from Hans?" I asked.

She smiled: "He wrote a quick note to his family and me. He is fine, but he didn't say anything about military activity. We were relieved to learn that he was well and optimistic."

I walked with Gretchen in silence for a while. The trail passed through wooded areas for about a half hour. We were moving on an uphill grade and eventually came to an open space. Below us cows munched on grass in grazing fields. I eventually found a spot to unload our packs, near some wild flowers, and we sat on the ground for a while. I was sweating a little, and she was breathing hard so I opened a bottle of beer and we both drank from it.

"The trees are getting smaller," she said.

I pointed to the East. "Can you see the lake?" I asked. It looked cool and inviting.

We had walked for about three hours. The sun felt good. I took a sip of beer and handed her the bottle. I stretched out feeling the warmth of the bright sunlight. We admired the lake, trees and pastures.

"Tell me about your college days," she said.

"Well," I said, "I went to a small liberal arts college in North Carolina, which is in the southern part of America. There were about a thousand students there. The buildings were made of red brick and constructed in the Georgian style. I played football and baseball, but these are sports that you probably are not familiar with. I studied history and had some excellent professors. I made a lot of friends and had a wonderful four years." I shifted my position on the ground and took a sip of beer. "Why don't you tell me about your youth?"

"Not so quick," she said. "Did you have lots of girl friends?"

"I dated a lot, but nothing serious."

"Now, tell me about your life," I said.

"I have a vivid recollection of my years in the Hitler Youth. Most Germans joined the Jung when they were ten. I was too old for that, but I served as an assistant to our leader. We met in a large three-story building in the neighborhood. We usually went there after school to play games, get help with homework or only to talk. On Wednesday evenings, we met there for a presentation given by our group leader, which was followed by a radio program called 'Young German Hour.' Sometimes we saw and heard a play performed or a discussion by a group of young people, or maybe a lecture presented by a person of national reputation. Each week we covered topics concerning German heritage, current events or international affairs. Also, we had booklets that focused on the topic of the week."

Gretchen paused to drink some water from her canteen. She wiped the corner of her mouth with her hand. Then she handed me her canteen. "Have a drink. My germs won't kill you." She touched my arm and smiled as I returned the canteen to her.

"Your Hitler Youth sounds a lot like our Boy Scout programs for American youth," I said.

She nodded and tossed her hair out of her face. She was really warming up to her topic. "We had weekend outings and summer camp with all expenses paid by the government. In the camp, the girls learned about German history, old traditions and folk dances. We played games and participated in athletics. We learned how to swim, ride horseback and shoot guns. My favorite job was to teach the girls how to use make-up properly, because it might otherwise attract the wrong kind of men. Also, I taught nutrition and the proper care of children, although my mother had to teach me first. It wasn't all serious. As teenagers, of course, we all had our moments."

As I looked at her, I thought I saw a hint of a blush. She continued. "Hitler became our role model, because he did not drink or smoke, and he was a vegetarian. We taught that Hitler respected women, worked hard and was honest. We taught the girls how the Teutonic Knights had defeated the Romans and used the swastika as their symbol. It was an ancient Aryan sign for the eternal circle of life." She stopped and looked up at me with a glint of humor in her eyes. "Of course, I had to learn all this before I could pass it on."

As I listened to Gretchen, I soaked up the warmth of the sun and partially dried out my sweaty clothes. I was impressed with how sincere she seemed. She could not hide the pride she felt about her part in helping to form these young girls.

Gretchen continued her description of the Hitler Youth program. She pushed back some loose strands of blond hair from her face and smiled at me. She seemed to appreciate the close attention I gave her. I smiled back at her, touched by the warmth in her voice.

"At age seventeen, we spent six months in the Labor Service working for our country. The boys worked on such projects as draining marshes and preparing land for the autobahns. The girls worked with poor families teaching mothers how to raise healthy children. We taught nutrition and sanitation to the poor. It was a good time, and we made many close friends within the Hitler Youth."

Much of this sounded similar to my experiences during the 1930's Depression in the U.S.

"We have a Civilian Conservation Corps and other groups that did much of the same kind of teaching and work. There are camps in America where young men work on land conservation projects. The Germans and Americans coped with the Depression the same way." I was pleased our countries had this much in common.

We were quiet for a while. I stretched out on the ground using my backpack as a pillow. I looked at the bright blue sky and watched the occasional white clouds. I was happy and contented.

After a while, Gretchen offered me some more water. I sat up to drink, and we decided to continue our trek. I stood for a moment surveying the countryside, the green hills and pastures in the distance. Offering her a hand, I pulled her up to a standing position. We adjusted the packs on our backs and trudged along the path. The trail narrowed, and we walked in silence in single file. Looking at her in front of me, I wondered what she was thinking. I admired her strong leg muscles as she walked. The terrain was more difficult, but she seemed quick in her movements. She set a fast pace, as we moved up the hillside into higher country.

In spite of biking and jogging around town, I was getting tired, but Gretchen told me we were only three-fourths of the way to her parent's mountain cabin. We stopped for a short rest and more water. I looked at her. She was a picture of health with sparkling blue eyes. She was solidly built and moved like an athlete.

"Are you tired?" I asked, hoping she shared my fatigue.

"Not really," she said. "We will be there in another hour."

She handed me her canteen, and I took a drink.

"You are doing a beautiful job of setting the pace and covering the ground," I added.

She seemed startled at my compliment and stepped closer to

me. Placing her hand on my cheek, she turned my head to hers. She kissed me quickly on the lips, and then moved off up the trail. I stood dumb-founded, shocked and in a fog.

That was a real kiss, I thought. Was her mouth open? I tried to remember. Did our tongues touch? It happened so fast.

I stumbled forward. Why did she kiss me? I reflected. Did she think I said she was beautiful? Perhaps she misunderstood me. I hoped this was a prelude to what was to follow.

I walked up the trail in a daze. What about her boyfriend, Hans? I had no answers, no clue. I don't remember much about the rest of the hike. Eventually, she led me to a rustic cabin in a valley. There was a small lake to the west, with pine trees and evergreens all around. The cabin was made of rough wooden planks, and there was a steep slope to the roof. Inside, a large stone fireplace took up one wall. To one side, there was a table and chairs. A sofa and chairs were around the hearth. An abundance of candles were on the table and mantelpiece. Outside, I had noticed a large pile of fire wood, neatly stacked against one wall of the cabin.

Inside the cabin, we shed our backpacks and placed the contents on the rustic dinner table. She tossed me a towel and led me to the lakeside. The water was cold, but we washed our face and hands and dried off. We refilled our canteens with fresh cold water and returned to the cabin.

I had no idea what was going to happen. I was excited and nervous.

Gretchen broke the awkward silence. "Are you hungry?" she asked.

"You bet I am."

She smiled brightly. "Why don't you light a fire, and I will get some food and drink ready?"

Firewood was already on the hearth, with old newspapers and matches. I crumpled the paper, and piled up small pieces of wood on top. Once I got the fire going, I stacked some larger slabs of wood on the fire. I pumped a bellows I found by the fireplace that forced air into the flames. Before long, there was a bright, warm fire going.

"That should take the chill off," I called out.

I returned to the wood pile outside the cabin, and loaded up an armfull of logs of all sizes and placed them on the long, stone ledge next to the fireplace. I made several trips to insure that we had a good supply of dry fuel. Gretchen busily placed food on the table: sandwiches, cheese, carrots, celery, grapes and pretzels. Four bottles of beer remained and a good supply of chocolate bars for dessert. I was famished.

"Yum," I said. "A feast fit for a king and queen."

I noticed a rug in front of the crackling fire. I took food and beer and sat by the flaming logs. She joined me and gave me another beautiful smile. We didn't say much but ate with amazing appetites. The food in front of us slowly disappeared. Gretchen got some pillows from the sofa, and we sat on them and used the cushioned furniture as a back rest. We sat in silence and gazed into the dancing flames of the fire. I felt at a disadvantage as she knew what was going to happen, and I only hoped I knew what was ahead.

Eventually, I got up and added more logs to the fire. When I returned, I sat closer to her and rested my arm on the sofa behind her back. The smell of burning pine filled the air. She looked at me and once again gave me that disarming smile. She pulled out a chocolate bar and broke off a piece. Instead of eating it, she put it to my mouth, and rubbed it on my lips. Then she handed me a piece, and I smeared it on her wet lips. Then she put the sweets away, and we began to kiss gently licking the chocolate off our lips. I pulled her close to me, and we continued to kiss. I licked her fingers, and we cleaned off the sweet candy. I touched her hair and face and kissed her for what seemed like a long time. I noticed that a piece of chocolate had dropped inside the front of her shirt. I unbuttoned the shirt, but I still could not get at the runaway sweet treat. I removed her shirt and unhooked her bra. In a flurry of kisses and licks, the candy was gone.

"I like that chocolate candy," she whispered.

I was breathing hard. It seemed like years since I had made love to a pretty girl.

"I feel like I'm all hands," I whispered back.

"It feels good," she replied.

I pulled her down on top of me. I rubbed her back and felt her spine and down further. We took off our pants and the weight of her body felt wonderful as we joined together.

I must have fallen asleep because when I woke, Gretchen was cuddled up beside me sleeping with her mouth open. I looked into the fireplace and realized I needed to add fuel. I got up and stumbled to the wood pile and added a few logs to the fire. Flames began to dance on the logs. Gretchen helped me pull a mattress in front of the fire and got a blanket and pillows. We cuddled as before in front of the stone fireplace and eventually fell asleep. We were both tired from our long hike and passionate sex.

Later, I awoke to a chill. The fire was about out. I poked at it with a stick and revived some small flames. I gathered more wood, and eventually the fire was roaring hot. My nakedness as my body glowed in the firelight did not embarrass me.

Gretchen was awake. "I'm cold," she said softly. "Get me warm."

As we kissed, she pulled me down on top of her. I could not get enough of her.

Later, I awoke again and the chill was back. I rekindled the fire. Her smooth skin and nakedness gleamed in the firelight. I wrapped her in a blanket for warmth.

I had worked up an appetite. "Do you want something to eat?" I asked. I found food and returned to the fireside. We ate and drank, as if we were starved. I stared into the fire and realized that neither of us had whispered a word about love. My mind wandered. We were a strange couple. She touched my leg, we embraced, and I rolled back on the mattress with her on top of me. We found paradise once again, before we dozed off.

Dawn was approaching when I awoke. Gretchen touched my cheek and pointed my face to the window. It was the most beautiful sunrise I had ever seen. The sky was filled with colors of many hues. I sat in silence witnessing this miracle of another day.

Eventually, I struggled to my feet and stacked more kindling and logs on the fire. I fanned the air with a cereal box and soon we had a hot fire. The room warmed up, and I noticed that I could no longer see our breath.

"Life is good," I said.

She smiled at me, but said nothing. I wanted to talk about the night. What would she tell Hans? Would she go with me to France? Did she love me?

"Shush." Gretchen placed a finger on my lips. "Enjoy the moment," she sighed and pulled me down to the mattress, and kissed me again and again. We rolled together and once again enjoyed our youthful bodies. Afterward, I lay in front of the fire breathing deeply. I must have dozed off to sleep for a short time. Finally, she woke up and announced that we needed to pack and prepare for our trip back to Bad Aibling and the real world.

I checked to see if the fire was completely out. She packed our backpacks and straightened and cleaned the cottage. We carried our belongings outside and stood in silence absorbing the surroundings.

"What a gorgeous sight," I said. "The mountains, lake, the quaint but rustic cabin are all like a dream place. You are like a dream."

"Maybe I am a dream," she said with a smile. "We need to leave now or it will be dark, and we will still be on the trail."

We shouldered our packs and began the descent from the highlands. Gretchen set a steady pace. Now we were using different muscles in our legs. It was easier, but I still needed to concentrate on what I was doing.

My mind raced in many directions. Should I stay in Germany? Should I try to take her with me? Could a German girl travel to France in time of war? Could an American move from Germany to France? Would the war spread, or would statesmanship rule the day? Would the U.S. try to mediate a peace treaty? Was it too late? While these questions danced in my mind, I followed and looked at the beautiful woman in front of me. She maneuvered almost effortlessly down the trail. Was I in love or just lonely?

We walked for a long time making good time. We should make it home before sundown, I thought. Later, we stopped in a clearing to enjoy the sun. We took the time to eat the last of our provisions. The last beer was warm, and the chocolates were starting to melt. However, the food tasted good.

Gretchen seemed a little uncomfortable and fidgeted with the last beer. We were sitting on the ground leaning against a large rock. The sun warmed me and I felt completely happy, satisfied, and more than a little proud of myself. She looked me in the face, not smiling, but serious.

"We received a message that Hans was wounded on the Polish front, during the third day of fighting." She paused. "His wound was not believed to be serious. He is coming home in a matter of days to recover for several months, before he can rejoin his unit. He was hit by shrapnel in the legs from a Polish artillery blast."

I muttered how sorry I was that he was hurt.

She continued. "I will have to be with him and help in his convalescence."

"What are you trying to say?" I asked in a reluctant voice. "We made love over and over again in what was probably the most passionate night of my life. And now you're saying you can't see me anymore?"

Her eyes teared up. "If you were staying in Germany and there was no war, it would be different. But there is a war and you will be leaving soon."

I was confused. "I could stay, or you could go with me."

"No," she said. "You are an American, and I am German. I must stay here and help Hans get well. You will be leaving Germany soon. I must stay here."

"I don't know what to say," I mumbled and kicked a few stones that lay nearby.

"We had yesterday, Mitch, and it was beautiful. I will never forget you, but today we are back in the real world."

"I will always remember you, Gretchen." I took her hand in mine and kissed her on the cheek.

CHAPTER 6
BORDER ESCAPE

Days passed and I tried to keep busy. I thought about Gretchen and Hans. I wondered how my parents were. Finally, making arrangements to leave Germany occupied my time. I found it would not be as easy as just getting on a train. I wrote to the American Consul in Munich, Mr. John Allen, and to his counterpart in Lyon, France, Mr. Jason Anderson. Both men replied with detailed letters, suggesting how difficult it would be to leave Germany and enter France. Many letters would have to be written. Permissions from both sides were mandatory. After all, France and Germany were at war.

During the gray days that followed, I took long bike rides into the countryside stopping often at my favorite spot in the foothills along the stream, a place I thought of as my second home. I felt safe in my secluded sanctuary where I rested my back and head against a fallen tree. I watched as chipmunks nibbled on seeds and berries. They scurried from place to place preparing for the winter weather. It was November. The tops of the distant mountains were already white with snow.

Now that I had decided to leave, I was in a hurry to depart, but German diplomats were not that anxious to bid me adieu.

One day I came upon Helmuth, at his usual spot in the park, playing a brisk game of backgammon. He welcomed me with a warm handshake.

"My wife and Gretchen have missed your visits. You have not been sick, I hope."

"No, nothing like that. I have been trying to make arrangements to leave Germany, but it is not so simple. There is much red tape to get the proper papers."

"Yes, yes, it takes time." He nodded. "Those bureaucrats have to have something to do to keep busy. Just be patient, and you will get your permission to leave."

I inquired about his wife, Ingrid's health, and that of Gretchen. They were both fine. I also inquired about Hans.

"His wounds were more serious than it was first thought, but he will be fine. An artillery shell exploded near him, and shrapnel hit him several places in the legs. "

"Sounds like Lieutenant Henry in Hemingway's *A Farewell*

to Arms," I mused.

"Yes, it does," replied Helmuth, "except Hans was in Poland, not Italy."

He invited me to dinner one night, but I gave him a lame excuse about being very busy. I shook his hand, looked him in the eye and thanked him for being such a good friend.

"Does this mean that you are leaving soon?" he asked.

"I don't really know, but it is time for me to go." I dreaded saying 'good bye' to him.

He gave me a knowing look and returned to his game.

■ ■ ■

The weather was turning cold. The leaves drifted down from the trees. Winter was not far off. There were snowflakes in the breeze. I began to feel frustrated about the prospects of leaving.

I decided to catch a train to Munich to see American Consul Allen. Maybe a personal visit would speed up the process and result in an exit visa. In the railroad station, people rushed from one place to another. They seemed business-like and serious. There were soldiers. Most were young, but smart looking in their military uniforms. I purchased a newspaper and made my way to the train. I found my seat across from a young couple. They looked tired and were trying to sleep. Next to me was a man in his fifties, I guessed. He looked prosperous, probably a business man. He nodded when I sat down, but continued to read his newspaper. I unfolded my paper, and scanned the headlines.

"Phoney War—No Military Action Reported."

I read the story reporting the military inactivity. It was

December and an unlikely time to start an offensive. Reportedly, the French were busy moving their vaunted artillery to the French-German border. Nazi plans were less clear, but there seemed to be a general movement of troops to the western front.

Another article caught my eye concerning a possible effort on the part of the U.S. to try and mediate a peace between the French-British coalition and the Germans. One view suggested that the Americans were too wrapped up in their isolationism to realize what was happening in the world. The journalist pointed out that America had entered the Great War in 1917 to help gain victory against the Central Powers only to realize at a later time that the war had settled nothing. Now the U.S. faced a divided Europe again. The disillusionment that many experienced after that war still hung like a dark cloud over the cautious 1939 isolationism.

Another view presented in the article was that President Roosevelt knew exactly what was at stake and was working diligently behind the scenes to somehow achieve stability. Just as President Teddy Roosevelt had stepped into the quagmire of the Russo-Japanese war in 1905 and produced peace and a Nobel Peace Prize for himself, perhaps F.D.R. could orchestrate the magic to end the "phoney war."

Eventually, a loud voice announced our arrival in Munich. While waiting my turn to disembark, I watched the people. I left the train station and walked the streets of Munich. The exercise felt good. The sidewalks were full of activity. As with my last visit to Munich, I saw Nazi flags and banners decorating the buildings. The main streets were a sea of red, white and black.

I was early for my appointment at the American Consul, so I strolled the streets looking for a restaurant where I might get some refreshment. A charming window display of pastry delights caught my eye. As I reached for the door handle to enter the bakery, I noticed a sign, *"Juden Unerwunscht"* or "Jews not welcome here." Stopping in my tracks, I looked at the sign in amazement. These people were cruel. I had heard that such signs existed, but now, here it was for me to experience. I entered, wanting to see what the general atmosphere was like. I ate my bread and drank my juice in solitude. These people seemed normal: smoking, drinking coffee and chatting. I noticed one man from the train, a guy with a slight limp in a dark overcoat. We made eye-contact briefly, but he quickly looked away. The waitress came to my table. She was young and pretty in her Bavarian dress. I paid the bill, and made my way outside.

It was only a short walk to the Consul's building. Mr. Allen's office was easy to find, and after a brief wait, his secretary escorted me into his office. John Allen was a tall, handsome man in his late fifties. He had on a dark suit with a red tie. His brown hair gave way to gray at his temples. His engaging greeting put me at ease. We talked of the war and lack of military action. He mentioned his home town of Durham, North Carolina, and told me of developments in the U.S. Eventually, we got down to business. He had a manila folder on his desk which contained material on my situation. It seemed to be a highly unusual case, and he was having difficulty gaining the proper clearances for me to leave.

He explained that while he understood that I was a student learning to speak and read the language and soak up the traditions and customs of the people, the German authorities found it surprising that I was not attending classes and had no tutors. They found it interesting that I had chosen Bad Aibling as my home, which was also the location of a Luffwafa training base.

"What do they think I am?" I questioned. "I am not a spy, just a graduate student trying to learn the German language."

"Have you learned it?" asked Mr. Allen.

"Yes, I have. I can write and read German very well. I also speak the language fluently, but I probably would not pass as a native German until I learn the nuances of the dialect. I would like to continue my studies in France in order to satisfy the foreign language requirements for my Ph.D. program at the university."

"Yes, yes, I understand," the Consul added. "But the Germans have questions. I do have the proper papers for Switzerland. The Swiss are not a problem, but the Germans and French are another matter."

"I should just sneak across the border into Switzerland," I said sarcastically.

"Oh no," replied Allen quickly. "That would be a mistake. I know of an American-Jewish couple who traveled to Oberammergau on holiday. They continued by train with tickets to Freiburg, but got off at Lindau where they hoped to catch a tourist sight-seeing boat across Lake Constance to Switzerland. They had papers for the Swiss, but they made one mistake. They caught the wrong boat, a German ship that did not stop across the lake. When they protested, they were arrested and never heard from again."

After a long silence, I looked Allen in the eye. "Would you give me papers for the Swiss and some sort of letter on U.S. Consul stationery for the French, explaining my capacity as a student? Then all I would need would be the German clearance. At least I would have those documents."

Allen agreed to this course of action.

"Thank you," I said.

He called in his secretary and they began to prepare the documents.

I read a magazine while I waited.

Later, with the documents in my coat pocket, I made the return trip to Bad Aibling. While on the train my thoughts wandered to Hemingway's *A Farewell To Arms*. The main character in the book, Lieutenant Henry, had rowed a boat across a lake from Italy to Switzerland, where he and his English nurse girlfriend gained their freedom from the war. Somehow, I didn't believe Gretchen would go with me, but I could try it alone. It didn't hurt to fantasize!

■ ■ ■

Back in Bad Aibling I returned to my old patterns of biking in the countryside, taking long hikes, reading newspapers, magazines and books, writing in my diary and talking with anybody I could engage in conversation, including waitresses and people at the backgammon tables in the park. Most enjoyable were my conversations with the Mullers. One day Fritz and Inge called me to their living room, and we sat before a warm fire. We talked about the long cold winters in Bavaria. Eventually, he told me that a government official had visited, and asked many questions about me and my activities.

"He asked if I noticed anything unusual about you. He inquired if you used the phone very often or traveled much. He seemed very suspicious about what you were doing. I told him you were a student, but he had many questions about that."

I told Fritz that I had requested papers from the German government that would allow me to travel to France, where I would continue my foreign language studies. Fritz looked skeptical.

"Fritz," I said, "I am not a spy. I am simply a student trying to earn a Ph.D. in history."

"I believe you," he assured me. "But I am not sure the official believed that. He asked if you spent much time at the Luffwafa air base. I told him you go on long bike rides in the foothills, talk to people in town, and read a lot. He wanted to know what you read. He wanted to look in your room. I tried to stop him, but he threatened to bring the S.S. in and cause a lot of trouble. He searched your room, but only found a biography of Frederick II by Ernst Kantoswicz."

"Frederick II was Germany's greatest medieval emperor," I said.

"Yes, I know," said Fritz. "He also found your diary, and read it carefully. He seemed disappointed in your lack of detail about your life here."

"This would never happen in America," I said disgustedly. "I feel violated."

Fritz put his hand on my arm. "I'm sorry this happened, but I could not stop him. I am not always proud of what my country does.".

I added quickly. "I love your Germany. It is a great nation. You have produced great leaders. The works of such men as Holderin, Goethe, Schiller, Beethoven and Wagner are some of the greatest in the world."

Fritz added the names of Frederick the Great and Bismarck. "It is too early to tell about Hitler," he said. "The Fuhrer has lead Germany out of the Depression a lot quicker than your President Roosevelt, although they used many of the same kinds of programs and technology."

"Yes," I agreed. "Germany has made great progress in recovering from its financial troubles."

We sipped hot tea in silence for a few moments. I gazed out the window and noticed that the snow flurries had stopped and the sun was shining brightly. It was cold, but not cold enough to keep me from taking a bike ride. I excused myself from the Mullers and went outside to the bike.

My destination was the Café Arnold. Biking down the street, I had the distinct impression that a person in a black auto was following me. I was becoming paranoid. Why would someone follow me? When I reached the Café, the car passed by going down the street. I gave a sigh of relief and joined the crowd in Arnold's. I sat at the bar and ordered chili, beer and bread. I noticed there was American music on the radio, and a few customers were singing the lyrics in English. The fellow next to me seemed to know the words, but when I engaged him in conversation, he spoke only in German.

"I have heard the music so often that I learned the words, but they mean nothing to me," he explained.

I told him I was from the States, which led to many questions about America.

"My idea of America is millionaires, beauty queens, stupid music and Hollywood," he said.

I tried to tell him of the economic depression and hardships of many Americans, but my voice was drowned out by the boisterous singing of "Horst Wessel," a popular German song of the day.

"Horst Wessel was a S.A. commander of a district in Berlin," he explained. "He wrote the lyrics of the song in 1929 and was killed in the street fighting between the brown shirts and the Communists the following year. Dr. Goebbels, the Nazi propaganda minister, made him a martyr of the Nazi movement. Now the song is like a second national anthem."

"What are the lyrics?" I asked.

My friend recited the words of the first verse.

"The street free for the brown battalions,
The street free for the Storm Troopers,
Millions, full of hope, look up at the swastika;
The day breaks for freedom and for bread."

"Wow, that's powerful stuff. The lyrics are moving," I said.

"I guess so," my friend said and shrugged his shoulders.

After much singing, my friend left. I watched him leave the café, and as I turned back to my beer, a man entered the café. He wore a dark coat and limped. He looked familiar. I searched my memory for where I had seen him before. Was it on my trip to Munich a few days ago? I vaguely remembered such a man but was not able to see his face at that time. My suspicions rose. Was he following me? I paid my bill and left the café to see if he would follow me. Outside, I waited at a spot where I could see the café door. He did not come out. After fifteen minutes or so, I got my bicycle and rode into the countryside heading for my mountain stream sanctuary.

The road was clear of snow, but the fields were covered with a thin layer of white flakes. It was a bright, beautiful day. A cold but not bitter wind hit me in the face, as I peddled down the deserted road. At my secret hideaway, I sat by the stream and thought about the guy with the limp. He was an older man, maybe in his forties. Had he injured his leg during the Great War? I wondered. I sat there in deep thought, and eventually closed my eyes. When I awoke I focused on a rabbit munching on a plant. It evidently did not see me, and I quietly watched. All of a sudden, a big bird landed on the rabbit and began choking it to death. I jumped to my feet and scared the bird away. It flew into the air clutching his prey in his claws. My serene moment had been lost by the vicious attack. I stood there watching the bird fly off into the distance. That was unsettling.

Picking up a few pebbles, I tossed them into the stream, trying to hit a piece of driftwood. I walked around and noticed footprints in the snow. Someone had been here earlier. Had a family enjoyed a picnic here? Had a couple made love here? Had someone searched my secret hangout? What were they looking for? Maybe they thought there was a radio hidden here. Maybe they suspected I had a cache of guns or explosives. Maybe my imagination was getting the better of me. I mounted my bike, and rode back to my room at the Mullers.

They were not at home. On the table I found some delicious looking cookies with a note for me to enjoy the snack. There was also a letter from my parents. I took it to my room and sat down to read about life in America. My thoughts drifted from one subject to another. Did the German authorities really think I was a spy? The idea was ridiculous to me, but maybe the man with the limp was building a case against me. Thinking back to my trip on the ship to Europe, I wondered how the nice German-Jewish family was doing. I remembered Leah's innocent smile, and hoped she was safe. Things were not good for people like them in Germany.

My mind skipped to Munich and Consul Allen in the embassy. While he had reacted negatively to my flippant suggestion that I should try to cross the border into Switzerland, he did lay out a plan of how others had tried to escape. Was he actually suggesting I should get out while there was time? I had no plan to actually do it, but I began to list in my mind the various steps I would need to take to escape from Germany. I ate some of the cookies while I calculated. Would I have to tell the Mullers goodbye, or should I just leave? I would have to figure that out. How would I travel to Lindau?

It was too far to ride the bicycle. I would have to take the train. I could buy tickets for another destination and get off at Lindau. That might work. I could go to the docks at Lake Constance and try to figure out which boat to take. If I got to Switzerland, what would I do next? Should I wait there until the war situation cleared up? Maybe F.D.R. would offer a peace treaty that all could accept. If not, should I go into France with the letter from U.S. Consul Allen? In frustration I asked myself, "how in the hell can I get out of this situation?"

■ ■ ■

The next few weeks dragged by, as I agonized over what to do. I kept hoping the world situation would improve, but the phoney war continued. After sending several boxes of books back to North Carolina, all I had left were clothes, my journal and several books I was still reading. I had a medium-sized backpack, but not all of my clothes would fit inside. I packed and repacked the backpack, but I could not take it all. If I left, I would wear my winter jacket, warm clothes and my boots. I could fit in my journal, toothbrush, toothpaste, a comb, shaving utensils, soap, and four changes of clothes including my tennis shoes. I would simply leave the rest at the Mullers.

I kept watching to see if I was being followed, but there was no one that raised my suspicions. Once I saw a man with a limp, but it was not the same person that I had seen on other occasions. Most of my actions were simply things to keep me busy. I had no intention of trying to flee Germany without the proper credentials.

One day I was out biking and came to a railroad crossing. A

train was coming and I stopped to watch it go by. Maybe, I thought, I could jump on a freight train, ride for a while, get off in a city and buy a ticket from there to Switzerland. That way if I was followed, I would be hard to trace. The train was getting closer, thus interrupting my fantasies of escape. It was noisy. A soldier sitting on top of a freight car waved with one hand while he cradled his weapon in the other. The cars smelled, and I wondered about the cargo. As the train swished by, it sounded like a voice called out for water, but I couldn't be sure. There seemed to be people locked in the freight car. I was stunned and felt a knot in my stomach. The last car whizzed by, but I stood in a daze, unable to move. The stench was overwhelming, and I thought I might throw up. What had I just seen? Why was there a guard on top of the train car? Were these political prisoners or forced laborers? Then I thought of the Jews, and I knew.

I mounted my bike, and rode to my stream in the foothills. The clear water rushed over the stones in the water. A squirrel scooted up a tree. I sat by the stream and gazed into the water. Eventually, I went to my bike and retrieved a newspaper from the bag on the handlebars. I returned to my seat by the stream and began reading the paper. The date was March 25, 1940. I found an interesting article on the Russian-Finnish War, which after bitter fighting in January and February had resulted in a Russian victory. The journalist was impressed by how well the Finns had acquitted themselves against the Reds. The writer's conclusion was that the Russian military was still operating at the speed it had adopted during the Great War in 1917. It had been badly trained and ill-equipped. The "sleeping bear" posed little threat to the Germans. He urged the German generals to consider stepping up the timetable in the West. It was a convincing article and woke me up to the fact that I was running out of time. Spring was just around the corner. The conditions would soon be right for the "Phoney War" to end. It was becoming clear to me that the U.S. would not be able to do anything to stop the coming onslaught. President Roosevelt had his hands full back home with the isolationist mentality of many Americans. I realized all of a sudden that I needed to get back to good ole North Carolina. But how?

■ ■ ■

By early April, I began to make real plans to leave. It wouldn't hurt to plan even if I never followed through. Today, as usual, I wore my backpack and rode to the train station. I examined every person I could see. The station was not crowded. I looked around and located the restroom. When I came out, I found the ticket booth. I read the schedules posted on the wall. I walked around the departure area and then returned to my bike. I searched for suspicious looking people, but no one seemed concerned about my actions. I bought a candy bar at a local store, ate it slowly and watched the people. When the candy was gone, I rode off to the countryside, constantly looking to see if I was being followed.

The next day, I walked to the park and visited with the backgammon players. I went to the library and ate lunch at Arnold's. As best as I could determine, no one followed me. The next day, I made a bike trip to my stream in the hills.

Later that day, I read in my chair at the Mullers and made my plans to leave. I decided to make a run for it. Diplomatic channels were too slow and uncertain. I was anxious to leave. I had overstayed my time in Germany. I filled my backpack with clothes, my diary and food. I would leave some books and clothes behind, as if I planned to return to my room. My well-worn loafers and some clothes were left in the closet. I wanted my room to look as if I would return to it shortly.

Nervous and unsure, I took my backpack and jacket and headed for the door. The Mullers were in the kitchen eating. I waved to them and told them I was going on a hike and would be gone for a day or two. I tried to look casual, but I wanted to hug them and thank them for all they had done for me. I walked out the door and into the front yard. Filled with a mixture of regret and excitement, I looked back to glimpse at what had been my home for over a half of a year.

I pushed ahead, and walked briskly to the railroad station. No one seemed concerned about me. I went inside the station, looked around and checked the schedule postings. Nothing had changed. The ticket exchange was still there, but I walked past it to the restroom. My heart was beating rapidly. No one was using the bathroom. I checked my backpack, washed my hands and pushed back my hair. The train I wanted was scheduled to leave in half an hour. I returned to the waiting room and got a cup of tea. I drank it slowly and watched for suspicious people. Was I some paranoid freak, or should I be more concerned than I was? I imagined that soldiers or police would come to arrest me. But nothing happened.

I purchased a ticket to Lindau, a port town on the Bodensee, as Lake Constance was called. The ticket master explained to me that I would have to change trains in Memmingen before heading south to the lake. I thanked him, and made my way to the departure platform.

When I boarded the train, I noticed the car was about half full. There were two soldiers, who appeared to be on leave. An older couple sat across from me and a very attractive young lady sat farther up the aisle. I looked out the window and tried to act normal. Two men in coats and ties were in front of the girl, and farther down the aisle there were others who looked like farmers. No one looked like secret police or S.S. I tried to relax and read the newspaper that I had purchased in the station. The conductor made his way through the car and on to the next.

The train moved forward, and we were on our way. I began to feel more confident. Bad Aibling slowly disappeared into the distance. I read the paper. The two soldiers were more concerned about the pretty girl than me. I avoided making eye contact with anyone. Instead, I looked out of the window as the landscape rushed by. We stopped at the station at Penzberg for ten minutes, and again at Kempten briefly. Austria was only a short distance away. Earlier the Germans had joined together with Austria in Hitler's 'Anschlus.'

Switzerland was my best chance to escape. The countryside rushed by. We were now heading in a southwesterly direction. After a short stop in Lindenberg, we moved on toward Lindau. Liechtenstein was close by, but my thoughts were on Switzerland.

Eventually, we pulled into Lindau. It appeared to be about the same size as Bad Aibling. I disembarked and went into the station to get my bearings. Armed soldiers were everywhere, some guarding doorways and others checking passports. Seeing no one suspicious looking, I went outside and found a taxi. The driver took me to the harbor. There I found more guards at the piers checking people as they boarded the ships. There was a small café facing the water. I entered the noisy café and took a table near a window, where I could watch the activity on the waterfront. Eventually, I spotted a ship heading for the Lindau dock. It looked like a tourist boat. Soon I could read its name: "Bodensee Queen" on the bow. I quickly paid my bill and made my way to the pier.

I waited off to the side carefully avoiding the police but watching the ship tie up and its passengers disembark. I followed the crowd of people who exited the ship. Some were met by friends. I was watching for anyone who might go into the bar next to the café. Many had joined their friends, but several headed for the bar. I followed and tried to remember their clothes color. I waited a minute or so outside the bar, giving them a chance to get seated. I entered and found one of the people at the bar. There was an empty stool next to him. I casually joined him. I ordered a beer and some nuts, and chatted with the bartender. The man next to me sipped his beer and checked his ticket. I offered him some nuts, and he gratefully accepted. We talked of the weather, and he told me about his trip across the lake. I allowed as how I planned to cross the lake to Switzerland. We ordered a second beer. He looked at his watch and said his boat was leaving in fifteen minutes for its return to Arbon on the Swiss side of the lake. I got up as if to leave.

"Where are you going?" he asked.

"I will need to buy a ticket," I replied.

"No need to do that," he grumbled. "I have an extra ticket. I was supposed to go with someone on this trip, but she did not meet me as planned. I have a ticket for her, but she did not show. You may have it," he said sadly. "Besides, you won't have to waste time with customs."

"That is very kind," I replied, "but I will pay you."

I handed him the money, and he in turn gave me the ticket. We quickly finished our beers, which I paid for, and we headed for the ship. We stood in line waiting to board the ship. As we got closer to the table where the agent sat checking passports, I could see his face. He had greasy hair and a thin mustache like Hitler had. His pistol hung in its holster on his side. My new friend advised me to tear my ticket as his was torn. I was nervous and began to sweat. Would he allow me to pass or would I be questioned further?

As I neared the table, I heard some shouts and the line surged ahead. The agent grabbed his gun, told us to wait where we were and hurried toward the disturbance. My friend pushed me forward and we quickly walked to the boarding ramp and entered the ship. The ship official checked our tickets and at the same time hiccupped unexpectedly, and we all laughed.

It was a beautiful late afternoon and warm enough to sit on

the open deck. We ordered two drinks and found two deck chairs. My friend told me about his business and where he lived in Switzerland. He asked me about my life in Germany.

"I live in Bad Aibling south of Munich," I said. "I have some personal business to attend to in Switzerland."

"Ha," he chortled. "I thought you were running away from Herr Hitler."

We both had a good laugh. He went on to talk about some trips he had taken in Germany and about the war situation in general.

When we arrived in Switzerland, I followed him off the ship. It was so easy. There was no military presence and no hassle. We shook hands at the end of the pier, and he was on his way, leaving me alone. I surveyed my surroundings. Eventually I found a cheap hotel across from the nearby train station. That night I enjoyed a wonderful meal of pork chops, beets, and applesauce. Later, I had a peaceful rest.

The next morning, I gathered maps and schedules at the train station and studied them, while I ate breakfast. I looked for suspicious looking people, but found no one who seemed interested in me. After careful study of the routes available to me, I developed a plan to take the train through Bern to Lausanne, then south to Montreux on Lake Geneva and further south to Martighy, a small town near the French border. Here I would investigate the train situation and check out what was involved in crossing by train to France. I decided to stay away from Geneva and try to cross at an unlikely place.

My train trip across Switzerland was spectacular. The

mountains and lakes were breathtaking. The idea of living in Montreux was appealing. With Mount Blanc in the distance and Lake Geneva in front of me, I could not think of a more beautiful place to live. But, I needed to go home and get busy in pursuit of the elusive Ph.D. I thought about doing the boat trip scenario across Lake Geneva to France, but that did not look promising. I figured that airplane travel would be watched closely and, besides, no one was there with a plane ticket to Paris. Finally, I decided just to buy a train ticket to Lyons, France, and see how that would work. I still had my letters from the U.S. Consul addressed to the French government officials. I wasn't convinced they would do the trick, but I had no other plan. I purchased my ticket from Martighy to Lyons and hoped for the best. The ticket officer only checked my U.S. passport, which was in order. He advised me that once across the border, the French would check out the passengers again. I thanked him and boarded the train. Goodbye Germany, goodbye Switzerland, and hopefully, hello France!

CHAPTER 7
WELCOME TO FRANCE

I boarded the train around noon and found the passenger car extremely crowded. I spied a seat next to an older man and made my way toward it. A lady stepped in front of me, and like a gentleman, I made room for her. She smiled and took the seat I had my eye on. I looked around the car and saw no empty seats available except one towards the end of the car. When I got there, I realized something was draped across both seats. It seemed to be a person. What looked like a head was covered with long, dark black hair covering the face. Then I discovered an arm and hand covered with bracelets and rings. There was jewelry everywhere. It must be a woman. I looked at other seats. They were all full. A couple across the aisle shrugged and smiled. I gently pushed the person to one side. She seemed to be asleep. There was enough space for me to wiggle in among the arms and legs. I placed my backpack on my lap and tried to turn away from her. In the crowded seat, I shifted around seeking a comfortable position. An arm flopped against me, and I gently lifted it back to her side. I could smell perfume. I looked at her hand. It seemed to be that of a young person. I sat and wondered how long it would take to get to Lyon.

I was also reminded of a film I had seen in America about two people on the backseat of a bus. It was Clark Gable and Claudette Colbert in some screwball comedy set in the early 1930s. She was very rich, and he was a newspaper reporter. I remember that she was inexperienced about real life and traveling on buses with the common people. When he realized she was from a wealthy family, he decided there might be a news story about her. He helped her when her suitcase was stolen, and they became friends.

"What was the name of that film?" I said out loud to no one in particular. Yes, I thought, it was directed by Frank Capra and entitled: "It Happened One Night."

The body moved next to me and her hand landed on my shoulder. This was no Claudette Colbert next to me, I mused.

My thoughts turned to America. I must be homesick. I missed my parents and the university atmosphere. Maybe I would spend a few months in France and then head home. I needed to brush up on my French. I could read it fairly well, but my conversational skills needed practice.

Soon I came to the border and then into France. At Chamonix, French officials boarded the train to check passports. The lady next to me roused and after considerable moving about located her travel bag. She did have a face, and I guessed she was somewhere between fifteen and thirty. She paid little attention to me and acted as if I were an inconvenience. The officer returned her passport and then turned to me. He read my passport and asked the nature of my visit to France. I produced my letter from the U.S. consulate. It was in English, and I translated it for him as best I could. He seemed unsure. He returned my papers and said I would be met in Lyon by police who would check out my story. This was not good. The truth was that I had illegally left Germany.

The French countryside zoomed by. I gazed out of the window in a stupor of lost thoughts and worry, but also appreciation of the fact that I was in France. I tried to talk with the person beside me, but she was not particularly interested in talking. All I could get out of her was that she had visited relatives in Switzerland and now was returning to her hometown of Abbeville on the northwestern coast of France near Amiens. She broke off the conversation when she turned her back to me and faced the window. It was quite a maneuver considering her long full skirt, coat and sweater, long hair and at least fifty pounds of jewelry including huge earrings. I might have exaggerated a trifle, but at least she was entertaining.

We stopped in Annecy for a short break. The mountains were

beautiful with some snow glistening in the distance. I had pastry and milk and returned to my seat on the train. I thought I should switch to wine now that I was in France. Maybe next time. My seatmate was sleeping, but she had left maybe a third of the seat for me to stretch out and relax. I was not getting much practice in speaking French with her next to me. The trip dragged on. We passed a beautiful mountain lake and a wide river. The train was now crowded with people, and I sensed we were close to Lyon.

As we pulled to a stop in Lyon, I felt uneasy about meeting with the French government officials. I waited in my seat, but no one came to me. Finally, I got off and into a sea of humanity. The station was packed with people, many of whom were military. It seemed that half of the French Army must be here. No one approached me. I had no luggage, only my backpack. Surprisingly the ticket office was abandoned. A sign said: "No Tickets Available." I asked a man who was standing near the ticket booth.

"When can I buy tickets?" I asked.

"I don't know," he replied. "The military has taken over all the trains to move men and equipment to the border."

"They must be expecting trouble," I said.

He nodded.

I walked out into the street. Lyon was renowned for being the food capital of France. I read somewhere that more chefs produced the best meals in the world right here.. After eating in a local restaurant, I judged that the meal I had was not prepared by one of those chefs. I walked around the city and returned to the train station. There were still no tickets to be purchased, and it seemed hundreds of people were standing around. Back out in the streets, I crossed the Rhone River bridge and caught the funicular up to the top of the hill to the Basilic Square. Later, I returned to the station. It was dark now, and only a few people remained. I learned that train service for civilians was discontinued indefinitely. The French Army was on the move. What to do now!

I wandered aimlessly through the depot. Then I spied the woman with whom I had shared a seat on the train. She was perched on top of several suitcases with her head bowed. I asked if she was all right, and she looked up, her eyes full of tears. I could see she was frightened.

"I don't know what to do," she said. "There are no trains."

"I know," I said. "Maybe they will run tomorrow."

"I don't know what to do," she repeated. "I have little money and no place to stay but here."

She had been snooty on the train, but now she was helpless. I wanted to leave her, but she seemed so scared. Being a southern gentleman did not help my situation.

"Okay," I mumbled. "I will stay here with you, and in the morning maybe the trains will be running. You will be safe," I added.

It was not a restful night trying to sleep on the hard benches in the railroad station. I used my backpack as a pillow and managed to get some sleep. She sat on the bench with her four suitcases on either side of her.

The next morning she was very quiet. A policeman came by

and told us there were no trains in the foreseeable future. "You should make other plans," he advised. He added that we could not sleep in the train station anymore. He wished us good luck and departed.

"I'm hungry," I said. "Do you want to get some breakfast?"

"I'll get some coffee," she said.

We left her bags in the empty ticket office and walked the street. She was anxious about her bags, but I convinced her they would not be stolen. We walked the street looking for a grocery store.

"We can get bread, fruit and juice," I said. "That should hold us."

We passed by several stores including a bike shop. I stopped and admired the bikes in the window.

"There," I pointed. "I used to ride a bike just like that one, except mine was red, not blue."

She nodded. A grocery store was two doors down, and across the street was a small park. We had breakfast sitting on a park bench under a tree with our food between us.

"My name is Mitchell," I said, "but most people call me Mitch."

"Mitchell," she repeated. Her French accent added a lot to my name.

She smiled. "My name is Brigit."

We shook hands. She actually was rather pretty, once she got all of her hair out of her face. She still had so many clothes on that she looked heavy.

"Aren't you warm wearing all those clothes?" I asked.

"I am, but there was no more room in my bags."

We studied the spring flowers in the park, the budding bushes and trees. "We should get back to the train station to see if there are any changes," I suggested.

We reached the station and found almost no one there. The ticket master was closing up his office. Brigit reclaimed her bags with a sigh of relief.

"Are there any trains leaving?" I inquired.

He looked at me and seemed to recognize me from the day before.

"There are no trains today. I have been told to go home, and they would call me in a few days. No one but the military can use the trains," he said in a firm voice. "You should make other arrangements."

I reported the news back to Brigit. She looked scared and helpless.

"I am going into town to look for alternate transportation," I said and began to walk away. I stopped and faced her. "What will you do?" I asked.

She shook her head dejectedly. A tear rolled down her cheek. She had so much luggage, she could not follow me. She touched my heart. "Stay here," I said. I will return with whatever information I can get.

She nodded, and I turned and walked away. I tried to rent a car but with no success. Things were too unsettled, and gas was of short supply. The bus situation was uncertain and was at a standstill. A boat trip seemed unlikely, and I walked back toward the station. I passed the bike store and got more food and drink from the same grocery, where I had purchased breakfast. I sat on the park bench and thought about my options. I could stay in Lyon and practice speaking French. I worried about seeing the authorities who were supposed to meet me at the train. I decided that I should be near the west coast, in case I needed to get out of France and go to England.

I saved some of the food for Brigit and headed back to the station. I passed the bike store again and looked into the window. I wondered if I could ride a bike to the coast, near Calais. England would be very close and only a boat ride away. I began to price the bikes and decided on the one I would buy, if I decided to ride. I could talk to people along the way and learn a great deal about the French and their language. I had been riding steadily for half a year and was in good shape. The weather would be fine. I convinced myself to do it. First, I would tell Brigit good-bye and wish her luck. When I returned to the train station, she was right where I had left her. She smiled and seemed happy to see me. I gave her the food I'd saved and while she ate, I told her my plan. She realized that I planned to leave her. What else could I do?

She looked at me with a frightened expression. Tears started to come. "What about me?" she asked.

"You can stay here until the trains start service again."

"I have no place to stay and very little money," she said softly.

"You can't ride with me," I said. "You have too much luggage." As soon as I said it, I realized that was a mistake.

"That's it!" She said brightly, wiping away the tears. "I will go with you. I will get a bicycle and tie the suitcases to it."

I was too stunned to speak. I shifted my feet and just looked at her with long hair almost to her waist, jewelry everywhere and layers of clothes. She didn't look like a biker. Then I made my next mistake. "I bet you can't even ride a bike," I said confidently.

"Yes, I can, I have one at home. I rode a lot as a kid. Please, please, please, I can do it. It will be fun! An adventure."

"No," I blurted out. "You have too much luggage, and I will be sleeping on the ground every night."

Her tears began to flow again. I felt terrible and was at a loss as to what to do.

"I will teach you how to speak French," she whispered, "like a real Frenchman. "You will learn the right way to speak and not from a textbook. Please," she said with renewed confidence. "I will help you get to the coast."

I could not help but smile. Now she was going to help me, when in reality I thought I would be helping her.

"I don't think it will work," but I grabbed her two biggest suitcases and started to move toward the station exit. She picked up the other two and off to the bike shop we went.

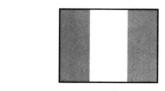

CHAPTER 8
BIKING THE BACK ROADS

An hour later, we emerged from the store into the bright sunlight pushing two bikes. We had tied two suitcases on the back of each bike. Also, I purchased an air pump and a tire repair kit. Brigit did not have enough money to pay for her bike, but I had convinced her she would not need her long, heavy winter coat. The salesman took her coat and some of her money in trade for her bike. I picked up a compass and a road map of France. My plan was to stay away from large cities and use country roads as much as possible. I wanted to get away from

Lyon quickly to avoid government officials. We headed west towards Vichy. I figured we could do about fifty miles a day under normal circumstances, but the bikes with so much weight on the back were hard to control. After an hour of hard peddling we were still on the outskirts of Lyon. I was wet from perspiration, and Brigit looked exhausted. We stopped to rest, and I sensed she was having second thoughts about the "adventure."

She surprised me, however. "This is fun! We can do it," she said. "Each day we'll be stronger and make better time."

"I hope you're right."

I looked for water, but all I could find was a wooded area that had a small stream running through it. We stopped and tried to find a place to sleep on the ground. We ate, drank and fell into restless sleep. At this speed, I figured we could make it to Calais in about a year.

■ ■ ■

The next morning was not good. I was dirty and wet from the dew on the ground and did not feel rested at all. Brigit was tired, but tried to be positive. She failed. We washed by the stream and splashed cold water on our faces. I decided we would ride for an hour and then get breakfast. We stopped at a farm. A teenage girl was by the road, and Brigit asked if we could buy some food. She took us to the farmhouse and called her mom and dad out to talk to us. They were very nice and agreed to give us some food and suggested we sit in their yard. I had some wine left from yesterday, and we washed down some bread, nuts and apple. I could tell the girl greatly admired

Brigit's jewelry. She went inside her house and shortly emerged with some homemade cookies. She handed them to Brigit and smiled. Brigit seemed surprised.

"Why don't you give her some jewelry?" I suggested.

"Oh, I couldn't."

"Sure you could and maybe a piece of clothing," I said, smiling.

"But I need these," she said.

"I'm sure the girl needs the cookie."

Brigit took a deep breath and sadly removed one of her many bracelets and held it out to the girl. She took it eagerly and tried to put it on her wrist. Brigit helped her. I thought the girl might cry, but instead she threw her arms around my surprised fellow traveler. She shook my hand and raced into the house to show the bracelet to her mother. We sat on the ground and rested for a while, before we continued our journey.

I tried to set a little faster pace, but Brigit could not keep up. We passed through L'rbresle and stopped in a park to rest. The village was small, but I found a fruit stand, where we purchased a variety of the fresh food. Brigit was getting low on money, and so was I. We pressed on, trying to get more miles behind us. I was wearing my shorts now, Brigit was still in her long skirt. She was a determined lady, but she was wearing down. Later that afternoon, she hit a hole in the road and sprawled to the ground. Her skirt protected her, except for her hands which were scraped. I realized we needed to stop to rest and get cleaned up. I worked on the bikes, cleaning them and rearranging the suitcases. This gave Brigit a little privacy, and she even changed clothes. The truth was, she had no clothes appropriate for cycling. Her long hair was kind of a mess, but I said nothing. She confessed her legs and shoulder muscles were sore as were mine.

That night we slept on some hay in a barn. We both realized we were having a rough time. I wanted to be on my own, but I could not just leave her. I wondered if she sensed my frustration. She said nothing, and we continued for several more days. We seemed to get into a routine of biking, eating, drinking as much liquid as possible, and resting. I wrote in my diary. However, there was little excitement to relate.

On the morning of the fifth day of our trip, we were in the outskirts of the village of Roanne. I noticed a group of young girls working in the fields. As we got closer, I saw several nuns with the girls. We stopped and talked with the Sisters. There were three of them dressed in their habits. I inquired if there was work for us in exchange for food and lodging. The Sisters were reluctant at first. I didn't push the issue but talked to them about the weather and the road ahead. I told them we were trying to bike to Calais, and they thought it was a joke. The spokesperson was a tall, lean nun named Paulette. She decided we could work for the morning, have lunch, and then she would decide if there was more for us to do. Brigit went over to work with the girls who were picking wild berries. I worked with the boys who were loosening the soil in preparation for planting. The youngsters seemed healthy and happy with working in the fields. They told me of the classes they took, when they weren't farming. It felt good to do something other than ride a bike. After several hours of this hard physical labor,

I began to miss the biking.

I heard a shrill whistle noise and learned it was the lunch signal. We gathered under a group of pine trees, and the nuns spread blankets on the ground. We had baskets of bread, cheese, and sausage. There were big pitchers of lemonade and bags of apples. I sat down on a log and enjoyed the food and the sight of the hungry workers eating. Then I noticed the girls. They all had jewelry on, as well as big smiles on their faces. Brigit looked different, also. She had hardly any bracelets and necklaces left. She actually had wrists and a neck. She was smiling, too.

I didn't realize I was so hungry. I was on my second glass of lemonade, gulping it down. It was embarrassing, but I needed liquid. I began to slow down and watch the people around me. They were quietly eating, relaxing and enjoying the rest period. My thoughts drifted back to the German Youth groups that I had seen. They had seemed healthy but much more disciplined and serious. The nuns had prayed over the food, but now it was almost gone. As I surveyed the group, I realized that most were lying on various blankets, and some had their eyes closed. Was it nap time?

After a half hour of sleep, I awoke to the stirring of the group. Our rest period was over. Brigit brought over a cup of water for me.

"I'm sore," she said. "Are you? Every muscle in my body hurts."

"Me, too," I murmured. "We need to get back to biking, or we will never get in shape."

She smiled at me and then rejoined her group. Sister approached me and indicated that there was wood to be split and stacked.

"It's hard work, but it will be worth it, because Sister Paulette is cooking her famous world renowned crepes for tonight's supper." She added, "I have arranged for you to stay in the boys dorm, where Brother Philippe lives with the boys, and Brigit can stay with me and the girls."

"That sounds great," I replied and went off to spilt logs.

■ ■ ■

Dinner was all that it was advertised to be and more. The lemonade, vegetables and crepes were delicious. After the dishes were cleaned up, the children played some games and sang songs to honor us as their guests. We sat around the campfire resting and enjoying the peaceful scene. The children had remarkable voices, and their French dialect made for a perfect night. I thought back to my youth and sitting with my parents around a similar campfire, cooking marshmallows and eating s'mores.

A while after the sun set, we were sent to our rooms. Mine was a small area with a table, chair, bed and a place to hang some clothes. The mattress was hard, but a welcome sight for me. I slept hard, until the light from the window woke me. I lay listening to the rain on the roof. I had wanted to cover a lot of miles today, but the rain put that idea to rest.

Breakfast was early. Apple juice, croissant rolls and cheese hit the spot. Brother Philippe joined me with his coffee.

"What do you hear about the war?" I asked.

He thought for a moment. "We are rather isolated and know very little. I believe there was fighting in Scandinavia, but I am unclear of the specifics of the conflict."

I changed the subject to the weather, and he reckoned the rain would clear by noon. I started preparing the bikes for a noon departure. Brigit arrived with only three suitcases.

"This is progress; this is progress!!!" I exclaimed.

The only problem now was that one bike would have one suitcase and the other would have two. I would have to carry two. I packed the bikes carefully, checking the tires. I toyed with the compass a bit and went over the maps again. Vichy was my destination for the night. It looked like about thirty-five miles. From there I planned to head north towards the distant city of Reims traveling east of Paris. Once in Reims I would go in a northwesterly direction toward the coast and Calais. But first we needed to get to Vichy.

It was time to tell the children and the sisters goodbye. Brigit hugged a number of the girls, and I shook hands with the sisters. One of the sisters gave me a letter to present at another convent located along the route we planned to follow. Perhaps we could spend a night there. It sounded good to me.

We were traveling, and it was good to be on the bikes again. Brigit and I did not talk much but concentrated on navigating the dirt roads and missing the pot holes. We got into a rhythm, and the sound of the bike chains was somehow comforting. We passed worn down farms and beautiful fields of bright yellow mustard seed plants and brilliant red poppies. At mid-day we stopped to eat by a stream. The nuns had packed us a lunch, and it was welcomed. I sat on a big rock near the stream bed. Brigit found a log to rest on. I washed my face and hands in the cold water, and she did the same. We ate without conversation, until we got our fill.

Bridgit mused. "I wonder if I would be happy as a nun."

"You sure looked comfortable with the children," I said. "I think you would be a good teacher and a nun. Did you ever consider doing that?"

"Not really," she said. "I couldn't stand to wear black all the time and little or no jewelry. That would be hard."

"Yeah," I half laughed. "Maybe you would be happier as a teacher, and you could wear what you wanted."

After a brief rest, we biked for several hours more. Brigit seemed to move better with the lighter load. It would be great if we could get rid of another suitcase, I thought.

Late in the afternoon we came to the outskirts of Vichy. We rode by orange groves and prosperous looking farms. The city was known as "The Queen of French spas" as one sign suggested. The spring waters were good to drink and to cure certain ailments. We crossed over the Allier River on the Passereille bridge and found ourselves in a different world of Spas, resorts, casinos and elegant restaurants. There were sporting facilities of all kinds and musical opportunities abounded. We found ourselves in the playground of the rich. After some sight-seeing, we headed north and back to rural France, where we felt more comfortable. We rode for about an hour, until we spotted a farmhouse. The building looked solid but in need of paint. Dogs barked to announce our arrival.

The whole family came out to see what was the disturbance. The man looked to be in his forties, bearded and weathered looking. His wife appeared healthy. There were four children, two boys in their late teens and two younger girls. They were pleasant and listened to our story. I offered to pay so that we might sleep in the barn. He offered us some food, as they were just beginning their meal. We gladly accepted, and we entered their home. After a meal of potato soup and vegetables, the head of the household and his two sons offered to show me around the farm. Brigit stayed with the women to help clean up the supper dishes. When I returned, I noticed the two girls with happy smiles and each in a new dress. I looked at Brigit, and she grinned playfully. I thought to myself that with about twenty more stops, she would not need any suitcases to carry her things. As it was getting dark, I retired to the barn. Brigit stayed with the girls in their room. I began to wish that I had more clothes, so I could give them away and sleep in the house.

It seemed we had settled into a routine. We biked about thirty to fifty miles a day. We ate fruit, bread, veggies, soup, cheese, sausage and eggs at a few farmhouses. Some of the time, we worked at the farms for our keep. Many times Brigit gave her clothes and jewelry away. We crossed the Loire River and shortly after we passed the little town of Dumper. From there we followed the river north to Deciza and on to Corbign. The villages became a blur in my mind. The Morgan Mountains were to the east of us, and we were glad we didn't have to cross them. Our sore muscles were turning hard. Physically, I felt strong. Brigit was doing a lot better. We were able to cover more miles. At Clambake, Brigit got rid of her second suitcase. Now we only had one tied to each bike. It seemed like half the young girls in France were wearing her clothes.

Somewhere around Auxevre, we came to the convent recommended by the sisters earlier in our trip. It was in a valley with grape vineyards everywhere. Many other crops were planted, also. The Sisters gave us a warm welcome, once they had read the letter from Sister Paulette.

Again, we found a number of young girls living at the convent. Sister Marie seemed to be in charge. She was attractive, although a little heavy. She had a wonderful smile and made us feel welcome. Brigit was assigned a room in the girl's sleeping quarters. I was given a room off one of the storage areas. They warned me about mice, but I was just glad to have a place to sleep. Sister invited us to stay several days. We were only too glad to accept her kind invitation. We worked in the fields; we ate and rested.

One afternoon it rained. I retired to my room to write in my diary. Brigit disappeared with the girls. At dinner that night, I was sitting at the big table talking with one of the Sisters. The girls arrived, but I could not find Brigit.

"Did someone notify Brigit that dinner is ready?" I asked.

The girls laughed and laughed.

"I'm here," said Brigit.

I couldn't see her until someone stepped out of the group of girls. This person had no hair in her face or matted down her back. I was too surprised to speak.

"Sister gave me a haircut. We tried to untangle my hair, but it was such a mess. We just cut most of it off. How do you like it?" she asked.

"I, ah, it's beautiful," I blurted out. "You look so different."

The girls laughed again at my reply. We all laughed. Then I noticed the lack of jewelry on her.

"What happened to your jewelry?" I asked.

The girls held out their arms and hands full of chains, glass and stones.

"We have it now!" they exclaimed.

Brigit smiled. "It was too clumsy to wear and got in my way all the time when I rode the bike."

"You look so different, I can't believe it's you."

I took her hand and held it high in the air. She smiled and bowed to the group. The girls cheered and clapped their hands. It was a happy moment.

■ ■ ■

That night as I lay on my straw bed, I thought of how changed Brigit was. She was adapting to the road. She was a biker now, not the helpless girl I had befriended in the train station. I began to have real hope, that I might make it to Calais and subsequently to England and then, to the U.S. I was gaining confidence. And I thought of my parents, how much I missed them, and how good it would be to see them. I thought of graduate school and the progress I had made in learning to speak German and French.

■ ■ ■

The next morning I was up early to check out the bikes. The tires were showing wear.

I oiled the chains and prepared to push on.

"Good morning," Brigit called.

She walked towards me. There was another surprise. She had cut the legs off some pants so that she might have shorts. She also had a small backpack. To my joy and relief, there were no suitcases.

"I've been busy getting my new wardrobe together. I have a few changes of clothes and other necessities. They are all in the backpack. We can make much better time," she explained.

"You are the best!"

Also, she had a bag of food. We mounted our bikes and waved good-bye to the girls and Sisters. We were off! I was amazed how much better we could handle the bikes without the suitcases, and how much speed we could muster on good roads. We probably reached speeds of ten to fifteen miles per hour. In shorts and T-shirts, Brigit looked like a real biker. It was late April, and the flowers were beautiful. We passed through St. Florencio, Bouilly and Troyes. We slept in barns and village parks. We drank wine and water. We ate fruit, bread and cheese. Every now and then, we celebrated a good day of travel with chocolate.

Near Romilly we came upon a gypsy camp along the road, where there was a river. There were a number of wagons pulled together. It was getting late in the day, and I wondered if we should visit with these people.

"They have a reputation for stealing things," Brigit said.

"I have heard that," I said, "but we do need a place to stay tonight."

"Well, let's stop and talk and see what they have to say."

The closest person to us was a bearded man, about forty,

wearing peasant clothes. He looked at us as we rode up to him. His dark features and dominant nose caught my attention.

"Could you tell me how much farther it is to Reims?" I asked.

He looked Brigit and me over and shrugged his shoulders. "I don't really know, but it is not too far."

A woman approached us. "Who are you talking to?" she asked him.

"Don't know who they are."

"We are trying to get to Reims," I said.

"Can't help you there," she said.

A group of children stopped playing and looked at us.

"May I give them some candy?" I asked the woman.

"Sure," she said and called the three girls and a boy over to us.

I took my backpack off, fished out some chocolate and offered a piece to each one.

"Would you like some water?" The man offered.

"Sure would," said Brigit.

We moved to the nearby stream and sat on a rock. The young boy dipped a bucket into the rushing water. I pulled out my cup from the backpack, and Brigit did the same. We drank, and I washed my face with a wet handkerchief. I noticed a couple of squirrels scampering about and the children went back to their play.

"We are getting ready to eat. Would you like to join us?" The gypsy man asked.

I looked at Brigit and she nodded. "That sounds great," I replied. "We have some wine that we can add to the meal," I said.

"You can rest here, and we'll be ready to eat shortly," he said.

I had watched our bikes closely, not knowing whether to trust the Gypsies or not. We had our backpacks with us. I looked over at Brigit. She looked good. Her arms, face and legs were sun-tanned and she looked strong. Her short hair looked great and she had on zero jewelry.

"How do you feel?" I asked.

"I feel good, like I am part of a biking team now. It took awhile, but now I'm in the swing of things."

She paused and smiled. "Your French is much improved. You might even pass as a Frenchman."

I smiled back, and she splashed a little water on me. It felt good. "Are you flirting with me?" I asked hopefully.

"I'll never tell," she smiled innocently.

Dinner that night was special. We ate around a fire with various kettles on tripods over the flames. We sat on rocks, makeshift benches and logs. We had soup, bread and apples. I didn't ask what was in the soup, but there were vegetables with potatoes among other things. It tasted good. We drank some wine and soon there was a toast to new friends. We were honored and made to feel at home.

Soon the music started. An accordion player sang along with tunes he played. Later, a guitarist joined in, and several of the girls danced to the music. In the candlelight, it was very entertaining. Brigit seemed to enjoy the spectacle, and I clapped along with the music.

When there was a break in the festivities, Francis, the spokesman of the group, approached us. "It is too late for you to find a place to sleep tonight, so I will offer you a wagon to use. Several of our people are off visiting relatives. We have an empty place for you to spend the night. I will show you where."

Brigit and I followed him to a wagon off to the side of the camp near the stream. We put our bikes leaning against the wagon and hoisted our backpacks onto the wagon. He showed us how to climb aboard and wished us a good-night.

We sat in the wagon and looked at each other. There was little room for anything but the straw mattress. Clothing hung on hooks at one side of the wagon, and a box of food was near the door.

"This should be cozy," Brigit said.

"They must think we are a couple," I said feeling awkward. That would be wonderful, if we were, I thought.

"Well, I can see why they would draw that conclusion," she said.

I thought of the movie I had remembered when I first saw Brigit. In the film the two main characters were forced to share a motel room because of a storm. Clark Gable hung a blanket between the two beds for privacy. There was little room to hang a blanket in this wagon. She moved in the close quarters and accidently bumped her shoulder.

"Ouch," she rubbed her shoulder.

"Sit beside me," I suggested, "and I will rub it and make it better."

I began massaging her shoulder gently, and it seemed to help. Her T-shirt was in the way, and I slid my hand under the shirt. I realized she wore no bra. I became aroused, and my mind was in turmoil. I should have noticed the missing bra, but realized that in my mind she was still the geeky-looking girl covered with make-up and jewelry. But she had changed. She had given all her makeup and jewelry away to lighten her load for biking. Now she smiled, and there was a natural beauty about her. Her face, arms and legs were tanned. Her skin was as smooth as silk. I was aroused by merely touching her. She turned and faced me. Her warm, brown eyes focused on me. I touched her face and hair. I pulled her closer. Our lips touched. We kissed hungrily for a long time. We were both breathing hard.

"I was wondering if you would ever do that," she said breathlessly.

"I'm glad I finally did," I whispered in her ear.

I helped her out of her shirt, and we cuddled on the gypsy's bed. We got out of our clothes and covered ourselves with a soft blanket. The firelight danced on the canvas walls of the wagon, but I hardly noticed. I was busy exploring Brigit's body, which was an exciting mixture of soft curves and hard muscles.

■ ■ ■

The bright sun of the next morning woke us. I felt a cooling breeze. We sat up and peeked out at the camp. It didn't seem to matter that we were stark naked. I looked at Brigit, and she at me. She seemed a bit self-conscious. My focus shifted to her mouth and I kissed her.

"Good morning," she said in a perky voice.

The smell of coffee drifted over us, and I began to dress. I touched her hand. "Last night was wonderful," I said in a husky voice.

"It was very special," she said.

"And today, May sixth, is my twenty-third birthday," I announced.

"We must celebrate," Brigit said in a soft voice.

"I thought we did last night."

"No," she said. "Tonight we will really celebrate, just the two of us."

Francis approached the wagon carrying two coffees. I jumped to the ground and greeted him. I handed one coffee up to Brigit.

"Will you travel today, my friend?" he asked.

"Yes," I replied. "Reims is close according to my map. We want to see the cathedral and try to go west to the other side of the city."

"You should have plenty of time to accomplish that."

We had a simple breakfast of fruit and bread. We bid the gypsies 'aux revoir' and were on our way. Luxembourg and the hill country of the Ardennes were to the northeast, Paris was to the southwest, and the Belgium border to the north. We would travel north and west toward Amiens and on to Abbeville, where Brigit would meet her family. I would continue on to Calais and across the channel to England. I worried about the possibility of military action in the area. The ground was drying up after the Spring rains, and it was the season for action. I wondered if a peace treaty had been signed. I was out of touch with world happenings. In Reims, I would catch up on the political situation.

My thoughts turned to Brigit. Was I in love or was it lust? Did she love me? If so, our timing was lousy. We could be in the wrong place at the wrong time.

We were a good biking team now. We had little baggage. We were now in shape for the grueling ride. I admired Brigit, as we moved quickly along the rough road.

My mind flashed from topic to topic. If the Germans attacked France, would it be the old Von Schlieffen plan with the German strength on its right along the Belgium coast or would they try to blast through the Maginot Line along the French-German border? I remembered my history professor from college and his vivid appraisal of the German offensive, during the Great War in 1914 and the resulting stalemate on the western front. What would the Russians do about all of this? I needed to learn what was happening.

I surveyed the countryside looking for an isolated place where we could rest. Am I nuts, I questioned? It wasn't smart to fall in love with a girl I was going to leave in France, while I returned to the United States.

We rode on. The bicycle chains made a humming sound as we moved down the road. Brigit rode in front and set the pace. I mechanically followed, lost in my thoughts. Late that morning, we arrived at the outskirts of Reims. We searched the horizon for the cathedral steeple. Eventually, we found signs leading us to our destination. The church was breathtaking. We had a feeling of peace and tranquility in the cathedral. The structure was massive and we wandered the grounds and the sanctuary. Finally, we emerged and found a nearby newspaper stand and outdoor café.

Brigit ordered food, and I purchased several newspapers. We

ate, read and sat in the sun. Germany had invaded and subdued Norway and Denmark sometime in April, thus strengthening their defensive position in the Baltic Sea area. French troops in large numbers were forming along the Belgium border and were joined by a British Expeditionary force. It looked to me as if they expected another version of the Von Schlieffen Plan. Perhaps the French and British would move across the Belgium line, if the Germans gave any indication of trying to move into Holland and or Belgium. Nothing, evidently, had set off the fighting, but it could begin any day. It was something to think about.

The food was good. We ate sweet pastry and drank good ole American Cokes. We held hands and admired the nearby cathedral. Later, we purchased some extra food for the night and returned to the road heading in a north-westerly direction. Many French villages lay ahead and eventually Amiens and Brigit's home in Abbeville.

The next few days were a blur. The rides were long and grueling. The nights were full of friendship and love-making. We passed through many villages. Some were run down. In others we enjoyed time in the parks, resting along the banks of fast-running streams. We massaged each others' sore muscles, and we talked. Bridgit wanted me to stay in her house in Abbeville. I had received letters from my parents earlier in Germany encouraging me to return to the U.S. as soon as possible. They feared the possibility· of all-out war. We talked and rode our bikes, on and on.

Eventually, we agreed on a plan. My parents would not

support me forever. I needed to finish school and begin supporting myself. If I stayed in France, what would I do? Brigit talked to her parents by phone and they agreed to pick her up in nearby Amiens. I would continue on to Calais. We would write letters to each other and plan to reunite, whenever it was possible. This was not a suitable answer for either of us, but it was the only one that made any sense.

Our trip was no longer much fun. The idea of separation was hard to accept after our time together on the road. We hugged and touched as if to assure each other of our love. We talked of the future. What would she do in Abbeville, and what would I do in North Carolina? One night we slept in a haystack outside the Village of Charles. The main roads had been crowded with trucks loaded with troopers, and the sky was busy with air traffic. As we lay in the hay trying to sleep that night, we thought we heard bombs and shells exploding far in the distance. Had the war started in earnest? Was our honeymoon over?

■ ■ ■

When we awoke early the next morning, the temperature was in the sixties, and there was a slight breeze from the east. That would help in our ride today. We had arranged to meet Brigit's parents on the cathedral steps around four o'clock. We had only our backpacks left to carry. We had a good laugh thinking back to her four suitcases of clothes. We quickly ate our bread and cheese and sipped our red wine. It wasn't much, but it would have to do.

We rode mostly in silence. By mid-morning we passed through the village of Reciters, and by early afternoon we rode past Villilers-Bretonneux. We were on track to arrive in Amiens at the appointed time. The traffic was heavy even on the country roads. Trucks carrying artillery and troops crowded past us. Supply wagons and troops, even on foot, crossed our route. Mules and horses carried their burdens. Something was going on. It was the middle of May. I hoped I was not too late to make my escape to England. I imagined that Calais must be a focal point of activity. I was losing confidence in my plan.

Finally, we reached Amiens and the cathedral. The building was magnificent. We walked our bikes in front of the sanctuary. Brigit could not find her parents. I watched a young girl sitting on the steps of the cathedral playing a flute. I recognized the music of Debussy. It was absolutely beautiful. I could have listened for hours.

"There they are!" Brigit excitedly proclaimed.

Pulling on my arm, she pointed to a couple on the top step. She waved, and they spotted her. I took Bridget's bike, and she ran to embrace her parents. I stood at the bottom of the steps, holding the bikes and watching the joyous reunion. They hugged, laughed and cried. Her mother was of average height, somewhat thin with long dark hair and middle aged. She was neat looking with an aristocratic air. Her father was tall with graying hair. Brigit had said he was a banker. He fit the stereotype of a well-to-do businessman. They descended the stairs.

"Mother and Dad, this is Mitchell." Brigit introduced me to her parents, Simone and Paul Sauveau. We shook hands vigorously.

"So you are the American who rode a bike across France with my daughter," he said.

Brigit interrupted, "It would be more accurate to say that I rode along with him."

"Where is your baggage, dear?" her mother asked.

"It's a long story, Mother. I'll fill you in later."

Paul pointed to a nearby café with outdoor seating and suggested we sit there. We ordered cold drinks. Brigit told our story to her concerned parents. I told of my plans to go to England, and her father looked shocked.

"The Germans have started their advance against us both in the hill country of the Ardennes and also into the low country of Holland and Belgium. It is too early to determine their objectives. We have both French and British troops by the thousands to meet them. It could be another stalemate like 1914."

I nodded. "I am running out of time, as I feared."

"If the roads are blocked and you cannot make it to Calais, I urge you to come back to Abbeville and stay with us," Paul said. He slipped me his card with his address on it. "Thank you for bringing our daughter home." He shook my hand.

I thought he seemed very emotional.

Mrs. Sauveau hugged me and kissed both of my checks. "Thank you so much and good luck," she whispered.

Brigit walked with me a short distance. She was tearing up and held tightly to my arm. "I love you. Please come back to me," she said looking into my eyes.

"I love you, too, and I will come back. It was a great ride, that I will never forget."

We embraced and kissed, and I walked out of the cathedral plazza, mounted my bike and headed north and east toward Calais.

CHAPTER 9
DUNKIRK

My route took me east of Vignacourt and to Beauval and Doullens. At night, I thought of Brigit, but more and more I listened to the noise of war. Hundreds of trucks passed me during the day and night. I constantly looked to the sky, sighting formations of planes. Most of the time, I could not identify them as British, French or German. Often, I heard artillery explosions. By staying on the back roads, I hoped to avoid the battle. I tried to understand if the action was north or east of me. Sometimes it seemed from the east, from

Luxembourg and the Ardennes. Other times, I was sure it was from the north and Belgium. I wasn't able to sleep much at night, but I did rest and doze off from time to time.

I rode from early morning until it was dark. My meals were hurried, and often I could find very little to eat. By the fourth day I reached the town Hazebrouck. Now it was time for me to head west. According to my worn map, I headed for the villages of Arques, St. Omer, Ardres, and finally Calais. If I was lucky, it would take only two days at most.

Almost immediately after leaving Hazebrouck, I became engulfed in a mass of British and French soldiers retreating toward the coast. I was swept up in this mass of humanity. I walked my bike as it was too crowded to ride. I fell in with a small group of British soldiers. They were dirty and unshaven. "Will you be making a stand somewhere down the road?" I asked.

"Who knows," said one of the men.

"Hell!" said another. "We've got no organization, and the officers are nowhere to be seen," added the soldier with a limp.

"This is a mob. There is no discipline here," added a third soldier. "It's every man for himself, mate."

Some French soldiers joined in with us. I overheard one telling how they would get to the coast as fast as they could. Later, I hooked up with another British unit, although there were many French soldiers and some civilians among us. At least the British had good rations that they were willing to share. The Luftwaffe was a constant menace. They strafed the clogged up roads and bombed British and French trucks and tanks. Riding a bike became dangerous. I rode half asleep dodging damaged vehicles and bomb holes in the roads. The inevitable finally occurred. I reacted slowly to a shell hole in the road, hit the hole in an awkward way, sprawled to the ground and rolled over into the ditch. My backpack had offered some cushion, but I was dazed. The breath had been knocked out of my lungs. I gasped for air and reached for my injured shoulder, as I sat on the ground. I looked up to see a lorry roll over my bike, severely damaging the wheels. I stood looking at the mess that once was my bike.

After a while, I started walking. All I had now was my backpack. Shells burst around me with unbearable noise. I walked in the cover of the woods when I could. My arm ached. Sometimes I got a ride in a truck until it ran out of gas or was bombed by the German air. I was frightened but had little choice except to keep on with the retreat. I fit right in with the British soldiers. Most of them were young, scared and inexperienced in battle. As we trudged on, I thought of the possibility of becoming a German prisoner or worse yet, a victim of a German sniper or Luftwaffe attack.

I hiked on and finally saw marshland. I was nearing the coast. At one point I fell in with some Frenchmen. They wondered if the wetlands would slow the German Panzer units. The tank treads might not be as efficient along the coast. The French were aware of the speed and armor of the German tanks. So was I, after listening to the soldiers. The French and British had nothing with which to stop them. Their tanks were no match to the German Panzer units. The Germans seemed unstoppable.

I wondered if we could make it to the coast in time to escape.

When it got dark, the Germans hit us with both air attacks and artillery. I found a place in the trees. There was a depression in the land with broken trees and logs piled together. I crawled into a cave-like place and watched carefully for fire. If there were flames, I would have to abandon my position. If German troops arrived, I would have to surrender. If the bombardment ever stopped, I would quickly head for the coast. All I could do was cover my ears and stay down near the ground. Debris constantly fell all around me. I think there was another soldier nearby, but I couldn't tell for sure. There were screams of pain and frightened soldiers scattered all around me. I thought of Gretchen and her soldier boyfriend. I wondered if they were married. I was glad that Brigit had gone home and didn't have to go through this hell. I remembered thinking about some of my college buddies and the stupid pranks we played on each other. From those thoughts I moved to Dr. Thomas, my favorite professor. He was organized, smart and very entertaining. He wore a sport coat and tie each day. Class began when he entered the room and walked to the lectern, where he placed his papers. The talking subsided to a hush. He greeted the class and explained the topic for the day, and how he would approach it. During the Nazi bombardment it helped me think of the past rather than worry constantly about where the bombs would hit.

I remembered how Dr. Thomas talked as he moved across the front of the classroom. He went to the chalk board and then he sat on the table next to the lectern. Some of the time he fiddled with his glasses. Often, he scratched the bridge of his nose with the edge of the glasses. To make a point, he would emphasize an idea by waving his glasses. I was not sure he really needed glasses to see, but he sure put on a good show. Sometimes, he used sarcasm. He had a funny comeback for students' comments, and he laughed with us. He had maps posted on the walls of the classroom, where he would dart from one to the other banging on them to make a point.

"You never heard of Bosnia or Herzegovina?" He asked in disbelief. Off to the maps he went. The next thing I knew, he was yelling, "Drang Nach Osten." This guy was crazy, I thought. But we rounded up some German language majors and got the translations. "Grossdeutschland" was easy for us to figure out.

A bomb exploded very close to me and I thought maybe my tree cave would collapse on me. I was frightened but forced myself to think about Dr. Thomas.

One day he got started on the German Chiefs of Staff before the War in 1914. It was a lecture that I memorized. It dealt with Germany's dilemma of a two front war with the French and British on the West and the Russians on the East.

Von Molke, the elder, served as German Chief of Staff from 1857 to 1888. He had been a great soldier in Prussia's wars against Austria in 1866 and France in 1870-71. His broad strategy involved lightning war on both fronts, hitting the Russians first, as they were slow to mobilize. Then a decisive battle would follow against the French, with a peace treaty to end the war. Thus he thought in terms of limited war with a quick treaty.

Frederick Von Schlieffen served from 1891 to 1905. He had

emerged as a heroic, mythic figure in Germany after the wars against Austria and France. As commander-in-chief, he developed an entirely new strategy to deal with a two front war. He was struck by the military weakness Russia had displayed at the turn of the century in her war against Japan. Also, he observed the poor transportation system in Russia, and the fact that they could slowly withdraw their troops into their vast interior. Von Schlieffen felt that they represented very little offensive threat, and that Germany should focus on the French first and the Russians second. This represented a complete reversal of German military thinking. The new Von Schlieffen Plan called for a strong right flank of seven armies to hit quickly through Holland and Belgium and south along the French coast, then to swing up under Paris and knock the French out of the war. Then Germany could deal with Russia.

In 1906, Von Molke the Younger took over the office as Chief of Staff. When the war began in 1914, he altered the Von Schlieffen Plan allowing only four armies in the German right flank.

In my mind, I could see Professor Thomas quickly move to the map and point out that right flank. First, he would wave his glasses at the map and then thoughtfully scratch his nose. The Allies, he would continue, were able to stop the weakened right flank of the Germans, and the Western front became a quagmire of attrition. The Germans eventually defeated the Russians in 1917, but were not able to successfully defeat the Allies when masses of fresh American troops landed in the West in 1917 and 1918. The Germans eventually sued for peace in 1918 and suffered the wrath of the Allies with the Versailles Treaty.

In military circles after the War, conversations centered on "what if?" Suppose the Germans had utilized the Von Schlieffen Plan to its fullest. Would the Germans have realized a quick victory in the West and thus changed the course of history? The more forward looking generals wondered about the next war and German war strategy. For me, a university student, that seemed years away and was the least of my concerns at that point in my life. Now I was living through the "what if." I guessed the Germans had faked a full-fledged drive through the Lowlands and instead launched an all-out attack from the Ardennes hill country through northern France. If that was true, it was working to perfection.

Sometime during this disaster I had fallen asleep. At daybreak I awoke. It was relatively quiet. I was hungry and dirty and slowly crawled out of my hole. When I stood I was shaky, but I soon adjusted to the situation. I looked all around and saw some corpses and got sick to my stomach. I saw body parts and deep craters in the ground. I came to a road and a partially destroyed lorry. It had been a supply truck with rations of food. I filled my backpack with rations and found a canteen. Some fires smoldered, as I continued my journey to the sea. Hopefully, Calais was close by, but I really had no idea where I was. A group of soldiers came my way. I hid until I realized they were British. I hailed them and joined their ranks. We walked, rested and talked. They were as confused as I was about our location. I shared some of my rations with them. They were headed west just as I was. A tall thin man named Harvey seemed to be in charge of the group. He was a lieutenant with reddish hair and moustache. All the men were as dirty as I was. Lt. Harvey got us going, and we trudged on towards the sun in the west. The roads were full of debris, stalled trucks and damaged tanks. Fallen trees blocked passage and pot holes were all around. Our progress was slow. We stopped to search the trucks for food, weapons and ammo, usually finding little of value.

We walked onward. Soon, two men emerged from the woods with their hands in the air. They were wearing remnants of French army uniforms. I conversed with them, and we swapped stories of our last few days. All of my new friends were somewhat skeptical about my story of being a graduate history student caught in the midst of this unfortunate retreat. We walked some more, seeing more destruction. Civilians clogged our passage. They pulled carts and carried small children. Other allied soldiers joined our ranks. It was not a raucous group. The soldiers were tired and dirty, solemn and quiet, but mostly serious as we made our way toward the coast.

Off to the side of the road the land was moist and swampy. One of the French soldiers said that he knew this area fairly well, as he had vacationed in this area as a child.

"This is not good tank country," he pointed out. "The Panzers will get bogged down in this muck."

It dawned on me that we hadn't heard any German tanks in the past day or so, only battered British and French vehicles.

"I hope you're right," I said to the soldier.

"But," the Frenchman pointed out, "that probably means

more German air."

We hiked on and caught up with a group of soldiers in front of us. They were holding up a sign they had found on the ground. It read, "Bergues City Limits."

"Ah," the Frenchman said. "It is a small town very close to the port of Dunkirk. We are almost to the coast."

"Finally," I uttered. "Which way is Calais from here?"

"It is a little southwest of Dunkirk. Why do you want to go there?" the soldier asked.

"Well, I want to get a boat to England," I answered.

"So do I," said one of the English.

"Me, too," chimed in another.

I realized how dumb my comment was.

Another soldier added sarcastically: "We'll follow you, mate. Lead the way."

The Frenchman added, "Dunkirk is a port like Calais, not much farther from England than Calais. But, you're not likely to find someone with a boat willing to take you to England."

"Yeah, I know," I said and studied my feet as I pressed on.

Airplanes that appeared to be German Stuka dive bombers passed overhead. In the distance to the west we heard explosions. German air seemed everywhere. Often we rushed to the woods for cover, so that the Luftwaffe would not spot us. I moved in a daze. I was tired. My arm hurt from the bike fall. I was dirty and hungry. I drank the last of my water from a canteen I had picked up from the road side.

"How much farther to Dunkirk?" someone asked.

"It can't be far. I can smell the smoke probably from the

Dunkirk harbor," was the reply.

An hour later our group stumbled into the city. There was much smoke and several fires burned out of control. Soldiers were everywhere. Some of us went into a bar. It was crowded with men in a quarrelsome mood. I ordered a beer and paid triple the normal price for it. A fight broke out in the bar, and I decided to drink outside. Several Frenchmen joined me in conversation.

"We just got back from the port," a Frenchman said. There are fires everywhere, but there is so much smoke that the Luftwaffe boys are having trouble spotting the ships. A lot of English vessels are taking on their soldiers and making ready for the return trip to Dover."

"Maybe I'll give it a try," I offered.

"No luck there," the tall Frenchman replied. "You need proof of your English unit before they will let you on."

"So what do we do, sit here and wait for the Germans to come get us?" I asked.

Another Frenchman joined in. "I talked to somebody who thinks he will go to the beach just outside of town and hope a stray boat will pick him up. Just north of here is a spot called Bray Dunes that he might try."

Another Frenchmen added, "Evidently there are lots of ships and small boats from England evacuating people from the beaches as well as the piers at the port. All kinds of boats: fireboats, launches, pleasure craft, hospital ships and destroyers, anything that floats."

"Sounds like it might be worth a try," I said.

Three Frenchmen and I decided to walk to the coast and hope to get lucky. It was getting dark. Drunks were everywhere. We followed the setting sun and eventually came to a sandy beach. Others were already there. Some had dug into the sand and had a fox hole to sleep in. Others were trying to use trucks and other debris to make a pier-like structure into the water.

A boat came along the shore apparently looking for survivors. A mass of men rushed to the water's edge yelling for help. About ten swimmers splashed into the deeper water, waving to people on board the boat. It looked like a pleasure yacht and only had room for the swimmers. I felt at a loss. My arm hurt, and no way could I swim into deep water.

In the dark, I walked farther along the beach where I found more men: British and French, and all kinds of makeshift structures that reached out into the sea. I heard some music and walked in that direction. I came to a fox hole in the sand, and there sat an Englishman playing "Roll Out the Barrel" on his harmonica.

"May I sit and rest," I asked and he offered me a nearby hole in the sand.

"There are enough foxholes," he said.

I was exhausted. I sat in the sand and tried to figure out what to do. The moonlight allowed me to survey the shore. There were all sorts of abandoned military equipment. I could see trucks, artillery pieces, backpacks, and weapons of all kinds. It was a mess, an army in disarray. "This place looks like a junkyard," I said.

Another boat came by and hundreds rushed to the shore. A

few lucky ones clamored aboard.

"If you are hungry, help yourself to any of the abandoned backpacks along the beach," offered the harmonica guy.

I followed his advice and rummaged among the debris. I found army rations, a half full canteen and a flashlight, which I stuffed into my own backpack. At least, I could eat for another day or so. I returned to my foxhole. I spread my newly acquired blanket in the hole and made myself a bed of sorts. Sleep came for short amounts of time. That helped. Other boats came during the night. I hoped my arm would be better the next day, and maybe I could join the swimmers. I drifted in and out of sleep.

The next morning was a repeat of the previous day. Hundreds of men were trying to decide what to do. A lot of small boats came during the day and many of the English soldiers were able to secure their escape. The Luftwaffe returned from time to time strafing and bombing the men on the beach. Fortunately, the sand deadened the explosives and diminished the effect of the bombs. I walked farther down the beach trying to get away from the large concentrations of men.

I walked on. The sun was hot, but there was a fresh breeze. Little smoke from the fires in Dunkirk drifted in my direction. Towards dusk, I came upon a practically deserted section of beach. Much equipment was strewn along the beach, and some makeshift piers dotted the shore line. The men who were here must have been picked up. It was peaceful. No swearing or drunken men appeared, only the tide washing ashore with seagulls and other birds searching for food. At sunset, I made my way out into the water along one of the makeshift piers that jutted out into the sea. Men had pushed trucks into the sea and piled other equipment on top to form these piers. When I reached the end, I held onto the remains of some sort of cart. It rested on a submerged truck that was in water over my head. I rested my pack on a pole that stuck up into the air. Eventually, I figured out how to sit on one of the wheels of the cart.

As I settled in, I heard the engine of a single airplane. It seemed to be flying along the coast looking for a target. I recognized the now familiar swastika painted on the wing tips. It was a Stuka. If it came my way, I planned to slide into the water and hide. I didn't realize the speed of the aircraft, and before I knew it, the plane was headed directly at me with guns blazing. I jumped into the water and tried to hide out of sight. The Nazi made one pass at me and flew on to the north. I breathed a sigh of relief only to notice that the water was red around me. I panicked and climbed back on the wagon. I had a flesh wound in my left thigh. I had to stop the bleeding. I rigged a tourniquet and eventually was able to wrap part of my shirt around my leg to stop the bleeding.

Now it was dark, and I sat half in, and half out of the water trying to keep my wound dry. In the dark, the moon and stars shown brightly. The water seemed calm, more so than before the attack. I got out the flashlight to make sure it worked. It did. I imagined sharks drawn to my blood and waiting to pounce on me. I had gotten too much sun during the day, and now I had the chills. What a mess I was in! I tried to stay calm. I looked out to sea and thought I heard something. Later I could see lights, but they were far out to sea. It looked like a large ship about a quarter of a mile out. I flashed my light and yelled but to no avail. I needed to get further out, but I couldn't figure how to accomplish that. I remember praying for a smaller boat to rescue me. It was relatively quiet. Small waves rubbed against the cart. I dozed off to sleep. I awoke later, but it was dark and calm. I found a safe place to put my flashlight and left it on.

■ ■ ■

I awoke with a gentle jolt. There was a motor and voices. "Is he alive?" one said.

"He just moved his head," said a female voice.

I could barely see one person leaning over the side of the motor yacht trying to get a grip on the cart pole that I was leaning against.

"We saw your light," the man said.

I reached for my flashlight and shown it on the man, an older person with gray hair. He looked strong and rugged. I shifted the light to the other person. It was a young woman, too young to be his wife.

"I must be dreaming," I said. "It's a dream come true."

"Give me your backpack. Can you get up and climb aboard the boat?"

I was stiff, but my adrenaline was flowing. I half stood and reached for the boat rail. Two other men grabbed my arm and helped me into the boat. I collapsed into a cushioned seat and looked around. It seemed to be a pleasure boat or perhaps a fishing vessel. Four other men were down below asking who I was.

"Is he French or British?" one asked.

"Neither," I said. "I am American."

"How did you get out here?" another inquired.

"Save that for later," said the older man.

They pushed off from the makeshift pier and out to sea we went.

"Do we have anymore room?" the woman asked.

A voice replied, "We have four below deck and five on deck."

"We could take two more," the older man calculated.

I sat in a dream world. I wanted to cry, and I wanted to shout out in celebration. I did neither.

"What's your name, mate?" asked one of the soldiers.

"Mitchell," I replied.

"Well, welcome aboard , Mitchell, or should I say Mitch?" asked the girl.

"Mitch is fine."

We were motoring along the coast looking for more passengers. I saw several trucks piled up on the beach. This looked familiar to me.

"I think I slept here last night," I blurted out. "Can you get in closer?"

We crept slowly toward the shore. Five men stood solemnly on the beach.

"Swim out to us," shouted the older man.

"We can't swim," called back one of the men. "Just leave us."

"Hell, no," said another man from the rear of the boat. "Captain, pull as close to shore as you can, and some of us will swim ashore and bring them back."

The captain of the boat did as he was told. Six men slid over the side and swam ashore. It took some coaxing, but soon they returned with the reluctant non-swimmers. We pulled them aboard. Blankets and towels were distributed to the wet soldiers. Eventually, the young woman handed out cups of hot tea. The captain once again headed out to sea.

"We need to get to buoy number six near Calais," said the captain. "To your left is Dunkirk, but it is too dark to see anything more than the flickering fires and the smell of smoke. From buoy number six, we head to Dover."

As dawn broke, we passed the buoy. I was startled by the sounds of a harmonica. It was my friend from yesterday on the beach.

"I thought I recognized you," he said to me.

"Keep playing; it sounds great."

As the sun rose, it became light enough to see other boats and ships.

"I've never seen the channel so calm," said the captain. "What a stroke of luck."

We were riding low in the water with the heavy load we were carrying. I enjoyed the smell of the sea. There were airplanes above, but they focused on the larger ships with hundreds of men aboard. The girl was looking at me now that it was light enough to see.

"You're wounded!" she exclaimed. "You're bleeding!"

"It's nothing but a flesh wound," I murmured.

She removed my makeshift bandage and began cleaning out

the open wound. She applied disinfectant and sturdy dressing from her first-aid kit. As she worked on me, I watched her quick efficient hands

"Are you a nurse?" I asked.

"I've had training, but I am not a nurse," she said softly.

She had long brown hair and a fair complexion. Her blue eyes were striking. She seemed shy but acted in a take-charge demeanor. She half smiled and sat back to admire her work.

"That should do it, Mitch."

"Thank you uh…" I stammered.

"Liz," she added.

"Thank you, Liz. I shall never forget you," I looked her in the eye. My reward was a big beautiful smile.

"What are you going to do when we get to Dover?" she asked.

"I'm not sure. I have been so focused on getting there that I am drawing a blank. Let's see. I will need to meet with the U.S. ambassador and make arrangements to return to America."

"You know, there is a war going on," she said, "and you need time for your wound to heal."

"I also have something wrong with my shoulder. I got hurt when I took a fall off a bicycle."

"You are a mess! Anything else wrong with you?"

"Nothing comes to mind." I wanted to add that I was tired, hungry, lonely and needed a bath, but I kept that to myself.

I must have dozed off, because I was awakened by a cheer from the men on board. They had spotted British planes above, and there was no sign of the Stukas.

"We are almost home," shouted the harmonica player.

"It won't be long," another yelled.

We continued our trip in silence. All eyes searched the horizon for land.

After a while a quiet voice said, "There they are." It was a sound of almost mystical reverence. I searched ahead with my eyes trying to determine what everyone saw but me. Then I saw the White Cliffs of Dover. I started to ask what was the big deal, but for once I kept my mouth shut. When I got a better view, I realized why this was such a cherished sight. I looked around the boat. Liz had tears in her eyes and several of the men wiped their moist faces.

One of the men spoke in a forceful voice. "We're home, laddies, we're home!"

CHAPTER 10
CONVALESCING IN SOUTHERN ENGLAND

Liz's father skillfully maneuvered the boat to a dock. He tied up, and we began disembarking. Each man thanked the skipper of the boat. By now they called him by his first name: John.

"Mate, you and your daughter have saved my life," one soldier said.

"Captain, we owe you everything," another added.

"You deserve a medal for this," a third man shouted.

"Good luck to all of you," John replied.

As I moved to leave the ship, Liz stood in my way.

My shoulder and leg both ached, and I felt weak.

"I've talked with my father," she said, "and we both agree that you should stay at our home until your wounds heal. I think your leg is infected, and a doctor needs to look at your shoulder."

I didn't know what to say. I realized I needed time to recuperate before I traveled to the United States. I was so surprised by Liz's offer that I wasn't prepared to answer her.

"At any rate," she continued, "we can go ashore and eat, while our boat is refueled and inspected."

"I don't even know where you live," I managed to say.

The two of us got off the boat and waited on the pier for her dad. I found a bench and sat down. It was hard to believe I had made it to England. For months, I had been on the run. Escaping from Germany, getting a glimpse of Switzerland from a train, and a long bike ride across France to Dunkirk proved quite an adventure. I wondered how Gretchen and Brigit were doing. I missed the wonderful people of Germany and France. My adventure was all behind me, or so I thought. I looked forward to going home. But first, there was England. I needed to call my parents and make arrangements with the U.S. Consul in London to get the proper papers signed and a ticket to America. I also realized that I needed to rest and get my shoulder and leg back in shape.

Liz interrupted my thoughts.

"Here comes Dad now. We can go into town."

It was a great feeling to step onto English soil. I felt I was among friends. They would help me recover. Then I could travel safely to the U.S. The streets of Dover were crowded. There were flowers in abundance. Members of the Red Cross welcomed the men. They lined up in units and marched like heroes returning from the battlefield. These men had lived to fight another day. From the determined looks on their faces, they would be a tough foe for the Germans.

We found a café on a side street and ordered a breakfast of eggs sunny-side up, toast, jam and meat. I wolfed down my meal like I hadn't eaten in weeks. I didn't normally drink coffee, but today I did. It was warm and delicious. John looked me over and asked about my leg. It hurt like blazes, and I knew I needed to see a doctor.

"Our family physician will take care of you." he said. "He will treat the infection. Soon you will be on your way."

John held out his hand, and I shook it gratefully. Without letting go of his hand, I took Liz's hand with my left hand and looked them both in the eyes. I got a little emotional and told them how much I appreciated everything.

"If the rest of the English are like you two, I'm afraid Mr. Hitler has taken on more than he can handle," I said in a soft, choked-up voice. My eyes were moist with tears. Liz hugged me, and her father put his arm on my shoulder.

"Let's go home, daughter," John spoke out, and we headed for the dock.

"Wait until you meet mom," Liz laughed. "You will start feeling sorry for ole Adolph."

The boat was refueled, and we prepared for the trip home.

John explained that they had a small farm just outside the town of Rye. It was located southwest of Dover near the Coast.

"It was once an important Channel port," he said, "but during the 1700s the river silted up to the extent the town is now several kilometers inland."

I tried to comprehend the description of the town, but I was drowsy and having trouble staying awake. My leg hurt, and I was hot with fever.

■ ■ ■

The next several days were a blur to me. I remembered I was in bed, my T-shirt and shorts were wet with perspiration, and I was burning up. Someone came to see me. I presumed it was a doctor. I vaguely remembered taking pills. At one point, I speculated I might lose my leg. It was a hellish time. Then one morning I felt better. I awoke, and I wasn't sweating as much as usual. My fever had broken. All I wanted to do was drink water or juice. I was weak and needed to sleep a lot, but I was feeling better.

I heard the door to my room open and in walked an older version of Liz. "My name is Anna," she said. "I am Liz's mother." She must have been in her late forties. She was of average height with long brown hair. She was attractive, energetic and quick in her movements. "How do you feel?" she asked.

"I feel better," I said.

"You had us worried for a while, but now you look better." She smiled and touched my forehead to check my temperature. "What can I get you?" she asked.

"I would like some juice or water," I replied. "I want you to know how much I appreciate all that you have done."

"You just take it easy, and we'll get you well in a jiffy. Besides," she said, "Liz has done most of the nursing."

Anna exited the room, and I was left with my thoughts. The room was rather small. I could see out of the only window in the room onto a lush garden with flowers and bushes in bloom. There were shade trees and a bench. The sun was shining brightly. It was a beautiful view.

A little later, Liz came in with juice and water and a bright smile. "Ah, you look much better," she said. "I brought a pile of London newspapers for you to read, so that you can get caught up on recent events." She placed the papers next to my bed.

"Was there a doctor?" I asked.

"That was Doctor Sullivan. He's our family doctor. He cleaned out your wound and put dressings on it. He showed me how to change it. You need to keep it clean so that it will heal."

"Are you my nurse, Liz?"

"You might say that, although mother helps also."

"Thank you so much for your help. I can never repay you for all your time and trouble." I drank some juice and ate soda crackers. The salt tasted good.

Liz took the glass and gave me a newspaper. "This is the oldest of the papers. You probably should read them in chronological order," she said.

I took the paper and began reading. It was about the heroic

French and British troops who defended the outer perimeter at Dunkirk against the Germans, buying time, while the rest of the men tried to escape. This was called Operation Dynamo, I learned. The British sent big and small ships to the rescue. I was one of the lucky ones. At this point, I lowered the paper and closed my eyes.

Hours later I awoke and looked into Anna's eyes.

"How do you feel?" she asked.

"Weak," was the first word that came to mind.

I thought for a while. "How long has it been since your husband and Liz rescued me?"

"Five days."

I was shocked. "It seemed like a day or so ago. I need to get out of here before I wear out my welcome; that is, if I haven't already."

"Don't worry about it," she answered. A mischievous smile came upon her pretty face. "Do you know that my daughter slept with you on several of those nights?"

"What?" I didn't know if she was kidding or what.

"Yes," she said, "you had the chills. We gave you lots of blankets but you continued with the shakes. She crawled in bed with you, and her body heat helped."

"I don't know what to say."

"Don't worry. I was here the whole time." She laughed. "You read your newspapers, and one of us will return shortly."

I read the part about Operation Dynamo. I thought about the troops returning to Dover and Southampton and various ports along the southeast coast. It must have been a wondrous time to have made it back to England, but it was a disturbing feeling to have been involved in such a massive retreat. I wondered if 25,000 men or even 50,000 had escaped. I read on about the various experiences that some of the men had. I looked out the window. A nice soft rain was falling on the yard. I noticed some plants and guessed they were raspberries or blueberries. I wondered if it was too early to pick the berries. I sure could eat some. I was beginning to get my appetite back. That was a good sign. I continued to read the newspapers.

Doctor Sullivan visited me the next day. He was a tall, thin man of about sixty years. He was soft spoken, professional and thorough. He carefully removed the bandages and inspected my wound.

"It's coming along nicely," he observed, "but it will probably take another ten days for a complete healing. You should walk around the house and gradually lengthen your forays around the neighborhood. Eventually you will regain your strength."

I thanked the Doctor and tried to make arrangements to pay him. He would have none of it.

He added, "From what I've heard, you deserve a medal, not a bill. I'm too old to fight the battles, but I try to do my part around here." He packed his bag and rubbed his chin. "You know I forgot to shave today. Anyway, your leg will heal nicely. I'm not sure about your shoulder. It might be partially dislocated. I would have a specialist check it out, if it gives you any trouble."

"Thanks, Doctor, I appreciate all you have done."

■ ■ ■

The next day I felt stronger. I walked around the house and sat up reading and writing letters home and to the U.S. Ambassador, Joseph Kennedy, for help in my return to the U.S.

The following day was sunny and mild. I took a short walk around the yard, and I admired the various flowers, fruit trees and plants. I spotted apple and cherry blossoms. It was a glorious day. I sat in the garden on a bench and read the newspaper. I couldn't believe it. Some estimates of up to 333,000 men were reported saved as a result of Operation Dynamo. It was a lot bigger effort than I had thought. I was very impressed by British efficiency and determination. Liz joined me in the garden, and I asked why she had been involved in Dynamo.

"Well, it's a long story," she said with a sigh. "As a teenager, I always went fishing with my dad. I learned how to maneuver the boat and do all the jobs to help him. I know I was a big help to him. When he decided to go to Dunkirk, I insisted on accompanying him. My mother was not thrilled about my going, but I convinced her that there was little danger. I could keep Dad awake and even spell him at the wheel, when we were on the open sea. We have a radio and we could keep in touch with her."

"Weren't you scared at all?" I asked.

"When I saw the German dive bombers, I was. But we were such a small boat, they didn't bother with us."

"Do you realize that you saved the lives of eleven men who probably would have died on the shores of France?" I asked, filled with admiration.

"Well, you eleven men had better start saving England."

"That's the problem. I can't do a damn thing with these wounds," I said out of frustration.

A fluffy kitten came around the path and sat at Liz's feet. She picked it up.

"This is Queenie," she announced. Liz rubbed the cat's nose. "She has been staying out of your way so far, but I think she realizes you are part of the family now."

"Wow! I'm honored," I said. scratching Queenie's head.

We sat in silence for a while.

"I'm planning a short excursion for us soon," Liz said.

"Where to?"

"It will be a surprise, but it will be fun."

"I can hardly wait." I beamed a great big smile.

■ ■ ■

It rained the next day, and I was confined to the house. I tried to do push-ups but that was painful because of my damaged shoulder. I did sit ups and read. I wrote a letter home and watched the rain. I wondered if the rain was a sign of trouble as in some of Hemingway's books. My brooding thoughts were interrupted when Liz returned from her job around noon. Her dad was working, and her mom was shopping.

"Would you have lunch with me?" Liz asked.

"I'd love to, I'm sick of lying around."

Liz poured lemonade. I remained silent, not at all happy with myself.

"We have chicken salad sandwiches and pretzels. Is that ok?"

"Lovely," I answered.

We sat in the screened-in porch and watched the rain.

Queenie, the cat, made her entrance and jumped into Liz's lap. Liz took a bit of chicken and gave Queenie a bite. I ate several bites and took a sip of lemonade. And then I realized how hungry I had been and how much better I felt after eating.

"Ah, this is the life," I said.

Liz smiled at me, and the cat got another piece of the chicken.

"What do you do during the summer?" I asked.

"I just finished college," she explained, "and since my dad is a school principal, I have decided to teach elementary school and work in the travel business on the side. Being a tour leader is a long range plan since the tourist business will not be active until well after the war ends."

"I would say you have plenty of time to prepare for your travel job."

"I have a lot to learn, but it is going well. In fact, you can help me out. I am preparing to lead tours around southeast England. I might have a busload of people to show Brighton, Hastings, Rye or Canterbury. I have to give a little background history to the group each time we make a stop. I specialized in history and education in college, so that helps. Otherwise, the agency gives me material to learn. I have to be ready for all kinds of questions."

"That sounds very interesting, but how can I help?"

"You can go with me to these places and listen to my speech and then make suggestions on how to improve it."

"OK, it's a deal," I said. "When do we start?"

"When it stops raining."

"I'm not sure that will ever happen," I said sarcastically.

The rain continued and Queenie ate most of Liz's sandwich. I ate all of mine. She asked me about my life. I filled her in on my interest in history and plans for the future.

"On second thought, I'm not sure I want to make speeches to you. You will ask me hard questions, and I won't know the answers."

"I will be kind, I assure you," I promised.

■ ■ ■

The next day was clear and sunny. Liz decided that we should go to Hastings, a coastal town southwest of Rye. The bus ride was not long and certainly delightful. The people on the bus were friendly and polite. In Hastings we saw a thriving fishing port. There were tall wooden buildings where fishing nets were stored. The nearby beach was rocky rather than sandy. When we walked along the shoreline, Liz told me about the cliffs and the caves where smugglers stored contraband at one time.

She got very serious and told me that in the year 1066 William the Conqueror and his French army had invaded England. They had landed along the southern coast of England with the idea of capturing the cities of London and Winchester. King Harold of England and his army confronted the French near Hastings, where a great battle took place. Harold was killed when he took an arrow in the eye. The French went on to victory. This proved to be the last successful invasion of England. Later, she explained, this battle was commemorated by a beautiful tapestry which is housed in Normandy, France, in the city of Bayeux.

We returned to the quaint port and the "old town" section of the city, where we saw interesting shops, a bakery and several tea shops. We enjoyed our walk and decided to have tea. The shop we picked had a blue and white theme with lace curtains and dainty table cloths.

"I don't suppose they serve hamburgers here," I said.

"No, silly, but they do have wonderful hot tea and scones. I'll show you what to order."

She smiled and ordered our food. It was a nice place, comfortable with colorful flowers everywhere. It was a very peaceful spot.

When we were settled in with our food and drink, she looked at me with a pensive smile. "OK, let's have it. What did you think of my presentation?"

"Well," I said, stalling for time, while I tried to think of what to say. "I learned a lot. I'm certainly no expert on local history or on public speaking, but it went well. You gave me the important information but not too much. You provided just enough facts, so that I might actually remember most of it, but not an overload of information. You spoke clearly and with enthusiasm. You sounded like you enjoyed what you were doing. You were very positive and pleasant to look at," I smiled and winked at her. My gosh, I thought, was I flirting? I cleared my throat and pushed on. "My only suggestions would be to talk a little faster and try to work some humor into your presentation. You have a great laugh, and you need to share it with the group."

She waited until she was sure I was finished. "Thank you," she said thoughtfully. "I expected something like that was 'ok' or 'good,' but the thoroughness of your comments was really very constructive. I liked what you had to say, all of it." She looked at me straight in the eyes, smiled and winked back at me.

Wow, I thought. Is she flirting with me? I was stunned and pleased. I must have been embarrassed too.

She looked at me. "You must be getting a little sun today. Your face is red."

"Yeah, that must be it," I said. "And, you must have agreed with my comments, because now you have added humor to your talk."

We both smiled. I paid the bill and we made our way to the bus stop. I held her arm and helped her onto the bus. It was crowded and there was only one seat left. She sat and I stood for the entire bus trip back to Rye. We walked in the rain back to her house. Like a good tour director, she had brought umbrellas along.

■ ■ ■

My daily routine started with breakfast with my new family and reading the newspaper. I tried to stay out of the way, while John went off to work and Anna and Liz left to shop, do volunteer work and their jobs. I wrote letters and followed the war closely by listening to the news on the radio. Germany had sealed off her northern border by occupying Norway and Denmark. Sweden remained neutral. Poland was split in half with Russia gaining the eastern part and Germany the western half. The Nazis occupied Czechoslovakia. Now Belgium, Holland, and France had fallen. As the Germans gathered men and equipment across the Channel, it seemed clear that England was next on the Nazi timetable.

I needed to get home. My wounds were almost healed. It was difficult to arrange transportation to America. The U.S. Ambassador, Joseph Kennedy, whom I had written for help, had passed my case on to a man named Waldo Bayley at the Embassy in London. He was to notify me when my papers and transportation were arranged. Until then, I filled my days with reading, working in the yard and trying to get back in good physical condition. I also helped Liz prepare for her part-time job as tour director.

"Today we are going to Canterbury," she announced.

"Great," I said, "I've always wondered what that was all about."

The bus trip was longer than that to Hastings. We sat close together. I felt that I wanted to touch her. I noticed that her hand was on her leg next to me. Without a word I took her hand in mine. I smiled into her eyes, and she put her head on my shoulder. This was a wonderful feeling. We squeezed hands, and I rubbed her arm and then sat in silence, contentedly looking out the window, as the green countryside flashed by. I was dazzled by her beauty and companionship.

When we arrived in Canterbury, we went straight to the cathedral. It was amazing. I walked through the structure in awe. Liz told me how Canterbury had been a Roman town in the early years. By 597 A.D. the Pope had dispatched St. Augustine to the town to convert the Anglo Saxons to Christianity. The Cathedral was built in 1070 and underwent many restorations. She showed me the medieval stained glass including that of Methuselah, the one-thousand year-old religious figure. I experienced the shrine of Saint Thomas Becket, the famous choir facility, Trinity Chapel, the great Cloister and many other interesting sites. I was amazed at Liz's knowledge of the Cathedral. Outside we saw the Bell Tower and parts of the old town.

Mercifully, we stopped for lunch. Since it was sunny outside, we ate our chicken salad sandwiches in the shade of a large tree. I collapsed into a chair, promising myself not to move for at least an hour. I sipped my tea, no ice, and relaxed with my favorite person. She seemed chipper as ever, unfazed by the morning's excursion.

"Don't you ever get tired?" I asked.

"I really don't think about it. I am concentrating on leading the tour and telling you the background on what you are seeing."

"Well, I think you are a perfect guide. Your rate of speech was just right, slow enough for me to comprehend what you are saying but fast enough to keep my interest. There were only a couple of times when I stopped listening and just enjoyed the beauty of the moment."

She smiled and turned red with embarrassment.

"I have good news," she said. "The Cathedral choir will give a short performance at one o'clock. Would you like to hear the concert?"

"As long as I can sit, I would love to go."

Back to the cathedral we went. I was surprised that it was a boys' choir. Their music was beautiful. The setting of the church, the acoustics, the quality of their voices, and the organ accompaniment all added up to a very pleasant time. A number of people attended the performance and willingly showed their appreciation of the music.

After the concert, we walked back towards the bus station. We had some time to kill before we could board the bus. We found a tea house, sipped some hot tea and talked of the day's activities. Later, we made our way to the bus depot. Liz remarked that it looked like rain, but it did not start falling until we were on board the vehicle. There were very few people on the bus. We chose to sit near the back. There wasn't much to see out the window, and it was almost dark outside with black clouds. We settled into our seats. Without thinking I took her hand. We faced each other. I gently pushed some of her hair out of her face and touched her face. Her hand touched my face, and I kissed her. I could not stop. She kissed me back.

"This is nice and cozy," she remarked.

"I'm having a hard time behaving myself," I whispered. "I've lost control of my hands."

"Your hands are fine. Don't worry about it."

I kissed her some more. No one on the bus paid us any attention.

"I think I love you," I said in a horse voice.

"I love you, too. I've been looking for the right person for a long time, and now I have found him."

I touched her face again, and she kissed my hand. The bus drove on in the rain.

■ ■ ■

Our dinner meal consisted of warm vegetable soup and meat

pie. The bombing had started, and black-outs were mandatory.

"We knew they would start, but we are not sure what the targets will be," John stated. "So far they seem to be aiming at air fields, port facilities and oil supplies. They are trying to bomb us into submission."

"We'll never give up," Anna said forcefully.

"The thing is," John continued, "we were expecting this and have or will have radar stations and spotters all along the coast. We can tell almost when they leave their bases in Europe. So we are ready."

This was interesting, but I wanted to talk about Liz and me. When the meal was over, Liz excused herself and left the table. Anna stood to clear the table. I asked her to be seated, as I had something to say.

"I asked Liz to give me a few minutes alone with you. That's why she left the table. I wanted to tell you both how much I appreciate your hospitality. You saved my life, nursed me back to health, fed me, housed me and have been like parents to me. I will never forget your kindnesses. Something has happened, however, and I want you to know about it up front. Maybe you have guessed. I am in love with Liz. I don't want to live in your house and sneak around behind your backs. We have made no plans as of yet. I wanted you to be part of the planning. Liz and I have not known each other very long and certainly, we need to give this some time. The war complicates everything. I will be going home soon. I realize the war will last, who knows for how long. I intend to come back to her as soon as conditions allow it. I hope you can celebrate our love for each other. If not,

I will understand and leave your home."

John was the first to speak. "We have suspected that you two got along very well. She helped you in the yard, and you have aided her with the travel agent business. You know we love our daughter dearly and will do anything for her. We supported her in her college education. She had several boyfriends, but no one she wanted to settle down with. Now she has been teaching and working on this tourist job for a while. She is bright, beautiful and self-supporting. We love her and trust her. If you are the right man for Liz, we will treat you like a son."

Anna had tears in her eyes, and she stood to hug me. John grasped my hand and shook it heartily. They called Liz back into the room, and all four of us hugged. John located some sherry and filled our glasses. John toasted his love for his family and welcomed me into it. That night we all sat in the yard listening to plane engines off in the distance and the sound of explosives down the coast. It seemed to go on forever. They must really be taking a pounding, I thought. The war was heating up. It seemed like I had been trying to avoid it forever, first escaping from Germany, bike riding across France, barely escaping at Dunkirk and now, ducking bombs in England.

After hugging all of us, Anna excused herself and turned in for the night. John was not far behind, and that left Liz and me. She asked about my conversation with her folks, and she thanked me for talking with them. We both seemed to understand that it was time for bed but in separate bedrooms. We hugged and kissed and went our separate ways.

CHAPTER 11
PICNIC AT ROMNEY MARSH

The next day, we were bound for Romney Marsh. It was a bright sunny day, and Liz thought we should take advantage of the surprisingly good weather. We packed a lunch and prepared to ride bicycles to our destination. I had mixed emotions about this trip. I had thought of Brigit many times since I had left her in France. I hoped she was well and safe, but my focus was entirely on Liz. She was unlike anyone I had ever met. She was very special.

We biked along country roads, where wild flowers decorated

the fields on either side of the rustic road. As we rode, Liz told me the history of the marsh. Evidently the land was under water during high tide in early times. During the Roman occupation the land had been drained. Now there was fertile land that provided grass for large sheep herds. Wool was in great demand throughout England. There were drainage ditches running through the land. Few trees were in sight but an occasional farm house could be spotted from time to time.

We found a quiet place along one of the streams and spread our blankets on the ground. We used our backpacks as pillows and lay on the blankets facing the sky. It was mesmerizing to watch the clouds. Liz talked of her school days for a while and then shifted the conversation to me.

As I started my story of college days, there was a drone of airplane engines overhead. They turned out to be German. I was getting familiar with the black cross superimposed over a larger white cross. These were Heinkels, the standard bombers of the Luftwaffe. As escorts, the Germans also had Messerschmitt fighter planes. As they flew gracefully overhead, I was moved by the sheer power they represented. Eventually they passed on and we could only guess where they were headed. We lay there beside the stream feeling very small and unimportant in the bigger scheme of things.

I held Liz in a tight embrace in Romney Marsh, and she clung to me. At first, I thought this was a sexual thing except nothing much happened. Then I thought it might be fear, as we imagined what must be happening farther inland when the planes reached their targets. Finally, I figured our embrace might be tied to comfort. Our next few years could be very difficult. We sought the comfort of each other that our embrace symbolized. My thoughts were broken by the now too familiar drone of airplanes flying north of us. The raw power of the machines drew our gaze to the north. I searched the sky for but could not see these hateful tools of destruction.

Then a new sound emerged from the picture in the sky. Two fighter planes darted out of the clouds, as if playing tag. It was a dogfight. At first, it was hard to identify which plane was the Messerschmitt and which was the British Spitfire. Then I saw the bright circles of yellow, blue, white and red of the RAF. The British plane was chasing the German. The Nazi plane had some difficulty trying to lose the Spitfire. They flew with lightning speed in and out of the clouds, constantly changing altitudes, quickly going right or left. It was a dazzling show.

Liz and I sat up, quietly pulling for the British pilot. He was able to stay on the tail of the Messerschmitt for short periods of time pouring machine gun bullets in the direction of the enemy. Finally, a puff of smoke came from one of the wings of the German plane. Soon, smoke engulfed the plane, and several fires flickered brightly. Our show was over quickly. We cheered, hugged, and saw a farmer and his wife cheering. We danced around, and then we saw a parachute fluff open. The German pilot had escaped the burning plane. The British plane dipped its wings several times and then disappeared. We watched the German descend slowly. The wind was blowing him toward us.

Liz grabbed my arm." The farmers around here will kill that pilot, if he falls on their fields. They'll run their pitch forks right into his gut."

"Let's see if we can get there first," I said.

We took off running down the road. We had to stop often to determine where the pilot would drop. We missed the landing spot by about three kilometers. We ran and eventually came upon several farmers and their families looking into the distance. I went to the man who seemed to be in charge.

"Have you spotted him?"

"Oh yes, he's over there in the tall grass by that group of white wild flowers along the drainage ditch."

"Is he armed?" I asked.

"We think he is, but we aren't sure," answered another farmer.

Liz was standing beside me holding my hand.

"He speaks German," she said, motioning towards me.

"Who are you people?" asked the leader farmer.

"My name is Liz, I live just outside of Rye on a small farm. My father is principal of the school there."

"And who is this bloke?" asked another farmer pointing his pitch fork in my direction.

"I am an American college student who came to Europe to learn French and German. I was picked up at Dunkirk. I have been staying with Liz's family recuperating from my wounds."

"You could be a German spy," another farmer added.

"Yeah, but I'm not," I said in a stern voice.

How ironical, I thought. When I was in Germany, they thought I was an English spy. Now I'm in England, and they think I'm a German spy. Really, I am only a dumb-assed American, who didn't have much of a clue about anything.

There was a lull in the conversation.

"Let me try to talk to him." I looked at the leader. "While I'm doing that, you could get your men to cut off his escape routes, if you think that would help."

"Yeah," he muttered as if a little hesitant to take my suggestions.

"By the way," I said, "my name is Mitchell," and offered him my hand.

"Yeah," he said, "I'm Paul."

We shook hands.

"Paul, we don't want anyone to get killed. He will be unarmed when I bring him out. If he got shot, that would be murder."

"Yeah," Paul said.

I asked Liz to wait by the farmers that had gathered.

"Don't do anything stupid," she said.

"Don't worry," I said. "I still have most of my lunch to eat."

As I made my way through the crowd, I realized it had grown rapidly. I heard one man say that the Home Guard would be here soon. I walked away from the crowd, as if to distance myself. I stood out in the open and waved my arms.

"Hello, German pilot." I spoke in German slowly to make sure he understood me. "My name is Mitchell. I am an American student. Before I came to England, I lived for six months in Bad Aibling, southeast of Munich." I paused. "What is your name?"

There was no reply from the German.

I continued my spiel. "There is a growing mob of people back there waiting to spill some German blood. They have pitchforks and hunting rifles. They mean business."

I paused again, but the German was still silent.

"If you will surrender to me, you will spend the rest of the war in a prisoner of war camp. You will be safe. Your medical needs will be taken care of. You will have food and warm clothing. Fighting this mob would be madness. What do you want to do?"

There was more silence and then a halting reply." Come forward, and I will talk."

I moved forward so that we were closer.

"My name is Gunther," he said. "I am a lieutenant in the Luftwaffe. I am married with two children."

"Are you hurt?" I asked.

"I sprained my ankle, when I landed in the parachute, but I can walk."

"Are you armed?" I inquired.

"Yes."

"Will you give me your gun?"

Gunther stood up and limped over to me and gave me his luger. I turned to the farmers who were still a good distance away from us.

"This is his gun, I will throw it away." With that I tossed it a good distance off to the side.

I turned back to Gunther. "Do you have any other weapons?"

"No," was the reply.

"Take off your pilot equipment and toss it aside."

He did as I asked.

"Take your jacket off and leave it on the ground."

Again he did as I asked. I looked him over. He offered me his watch. I guess he figured the farmers would take it anyway.

"I want you to have this," he said.

It appeared to be a valuable item. I thrust it into my pocket.

He reached into his chest pocket and pulled out a letter and several photos, one of his teenaged daughter and son and one of a smiling, pleasant looking woman I took to be his wife.

"I will keep these," he said.

I nodded in agreement. Then I turned to the farmers and spoke so that they could hear. "The German is unarmed and has surrendered to me. He will go peacefully with the authorities. Do not harm this man, as that would be pure and simple murder."

When there was no hostile response, I walked, and he limped, toward the crowd. The gathering of people had grown even larger. Home Guard men had joined the group. A couple of farmers sprinted to the place where the German left his gun and equipment. One of the Home Guards stepped forward and offered to take the prisoner. They placed handcuffs on his wrists and marched him toward a police truck. Several people tried to spit on the German, but the Guards rushed him through the crowd. Liz joined me as the crowd began to disperse. A man with the Home Guard thanked me for a job well done.

"Nice day for a picnic," I said as I greeted her. She hugged me.

"I was worried about you," she said.

"The German, Gunther, was more scared than I was," I said. "Speaking his language helped a lot."

We made our way back to our picnic spot just off the road by the stream. We spread our blankets again and used our backpacks as pillows. We settled back down looking into the sky. Thank goodness there were no more planes in the sky. I felt my pocket and pulled out the German pilot's wrist watch. I showed it to Liz. I examined it and realized that there was an inscription on the back. It was Gunther's name and address in Germany. Liz looked it over and guessed it had been handed down by his father to him. I put in on my wrist and wore it. It felt good.

It was peaceful and quiet, until we heard a car pull up by our bikes. We sat up. It was a woman who waved and made her way over to us.

"I'm sorry to interrupt you, but I'm a reporter from the local paper. I am Jane Pulling. Some farmers down the road told me where to find you."

"How nice," I said somewhat sarcastically.

"Yes, well…" she smiled. "I would like to write an article about you and the capture of the German pilot."

I offered her a spot on the blanket, which she accepted. She had a note pad and pencil and was ready to write. I introduced myself and Liz, putting in a plug for her new business of promoting tourism in the area. Jane smiled and waited patiently, while I gathered my thoughts. I told her of our picnic, the dog fight, the British victory and the rush to the spot where the German pilot landed. Here, she interrupted me.

"Did you want to grab a gun and shoot him?" she asked.

"When I saw him scared and crumpled up on the ground, I realized he should be treated like a prisoner-of-war, as I expect the Germans to do with our downed airmen."

She had other questions about my American background, my studies and my plans for the future. I was a little vague about my future. We chatted for a while, and then she finally left. Liz and I settled back down on the blankets and backpacks, but it wasn't the same.

I looked at Liz. "This is hardly our secret little rendezvous spot. I feel like every farmer in southern England knows every move we make, every word we speak."

"You're right," she sighed. "The mood is broken, let's hit the road."

■ ■ ■

When I came down to breakfast the next morning, John sat there with a sheepish grin on his face.

"Well, I see you were busy yesterday." He read, "The American Superman caught a Nazi pilot in the wilds of Romney Marsh. Although unarmed himself, he disarmed the warrior and turned him over to authorities." John put down the newspaper and sat there smiling.

"John, you know you can't believe everything you read in the paper. Besides, I was just defending this beautiful fair maiden from the evil forces of the dark world."

We shared a laugh.

"What new conquests of the evil will there be today, or is it tourist time?" John asked.

Liz chimed in. "Come on, Dad. Mitch was Superman for a day. Now it's time to visit Brighton."

John wished us well and gave me the newspaper, so we could read the story about the German pilot. Since it was raspberry season, Liz and I had cereal and fruit for breakfast. Anna saw to it that we had all we needed.

The bus trip followed a southwesterly direction along the coast. The scenery was picture-book beautiful. In Brighton, we stopped in what appeared to be the center of town and walked following the New Road into the arts section of the city. We saw the Theatre Royal, the Brighton Museum, and the Art Gallery which housed the well-known 1920s Art Deco lamp and other valuable pieces of art work. Across the green was the main attraction of the city, the Royal Pavilion, a famous oriental palace established by the Prince Regent. The Royal Palace Pavilion was England's equivalent to the Versailles Palace outside of Paris.

From here, we walked to the shore, where the popular Brighton Pier was located. Built in 1899, the structure was a typical late-Victorian amusement park with arcades and attractive vistas of the sea. The sandy beach was wide and colorful with blue and white furniture. We walked the promenade and eventually made our way to the old town, where there were an abundance of antique shops and various fashion boutiques.

Facing utter exhaustion, we staggered to the renowned Old Ship Hotel for lunch and tea. The hotel, built in 1559, was four floors high and painted white. It was a welcome sight. We located the restaurant and ordered food, lots of it. While we waited to be served, Liz played tour leader again.

"Do you know that Laurence Olivier lived his final days in Brighton? This city also lured thousands of tourists from nearby London. The more refined travelers choose Brighton, while the younger, less particular, settled for more rowdy resorts like Margate. Both cities served as a place for adulterous weekends spent in hotels, where the management was very discreet."

"Wow!" I ventured. "That got my attention."

Liz smiled and continued with more information than I could digest. Eventually, our food arrived, and the travel dialogue ended. I didn't realize I was so hungry, but we both put away our lamb dinners quickly. After tea, we looked around the hotel lobby. Now that I was rested and fed, I felt frisky. I spied a phone booth and escorted Liz over to it. I squeezed in and reached for her hand and pulled her in. It was tight, but we both fit. I looked into her eyes and kissed her lips.

"There's a question I have to ask you," I blurted out.

She looked surprised. "What?"

I paused for a few seconds. "Is this hotel one of those where people had adulterous weekends, and where the management is very discreet?"

Liz blushed and seemed speechless for a moment. "I'm not sure."

"Well, your mom told me that we had slept together before, when I was sick, so I thought you wouldn't be too shocked if I asked you."

Liz smiled and then laughed. "Yes, but nothing happened that night, so I figured you weren't interested in me."

"But I am," I protested. "Give me another chance," I said in a determined voice.

"Right here in the phone booth?" she asked.

"Wait here, I'll be right back."

She laughed and made room for me to exit the phone both.

As I walked toward the desk clerk, I realized I had no clue as to what to say, but I would quickly have to figure out something. A few minutes later I signed the registration book and took a room key. The clerk smiled, and I wondered if he was being discreet. I hid the key in my hand and returned to Liz in the phone booth. She was still there. I joined her, but kept the key hidden. She looked at me, but I did nothing.

"No luck?" she asked. "Is the hotel sold out?"

I held up the key and dangled it in front of her. "There was at least one room left."

"Oh my gosh, you really did it."

I squeezed out of the booth and offered her my hand. Up the stairs we went arm and arm to Room 303. I managed to open the door and then lock it, after we entered the room. My heart was racing. We kissed and hugged and touched.

"I want to take all your clothes off, " I said.

"I'm too nervous to take them off myself," she said. "It's up to you."

I slowly began to unzip, unbutton, kiss and hug her. I noticed some of my clothes coming off, too. We sat on the bed, and I took off her shoes and socks. She did the same to me. She pulled me up from the bed and pulled back the covers. Soon we were both under the covers. Her voluptuous body felt warm and sensuous under mine. I breathed in her pure fragrance and slid my hand over her silky breasts. We explored each other with sexual curiosity. Our mood changed from playful to full passion. We stayed in bed most of the afternoon. We even took a shower together and dressed just in time for tea.

"Timing is everything," I allowed.

Liz smiled.

■ ■ ■

We finished tea and made our way to the bus station and the ride back to Rye. We got home just in time for supper. There was a letter for me from the U.S. Embassy in London. Mr. Waldo Bayley had news. He had papers for me to sign, which would clear the way for my return to America. Also, he was closer to arranging transportation for me to the U.S. He wanted me to come to London in two days. I could catch the train to the city and take a cab to his office. I could then return to Rye while he finalized the particulars of my trip.

At dinner we talked of the war news. The Germans had mistakenly bombed London in late August, and the British had retaliated by bombing Berlin. By early September, the Germans were so irritated that they changed their military focus and began to bomb London relentlessly. Some Germans theorized that they might be able to break the English will to fight by destroying the capital and killing many civilians. Instead, it made the British more determined than ever to hold out against the ruthless Germans. I was hesitant to go to London, but there was no other alternative. Heck, I wasn't even sure I wanted to leave England at this time with Liz in my life.

After dinner, Liz asked me if I wanted to go to Rye the next day. There were sights to see, and I did need to get clothes for my trip to London. I had already purchased some clothes in Rye, but I needed more. I had loafers, khaki pants and a light blue shirt, but I needed a blue blazer and a rep tie with red and blue stripes. It would feel good to get dressed up after the rags I had been wearing across Europe.

The next morning we rode bikes to Rye. We walked along Mermaid Street and marveled at the quaint cobbled-stone roads and the half-timbered houses. It was like we had stepped back in time about three hundred years. We saw the Mermaid Inn, which was built in medieval times. At one time, the famous Hawkhurst smugglers operated out of it. Today it was a popular tourist destination.

"I wonder if they have discreet management in there?" I commented.

"You are misbehaving again," she added with a big smile.

We moved on to the Lamb House around the corner.

"Henry James, the well-known author, lived here for many years," she remarked. "Have you read any of his books?"

"I read one," I remembered. "It was entitled *Washington Square,* I think. Not my cup of tea. Hemingway is still my favorite."

Next, we came to St. Mary's Church and the turret Clock, one of the oldest working clocks in England. We returned to our bikes, and Liz suggested that we check out the family boat. It was about three kilometers outside of town. Liz explained that in the sixteenth century the old harbor began to fill with silt to the point where boats were kept away from town. We biked along the Rother River to a small harbor where the boat was kept. It brought back memories, seeing that boat again.

Liz seemed to realize that my mind was on the Dunkirk rescue. We parked our bikes and went on board. She began to clean up the deck area, and eventually I joined her. We talked about the men that she and her dad had rescued from the beaches of Dunkirk.

Liz had packed some sandwiches and removed them from her backpack. We sat on deck and enjoyed the food and the view. She had stored some Cokes on board, and we added them to our lunch. The food was good, and we relaxed in the sun. The Cokes were warm, but she didn't seem to mind. The boat rocked gently in the water. Eventually, Liz stood up and held out her hand. I took it and she pulled me up.

"Let's check below to make sure all is well," she offered.

Below, there was a small kitchen, seating area and a bed.

"Do we need to clean up here?" I asked.

"No, we don't, but I understand the management is very discreet," she added with a smile.

We were passionate, but much more relaxed with each other than we were in Brighton. I took off her shirt and bra and exposed her ample breasts. The bed was cozy. We took our time and eased into our love making. The boat rocked gently in the calm waters and the sea birds circled above.

CHAPTER 12
BATTLE OF BRITAIN

The next morning, I gathered my travel papers and prepared to take the train to London. I had on my new clothes and was ready to meet Waldo Bayley at the U.S. Embassy. I was not looking forward to the trip, because it meant that I might be leaving England soon. I thanked Anna and John for the healthy breakfast, and Liz walked me to the car. I kissed her good-bye and told her how much I loved her. Her father took me to the train station.

The train trip was not bad, but there were a lot of local stops.

At Victoria Station in London I found a cab. Soon I was on my way to the American Embassy. The day was warm and sunny. I had expected rain but not today.

In Mr. Bayley's office, his secretary offered me a chair. After a short wait the consul escorted me into his private office. He insisted that I call him Waldo and I was Mitchell. We talked about the war and the news from Washington, D.C. He asked about my parents in North Carolina, and finally we got down to business. He was in the process of making arrangements for my passage on a ship that was taking several American families back to the U.S.A. Two of these people had been injured in the bombings of London, and he had arranged for a nurse to accompany them. There was room for me to go, but the departure date was uncertain. He promised it would happen in the next five to seven days. This would give me time to complete my arrangements tomorrow, and then I could return to Rye until the day before the departure.

Waldo had some papers for me to sign. We talked for a while longer, and I made a down payment on the ship ticket. He had reserved a hotel room for me for that night. We agreed to meet the next day. When I left his office, I walked the streets for a while and ate lunch. There were posters everywhere attached to lamp posts and on the sides of buildings. One that caught my attention was that of a pastoral scene with a farmer and his dogs driving a herd of sheep over a beautiful landscape. The caption read: "Your Britain, Fight for it now." Another poster was of a phone booth with a man inside making a call, but with many people listening. This caption was: "Careless talk costs lives."

That afternoon I visited the War Museum and walked around Piccadilly Circus. I noticed an entrance to a bomb shelter there. I saw some damaged buildings and wondered if the Luftwaffe would hit the city during the night. After a late dinner of beef pie and ale, I returned to my hotel. It was dark outside. I decided to have a beer before I retired to my room.

The hotel pub was crowded with patrons. A man at the bar with freckles and red hair engaged me in conversation. He was smoking and drinking a rye malt.

"I wonder when the Germans will hit tonight," he stated, while blowing smoke into the air.

"Do they bomb every night?" I asked.

"Pretty much so."

As if to answer my question sirens sounded loud and clear.

"Where is the air raid shelter?" I inquired.

"I'm going to sit right here," he responded. "No German bastards are going to interrupt my drink."

I looked around the room and few seemed to be leaving. The bartender was busy fixing a drink. The couple next to me took their drinks and moved toward the exit. I was uncertain what to do.

Freckles, next to me, started talking as he lit up another cigarette. "The Nazis drop their bombs in sticks of five or six. When you hear the first one explode you wait to see if the next one is louder. If it is louder, that means it's coming your way. If you hear a swish, look out."

Most of the lights were out, and it was difficult to see very far. Cigarette smoke filled the air. Several bombs hit fairly close to the hotel. The chandeliers swayed over our heads. Dust was in the air. I got up and moved toward the exit. I opened the door and there was a terrific blast of hot air and a roaring noise. I was lifted off my feet and thrown outside onto the sidewalk, which was full of shattered glass. I was semi-conscious. I was bleeding from many cuts made by the glass. There was a loud explosion from inside the hotel. Bricks and other debris were flying everywhere. One hit me in the arm and there was a sharp pain. I was covered with pieces of brick and other building materials. I felt a piercing pain in my head. There was fire everywhere. I touched the back of my head. Blood covered my hand. I faded in and out of consciousness. I tried to stagger away from the hotel. The walls of the building were still there, but the inside had given way and crumbled one floor on top of the other. There were explosions all around, people screaming and firemen trying to fight the flames. I lost consciousness and crumbled in the street. Later, I revived. I heard fires crackling, alarms sounding, and I felt the heat. There were no more explosions. A fireman walked up to me. I was sitting in the road.

"Are you all right, Mate?" He asked.

I just looked at him. My head was killing me. I couldn't speak.

"Red Cross over here!" He shouted.

Two men with a stretcher came. One bandaged my head. They placed me on the stretcher and carried me to an ambulance. When I was placed inside, I looked to see if there was somebody above me on another stretcher. Is this *A Farewell to Arms* all over again? Hemingway strikes again. At least I wasn't eating cheese when the explosion hit, and no one was bleeding on me from above. My head throbbed, and I wished I was dead. I must have passed out again, because the next thing I remembered was being in the hospital.

I looked at the ceiling. There was a light. I tried to look to my side, but my neck was sore. My head still throbbed. My arm hurt, and I felt like I wanted to die. Later, a nurse arrived.

"My name is Betty. I'm one of the nurses on this floor. A doctor will be here soon to talk with you," she said smiling. "How do you feel?"

"Not good," I replied.

My vision was fuzzy and I felt like I had been run over by a truck. Later the doctor came and told me I had a broken arm and a serious head concussion. I had many cuts and bruises all over my body. I would have to stay in the hospital until further notice. At that point, I drifted back into sleep. I was in and out of consciousness for a number of days. I vaguely remembered a visit from Waldo but no details of the conversation.

I thought it was the next day, but in reality over a week had passed. My memory was non-existent, and my eyesight was still blurred. My cuts and bruises were healing nicely, but my head was heavily bandaged, and my arm was in a cast. Betty helped me get dressed, and I sat in a wheelchair. My head did not hurt so much. She told me I was going on a trip, a long trip back to America. She wished me luck and gave me a small traveling case.

"Your friend, Waldo, gave me this," she explained.

I paid little attention to it. The ambulance took me to the

docks, and I was wheeled aboard a large ship to my room. It was small but had a porthole, a bed and a comfortable chair. I also had my wheelchair. There was a knock on the door. It opened, and a nurse came in.

"My name is Katherine," she announced. " I will take care of you on the trip until we get to America. I have several other families to look after, also. I will take you to your meals and anything else you might need."

"Your last name isn't Barkley, is it?" I asked.

"No, it isn't. Why do you ask?"

"No reason," I said. She was tall with long blond hair. She seemed nice and tried to be upbeat.

"Oh, I get it," she said with a knowing smile. "No, I'm not Hemingway's Katherine Barkley. Sorry."

I recovered quickly. "Have you read his work?"

"Some of it, but I got tired of his sad endings." She tidied up the room and placed my travel case on the table next to the bed. "I will check on you every two hours or so," she stated and left the room.

I was quite tired. I slept, ate and slept some more.

The second day out, my appetite came back, and Katherine was able to find a cheeseburger and Coke. I was in Heaven. Eventually I was able to take my meals with the other American families aboard. One of the men enticed me into a backgammon game. He had worked in the embassy and had broken a leg in one of the air raids. He sure knew the game. That night I had a dream about an older man throwing double sixes with the dice. He seemed to be in a park somewhere. I couldn't remember much about my stay in Europe, but there seemed to be a tie with my experiences there and this game. I kept playing, losing and wondering.

One day I opened my traveling bag to see if I had a change of clothes. There I found a long letter from Waldo Bayley. I did remember him from the Embassy. His letter answered a lot of questions that had been nagging me. He explained that my memory was probably not good, and that he would clear up some of the questions I might have. He described the air raid and how I had been found in the road outside the hotel. Many had been killed inside, and I had been lucky enough to have been blown out the door and onto the road. A fireman saw me sitting in the street, but I was unable to speak. He found my wallet and identified me. He found the papers from the Embassy with Waldo's name and address in my coat pocket. Waldo was contacted and told where I was in the hospital. He had taken over at this point. He bought me clothes, using the torn and tattered shirt and pants that I had been wearing for size. He could only find one shoe as the other had been blown off in the explosion. Also, he had purchased socks, underwear and some toiletries that I would need.

In the letter, he also reported on my medical condition and shared the attending physician's prediction that I would eventually regain full memory of my eventful year in Europe. In a post-script, Waldo related that he had remembered that I was staying in Rye with an English family. He had their address from earlier correspondence with me. He promised to contact them soon and relate my "bad luck" in London. Also, he told them to discard my belongings, as they would easily be replaced for my voyage to the U.S. He cautioned them that I had little memory of the events in the past several months. Good ole Waldo had taken care of everything. I tried to remember the English family I had stayed with, but nothing came to mind.

My days at sea drifted by. I began to sun on the top deck, read and watch for German subs. I saw none, thankfully. I played backgammon, ate and learned of the American families' lives in London. It, no doubt, was a time they would never forget. For me, it was a time of trying to remember. One of the American ladies spoke French, and I talked with her in that foreign tongue. It came slowly back to me bit by bit.

One day we spotted sea birds. Later that day, we pulled into Norfolk Naval Station in Virginia. It had been over a year, since I had left home to go on this marvelous adventure. It would be good to see my parents and learn of their lives during the past year. I walked down the gangplank into the embrace of my parents. I was back home in America, and it felt good.

CHAPTER 13
GOOD TO BE HOME

My old room was just as I had remembered it. The bed, closet with some clothes, dresser, reading chair, lamp and several bookshelves full of books were all there. They were like old friends to me. Hemingway, Fitzgerald, Steinbach and Dos Passos were all there. Also, there was my Graham Greene collection and lots of classics by German, French, Russian, Italian and Spanish writers. In addition, I had my old college texts especially history and language books. I felt comfortable with so many books in my presence.

My parents had been fantastic. They had been extremely supportive and generous. I had missed them very much. We sat and talked a lot. They drank their coffee and listened to the stories that I could remember. They wanted to hear all about my adventures, and I was anxious to share them. The American Embassy staff had sent my papers and reports from the London hospital, and Dad had lined up a series of appointments with doctors to check my arm and head. I was sick of the arm cast and ready to toss it aside. My memory was getting better. I could remember most of the German and French I had learned. I could recollect some of the things I had experienced in Germany. It all seemed so long ago.

Some of my friends came over to see me. We played cards or just talked and ate. There were a few movies we enjoyed. The fall season was upon us, and the colors were magnificent. I took a biking and hiking trip one day, and physically I was beginning to feel good. In the past, I had walked down by the river, and I went that route again. Leaves were on the ground, and the squirrels were busy gathering nuts. I walked aimlessly along the Falls Lake trail. I came to an abandoned bridge. Part of the cement structure remained. I sat down and studied it. It seemed familiar to me. There was much graffiti on it. My eyes came to rest on the place that said: "Mitch Loves Sue," painted in red. I remembered doing that.

Sue was a high school girlfriend, and I got a little carried away one day. As I sat there, I began to think about the various girls that I had dated. I was really more interested in sports than girls in high school. When there weren't games on the weekends, I went out with girls. During my senior year, it was mostly with Sue. She seemed more of a real good friend, who I enjoyed being with, than a serious relationship that might lead to marriage. That was the last thing on my mind.

Then my thoughts turned to Gretchen and my stay in Germany. That time in my life was beginning to clear up in my mind. She was the blond, athletic beauty with the pleasing smile. I wondered if she had married her German soldier. I had never dated Gretchen but had spent that memorable night with her in the mountain cabin. I hadn't totally resolved in my mind why we had been together, but it seemed clear we had no long-range possibility of seeing one another again. Also, I thought about her grandfather, Helmuth, and hoped he would make it through the war. I had an urge to think about France and England, but my time there was not clear in my mind.

Looking at the bridge again, I noticed the many colors of paint in the letters on the cement. The whole scene was bazaar. There was nature at its finest with the color changes of fall and the crumbling bridge with many love stories decorating the white canvas of cement. I read the messages to myself. On and on, the names swept before my eyes. I wondered if any of these people actually got married. Did I know any of them? Were any divorced? I imagined that each story was compelling. Had any died? My thoughts raced from one name to the next. Then a deer appeared next to the bridge. It apparently did not see me. When I moved, it dashed away.

Hiking and biking again became a way of life for me. Also, I continued to brush up on French and German and paged through all the notes that I had taken in my graduate history classes before my trip to Europe. My visits to doctors' offices continued through the fall. Dr. Hampton in Durham pronounced my shoulder healed. It had hurt for a while after my bicycle crash outside of Dunkirk, but now I had full movement. He also removed the cast from my broken arm and pronounced it healed. Now I needed to rehab vigorously.

Dr. Baker was the specialist dealing with my concussion. At my last visit he gave me a thorough examination and afterward we sat down for a talk. There was a flourish of big words and Latin or some language I could not understand.

"Doctor, Doctor, please slow down and talk in plain English,"I said "Is it good news or bad?"

"I thought you were a college boy."

"Yes, but I'm in history not medicine."

"Well, he said slowly, you will be fine, but it will take a while to heal."

I was getting impatient. "How long is a while.?"

"Don't know for sure." He rubbed his ear and thought. "Probably take months or even a year, but you should be 4F for the military draft and not available for the war. Just stay away from bomb explosions and your memory should slowly come back. You can expect a complete recovery in one or two years."

"I was an accidental soldier in the Battle of Britain and I have had enough of war to last me forever."

"Come back in a month and I'll take another look at your skull, but everything looks good."

■ ■ ■

By Christmas time, I had firmed up my graduate school plans

at the University of North Carolina. During the second semester, beginning in January, I would take a course in Mexican history for credit and audit two others. One was on Russian history. The second had to do with the coming of the Great War of 1914 and the war itself. My main area of concentration was modern Europe with an emphasis in German history. I would eventually take courses in American history and Latin American affairs to round out my other fields of interest. My main objectives during the semester would be to pass my foreign language requirements in German and French. I would also apply for a teaching assistant job at the university. This would pay for my tuition and cover some of the food and lodging expenses that I would have.

The holidays were a time of joy for me, spending time with parents and friends, but it was also a period of loneliness. Some of my friends were married. Others had moved to various places in pursuit of jobs. Several had joined the military. I was anxious to move to Chapel Hill and settle into my own apartment which was within walking distance to the university. I had found a place in a former tobacco warehouse that had been remodeled. There was a small bedroom, bathroom, tiny kitchen but a decent sized living room, which I converted into a study-library. I had a large desk, lamp, typewriter, phone and floor-to-ceiling bookcases. Also, there was a sofa, coffee table, radio and record player for music. It was fun moving in and collecting all my things.

I met my neighbors. On one side of me lived two artists. We bumped into each other in the hallway, and they invited me into their place. It was a mess of painted canvases, easels, paints and tables. The walls were covered with their work. Beth was the tall, thin one with straight blond hair in a ponytail and freckles. She liked landscapes and flowers. I admired her work, and she explained what she was working on. Sarah, her roommate, came from the kitchen with red wine and cheese. She was the opposite of Beth in appearance. She was southern European or Mediterranean, rather short and quite animated with a loud voice and gestures to highlight what she was saying. They both laughed a lot and were fun to be with. They told many stories of the art department at the university.

Soon the wine bottle was empty. I had consumed about a half of a glass, and they took care of the rest.

"We'd offer you lunch, but we don't have any food here," Sarah said.

There was an awkward pause. "I've just come back from the grocery store where I bought sandwich fixings," I said.

The three of us moved to my place for lunch, but they seemed more interested in my walls than food.

"Your walls are empty," Beth remarked.

"Yeah," I replied. "I'll get something to hang one of these days."

"No problem," said Sarah. "We'll loan you some of our works, until you can get your own."

Before I could respond, they were gone. A few minutes later Beth hauled in a couple of her paintings, and Sarah did the same. They asked me which ones I wanted in the study, but after I stumbled around for a while, they decided for me. My apartment was now complete. I had a landscape painting including an old barn in my bedroom, two smaller pictures of flowers on my kitchen wall over a small dining table, and a portrait of an older Mexican woman over my desk looking down on me.

I could hardly wait to meet the rest of the neighbors.

■ ■ ■

I spent most of my time at the university library. I was assigned a carrel on the third floor where many of the history books were located. I read newspapers and *Time Magazine* to keep up with the current events. I also attended my classes. Of my classes, the Russian history class was just okay. The Mexican history class was much better. Professor Myerson was my idea of a perfect teacher. He was well organized with a short outline on the board highlighting the main topic that he would discuss in class. He had interesting stories to tell in bringing the material alive. He had traveled through Mexico extensively and spoke Spanish fluently. He assigned interesting books to read and even used novels as assigned reading. I was relieved that I could learn and remember the material.

The Europe and the War of 1914 class was great. It just blew me away. I worked harder in that class than ever, and it wasn't even for credit. I was fascinated to learn of conditions in Europe at the turn of the century. The alliance systems that developed in Europe leading to war, the rise of nationalism, the arms race, the new modern military staff organization and technology that led to total war, all captured my interest. The assassination of the Austrian Archduke Frances Ferdinand and the role the Serbians played in the whole mess added intrigue to the war that followed.

Dr. Frank Hoffman was the professor, and we struck up a friendship. He enjoyed speaking to me in German, and it also was good practice for me. One day he invited me to coffee in the faculty lounge.

"How's your health, Mitch?" he asked.

"Most everything is good. I can remember all the new information I learn in class. I still have some difficulty in remembering some events in my life from my time in Europe. It's coming back slowly."

"Do you think you have time for a part-time job in the History Department here at the university? To be more specific, I need an assistant to help me with grading test papers and in doing some of the research for my next book. : You are well grounded in the subject matter of my course and you are already sitting in on the lectures. Your language skills are first rate. You have all the background necessary."

I was surprised by his offer, but delighted at the opportunity. "I would love to work with you. It would be different to have an income and pay some of my bills." We shook hands.

"It's a deal," he said. Dr. Hoffman excused himself from the table and I was left to reflect on this new development in my life. I thought about Dr. Hoffman. He was married and had two grown children. I guessed he was in his late forties. He was a handsome man and seemed to get along well with everyone. He had written two books about Europe in the early 1900s. They were scholarly works and well received within the academic community. I had read his works and began to realize how fortunate I was to be working with him.

■ ■ ■

In the summer of 1941, I took my German and French language tests. I made an appointment with Dr. Hoffman and we met in his office. We talked for a while and then he casually took a book from his shelf and handed it to me.

"Open it up anywhere and read to me in German," he said.

I did as he instructed and then he asked me in English what I had read. Then he chose another book written in German and I repeated the exercise. Then we had a conversation in German. After about forty-five minutes of this he stood and we shook hands.

"Congratulations," he said with a smile. "You just passed your German foreign language exam."

I took the French exam from a professor in the Foreign Language Department. The procedure was about the same.

I really wasn't worried about passing the exams, and I did very well. I was now another step closer to my goal of earning the Ph.D. Maybe my decision to study in Germany and France had paid off. I was also pleased that my memory was restored well enough to retain the languages, which I had learned before the war.

That spring and summer of 1941, I began to follow Major League baseball with great interest. This was my present to myself for passing the language exams. I had no favorite team at this point but had read about such heroes as Ted Williams and Joe DiMaggio in the newspapers. It was thrilling to listen to the radio broadcasters who made the games seem so exciting. It was impressive that at age thirty, Detroit's Hank Greenberg

was drafted into the army. At the peak of his career, he went off to serve his country. I had recently learned of my draft status as 4-F, because of the injuries I had suffered during my time in Europe. I read about Cleveland's Bobby Feller and his blazing fast ball and Brooklyn's star outfielder Pete Reiser. I was sad when Lou Gehrig died in June of that year. I was particularly impressed with Stan Musial, when he was called up from the minors by the St. Louis Cardinals during the season.

My favorite player was Ted Williams, because I had seen him during spring training. The Red Sox played an exhibition game in my Carolina hometown on their way from Florida to Boston to start the regular season. I have a vivid picture in my mind of him kneeling in the on-deck circle swinging his bat. He had a beautiful swing, and that year he hit .406. During the All Star game at mid-season, he hit a three run homer in the bottom of the ninth inning to win the game for the American League.

This was also the year that Joe DiMaggio hit safely in fifty-six straight games. It was full drama for several months, but Joe always seemed to keep the streak alive. However, not all memories were of heroic feats on the diamond. This was also the year that catcher Mickey Owen dropped a third strike during the fourth game of the World Series, allowing the Yankee's Tommy Henrich to reach first base and eventually paved the way for New York to win the series over the Brooklyn Dodgers.

■ ■ ■

During the fall, I began to meet some of the T.A.s, as we called those who assisted the major professors. It was an interesting bunch of ten individuals. Several were married and did not interact with the rest on a social level. The rest of us began to meet every Sunday evening at one of our apartments. Also, we did social activities like eating out, going to the movies or attending various events that the university sponsored. It became a support group and brought us close together.

One of the T.A.s was named Herman Kennedy or 'Herm the Germ,' as he was called. He was a sports nut, and we sometimes saw the university football games together. Tickets to games were very inexpensive for students, and I became a fan. Herm lived and died with the wins and losses of the university teams. I developed pride in the success that our athletes achieved. I enjoyed the excitement that came to the campus on game weekends. Crowds of people, parties, marching bands, cheerleaders and mascots all added to the festivities.

Charlie Johnson was another of the T.A.s. This was his third year in the History Department, and a person we looked to for advice. In one of our Sunday night sessions, a new T.A., Tom Harding, described a problem that he was trying to deal with. One of his students, an attractive sophomore was very friendly towards him. Tom wanted to date her, but first sought the group's advice. Johnson immediately gave us his answer.

"Don't."

"Don't what?" I asked.

"Don't ask the lady out."

"But we're attracted to each other," Harding said.

"Then resign from being a T.A. and ask her out," Charlie advised.

"I can't resign," Tom replied. "I need the money to stay

in school."

Charlie thought for a moment. "Wait until next semester, when she's not in your class and invite her out."

"What difference does it make?" Tom asked in frustration.

Charlie paused. "Suppose she earns a C+ in the class, but she needs a B to keep her scholarship. What do you do then?"

There was silence in the room.

Charlie pushed on. "Suppose she was sexually forward with you, and you felt pressured to be nice to her with an A grade?"

Tom nodded his head, conceding the point.

There was silence. I learned a lot about things that I had never thought about.

"Anybody for a movie?" I asked.

Molly, another one of the T.A.s, inquired: "What's showing?"

"It's a movie from last year called 'The Great Dictator' staring Charlie Chaplin."

"Count me in," Molly said..

"Me, too," added Kim.

Charlie and Tom joined us, and we trudged off to the film.

The theater was about half full, but it was a loud audience with much laughter and a few remarks called out at Chaplin, who played a comic version of Adolph Hitler. The highlights were many. I really enjoyed the Hitler speech made at a Nuremberg rally. It was hilarious. I marveled at Chaplin's facility with words. The other scene we all liked showed Hitler in his massive office, kicking an air-filled balloon in the air, while he danced around the room. The balloon was like a globe and illustrated his mastery of the world. It was stupid but funny. We also enjoyed popcorn and cokes, but they were gone all too quickly.

After the film, we adjourned to a nearby ice cream parlor. Business was slow, but that allowed us to take our time and enjoy the food and conversation. The five of us seemed very serious about eating our ice cream cones. I had a scoop of vanilla and one of chocolate. I noticed the two girls. Kim was blond and wore glasses. She was fun to be around and laughed a lot. Molly had brown hair and came off as rather quiet and intellectual. Both wore sweaters and skirts. Both were attractive and fun to be with, but Mollie especially caught my eye. She was bright, attractive and we hit it off. She was very special to me and I liked to share time with her.

Tom asked me about the depiction of Germany and the people in the film, since I had recently returned from there. I told them about the wonderful people I had met, the families, the national spirit, and the youth groups. I raved about the opera I had seen in Munich, the health of the people, and the many activities they loved. Charlie asked about the 1936 Olympics and the treatment of our Negro athletes. I had little to offer on that topic, but I did share my concerns about the rampant nationalism and the dark side of the race question. I worried about the treatment of the Jews, but I had no specifics about that, except the anti-Semitic signs that were posted in Munich.

■ ■ ■

Today was December 7th. I had spent the day listening to the radio. Molly and Kim stopped by to borrow a book, and we all listened together.

Kim was mad. "Who the hell do those Japanese think they are?"

"I thought Hitler was the bad guy. Now we have the Japs to contend with," I muttered.

"Will you be drafted?" Molly asked me.

"I don't know," I answered. "I am 4 F now, but that could change. And, I might just enlist and pray they take me."

"But what about your studies?" Molly asked. "You were making great progress, and that would be lost."

"The Japanese are allies with the Germans and Italians. No doubt we will be at war with all three countries before long," I said.

There was a long silence. The girls were sitting on the sofa with me in the middle. I put my arms around them, and we listened to the radio. The news was bad from Pearl Harbor in Hawaii. We had lost lots of ships, but none of them seemed to be aircraft carriers. That was the key in my mind. We needed carriers to fight in the Pacific. Also, there were no Japanese troops landing there. We would need that location as a base to fight, both as a naval and air base. The day dragged on. The attack was a surprise and came early on Sunday morning. Needless to say, we were unprepared for what had happened. Since our navy in the Pacific had its headquarters at Pearl Harbor, it was obviously the Japanese target. There wasn't much military strength in the Far East, except for Japan and the U.S. The French, British and Dutch all had colonies there, but the home countries were either under German rule or held on for dear life in Europe. If the Japanese knocked out the American fleet, they would have free reign in the Pacific. It was a helpless feeling sitting listening to the gloomy news.

The phone rang. It was Charlie. "Those damn Japs just hit Hawaii. The party is getting rough! Do you care if Tom, Herm and I come over?" he asked. "We need to talk."

"No problem," I said, "but pick up six or seven hamburgers from Dave's Barbeque place and some potato chips. Molly and Kim are here. We have beer, soda and a salad. I also have a quart of ice cream."

The guys arrived about a half hour later and we enjoyed the good food. Beer and hamburger were always a favorite for me. Judging how fast the food disappeared, it was popular with everyone.

The radio news continued to be discouraging. One commentator predicted that it was a matter of hours before we would declare war on Japan. Would we declare war on Germany and Italy, the other axis powers? Another commentator wondered if F. D. R. was secretly glad the Japanese had gotten America into the war, before it was too late to help save the British. The news was endless. The group decided to sleep over. There were bodies on the floor, on the sofa, and in my reading chair. It wasn't very comfortable, but we enjoyed each other's company on such a chilling night. Our futures were uncertain. Did the nation have the resolve to stick it out? The Russians and British were hanging on by a thread in Europe. The Japanese would run unimpeded in the Far East. The Italians had more modest aims. Uncertain times lay ahead.

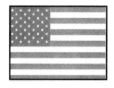

CHAPTER 14
THE PH.D.

My goal for 1942 was to earn my master's degree prior to a Ph.D.. I had finished my foreign languages and most of the course work I needed. Now I was ready to write my master's thesis. Dr. Hoffman had agreed to serve as my thesis advisor and we had settled on a topic. I would study the Versailles Treaty that ended the Great War. In particular, I would focus on the War Guilt clause that the Germans were forced to sign, admitting their responsibility for starting the war. The Treaty itself was very complicated in setting the stage for the War Guilt clause.

My primary source materials were the Treaty itself,

newspapers, personal memories, and letters found in the U. S. archives. To accomplish my research, I took several trips to Washington, D.C., to the National Archives and the Library of Congress. Inter-library loans were exceedingly helpful, also. It was a matter of plowing through what looked to me to be mountains of material. There was pleasure, however, in the mind numbing intellectual activities involved. It was a thrill to read the actual documents of the events I was writing about. Dr. Hoffman was a great help in all of this. He gave me advice on which materials were important. When I finished a chapter, he promptly went through the work and gave me constructive criticism.

While I studied the events of World War I, I followed World World War II through newspapers, news reels in the movie theater, and by reading *Time Magazine*. The war news was depressing. The Nazis were biting off huge chunks of Russian soil and taking hundreds of thousands of prisoners. But there always seemed to be replacements in the Soviet ranks. The Japanese were having their way in the Pacific. Was there any way to stop these two powerhouses? Hopefully, in a war of attrition, the numbers of Germans and Japanese did not measure up to the vast numbers of Russians, Chinese, and Americans. On the bright side, England still held out against the Germans, and the Hawaiian Islands remained under American control. The other news was that American production of war goods had picked up dramatically. Women were taking jobs in the factories and proving to be remarkable workers. I was sure that in the long run, this would pay dividends.

I became interested in big band jazz. I couldn't get enough of it. Glenn Miller, Artie Shaw and Harry James were household names. My favorite was Stan Kenton. The T.A.s liked to get together at Kim and Molly's apartment, because it was large, and they had a phonograph player. We had long playing records or LPs and we loved to jive and eat there. This music seemed to be popular throughout the U.S. Our university student government decided to bring the Stan Kenton Band to campus. We T.A.s eagerly got our tickets and anxiously awaited the day.

We met at the girls' apartment several hours before the concert. Everyone had been assigned to bring certain dishes. We had a tasty meal with great background music. We listened to Deanna Durbin's "Always," Jo Stafford's "I'll Be Seeing You," "Lili Marlene" by Perry Como, "Marie" by Tommy Dorsey, "Embraceable You" by Jimmy Dorsey and "You'd Be So Nice To Come Home To" by Dinah Shore. These songs and many others entertained us. Sometimes we sang along with the Ink Spots or Bing Crosby. Other times, we just kept time by tapping our feet or snapping our fingers.

An hour before concert time, we cleaned up the dishes and walked over to the auditorium. The hall was almost half full. We found our seats and waited impatiently for things to begin. Eventually, musicians strolled onto the stage, took their seats, and began to tune up. After a few minutes, Stan Kenton walked onto the stage to a rousing welcome. He started the band and then took his seat at the piano. I immediately recognized their first offering: "Take the A Train." It was so exciting. I was uncomfortable with the whistling from the crowd. Some students tried to dance in the aisles to the music. I preferred to listen quietly. My concentration on the music consumed me. I was sitting next to Molly, and without thinking, I took her hand. Two songs later, I realized I was holding her hand. I didn't know what to do.

Finally, I turned to her and said: "Thanks for sharing this with me. It's really special."

I'm not sure what all that meant, but I disengaged our hands. Molly smiled at me. I liked her. She was good company, but I wasn't ready for a serious affair. I hoped she understood.

After the concert, we all trudged off to Herm's place. He had beer, and we all settled down to critique the Kenton Band. At various times he had featured solos by members of the band. They were all good. I couldn't remember their names, but the sax section was outstanding. I decided to read about them from the expensive program I had purchased. Everyone seemed to enjoy the concert and vowed to go to the next one.

■ ■ ■

Herm the Germ had finished his thesis on the Berlin Olympics held in 1936. The T.A.s gathered at my apartment to go over his work, before he turned it in to his Master's Committee. The plan was for him to give a short summary of his work, and then we could ask questions.

"Adolf Hitler had planned that the 1936 Olympics would be a showcase of Aryan supremacy. German athletes would certainly excel," Herm explained. "Nazi propagandists led by Joseph Goebbels and film maker, Lei Riefenstahl, gathered to ease the blow delivered by ten African-Americans who won thirteen medals, including eight gold medals. Jesse Owens won four of the gold medals and was declared 'Athlete of the Games.' Hitler was furious. He refused to offer congratulations to the track star from Ohio State University. Owens graciously accepted the laurel wreath and medals, while Hitler sulked. There was no happy ending, as the athletes returned to a racially torn America. To support himself, Owens had to run races against dogs and horses, travel with the Harlem Globe Trotters around the country and worked as a playground janitor."

Herm bowed from the thunderous applause of the five of us. We paused to think of questions to ask him. Kim had the first question.

"What did Owens think of Germany? Were they dealing with the depression in a sensible manner? Were the people warm to him or did they avoid him?"

"Wait," said Herm, "that's three questions. Anyway, Owens seemed impressed with Berlin, the giant sports complex, the huge highway system, and the massive buildings. He had little contact with the people other than a few German athletes."

"Well, I thought it was an interesting project," said Molly. "Since I read the whole thesis, I made a list of a few grammar problems, two misspelled words, and one incomplete sentence."

"Thanks," mumbled Herm.

It was my turn now. "What made him such a great runner and jumper?" I asked. "Was he just a natural, was he a smart runner, or did he just work out and train all the time?"

Herm pulled out a piece of paper from a book.

"Let me read you something that Jessie said about his running technique. 'I stick with the field, breathing naturally until thirty yards from the finish. Then I take one big breath, tense all my abdominal muscles, and set sail.'"

Charlie asked the next question. "What was Jesse's background before the Olympics?"

"Well, he grew up on a farm in Alabama. His father was a sharecropper. It was a difficult life," he added.

"Wait," I said. "Something bothers me. We are appalled by Hitler's racism and his refusal to recognize the greatness of Owens because he was a black man. Yet, how are we any better? Owens has to race dogs and work as a janitor to survive in America."

"Yeah," said Herm, "but at least we let him run in the Olympics for his country."

"Right," I said. "We used him."

"Look, Mitch," Herm said. "I appreciate your insights, but the focus of my thesis is to celebrate Owen's achievements and not to delve into the quagmire of racism."

"Sorry," I said

Now it was Tom's turn. "What's next in line for Herm Hamilton? Do you get a high school teaching job, or do you set your sights on a Ph.D.?"

"None of the above, my friends. It's time for ole Herm the Germ to answer Uncle Sam's call. I'm going to join the Army Air Force."

"Great! Where do you think you might be stationed?" Tom asked.

"Possibly at Randolph Field in Texas," said Herm, "but I'm not sure."

"Well, we sure need pilots after the Battle of Midway in the Pacific," said Charlie.

"We socked it to those Jap bastards," said Herm.

"Yes," I said. "The key in the Pacific is carriers and airplanes. We got four of their ships and lots of planes at Midway."

"Not to change the subject," said Herm, "but let's eat."

Kim and I were in charge of the food. We had decided on grilled cheese sandwiches with lettuce and tomatoes on the side along with potato chips and Cokes. Rationing was in full force, but we pooled our food stamps and rode bikes to save on gas. At dinner, we all told Herm how much we would miss him and to keep in touch.

Several weeks later, Herm learned that he had met all the requirements for the master's degree. Then, he was notified to report to the Army. We planned a going-away party for him. Molly had heard great things about a movie in town called "Casablanca." We decided to take Herm to the show with dinner afterward.

We agreed to meet at the theater. Herm was always late, so we had time to buy him popcorn before the movie. I imagined that Herm would learn to be on time once the Army got hold of him. The five of us sat munching our popcorn. The film began, and I was swept away by the magic of Hollywood. The time was World War II, and the setting was French Morocco or more specifically, the city of Casablanca. Here anything could be bought, and it also served as a way station for people escaping from German controlled Europe to neutral countries such as Portugal. Casablanca was a sink of corruption, where Vichy officials and sometimes Nazi authorities tried to maintain order.

The story line was that of a romance and a political thriller. Rick, played by Humphrey Bogart, was an American who owned a café in the center of the film's action. Ilsa, played by

Ingrid Bergman, was the wife of a heroic resistance leader, who had escaped from a German concentration camp. The couple arrived together in Casablanca and asked Rick's help in escaping to freedom. In Paris, Rick and Ilsa had a romance prior to Casablanca. The story of the romance is skillfully interwoven with that of political intrigue.

Some of the scenes were memorable. One was set in Rick's Café with a full house of German and French customers. To add to the confusion, the band played. The loud, boisterous Germans began to sing Nazi patriotic songs. The French answered with their National Anthem and the support of the band. The French could not win on the battlefield but held their own in the café.

Another scene was also in the café, where Ilsa asked Sam, the piano player friend, to play: "As Time Goes By." This was the song that Rick and Ilsa had enjoyed so much in Paris before the war. Rick had told Sam never to play that song again, as it is the background with which the two lovers meet after a long period of separation. At the end of the film, the evil Nazi commander is killed at the airport. Ilsa and her husband fly off to freedom, and Rick, now a patriot, goes off to join the French Resistance. Rick had sacrificed everything for the cause.

I had the annoying practice of picking up what I thought were cool quotes from movies and saying them long after I had seen the movie. "Casablanca" proved fertile ground for me to gain many new sayings. When we wanted to get the T.A.s together, I might say: "Round up the usual suspects." Or if we were drinking Cokes or beer, I might say: "Here's looking at you, kid." If I was meeting Kim and Molly somewhere, I would say, "Of all the gin joints in all the towns in all the world, she walks into mine." If someone is running out of time on a project, I would say: "If its December 1941 in Casablanca, what time is it in New York?" If Molly offered to buy me a Coke, I would say: "I think this is the beginning of a beautiful friendship." If the two girls and I had a bad day, I might say: "I'm no good at being noble, but it doesn't take much to see that the problems of three little people don't amount to a hill o'beans in this crazy world."

I certainly went overboard, but I loved the film. Molly liked it, too, and we must have seen it four or five times during 1943. We were able to repeat many of the lines with the actors during the film.

■ ■ ■

In May of 1943, I received my master's degree. It was another step toward the Ph.D. Now, all I had to do was take a few classes and write the dissertation. Dr. Hoffman had agreed to advise me for this last leg of the journey. We agreed that I should continue my work on the Versailles Treaty with a special emphasis on the War Guilt Clause. This meant that I would have to follow each country involved in terms of the role it played in the coming of World War I, as they called it now. When did each country partially mobilize their forces, fully mobilize, and then declare war? I had to follow the events in Serbia, the Austro-Hungarian Empire, France, Britain, Germany, Russia, Italy and even Turkey that led to war.

In addition, the university offered to have me teach my own course on Modern Europe. It was an honor to be chosen to do this, and I was excited. There was no doubt that Dr. Hoffman was behind this offer. His support was very important to me, and I was determined not to let him down.

I loved teaching and the whole intellectual process involved. It was challenging to take a huge body of historical information, shape it and organize it, so that my students could enjoy learning. I wanted them to be as passionate about history as I was. Sometimes I used fiction as assigned reading for class, in order to understand the lives of those living during the period of study. Often it worked. Many of my students thought I had unusual teaching methods. We all agreed that this was better than reading a dull text book.

The downside of teaching was grading papers, exams, book reviews and taking class attendance. Put simply, I did not enjoy reading the same material over and over again, and that's what happened with exams. Given forty students in a class, it became monotonous reading exams. Some were eloquent, and some went right to the point. Others were vague, and some might even miss the whole point of the test question. It was difficult to distinguish between the grades of A, B, C and D. The F student was easy enough to spot.

Many of my students came to every class session. Others became quite creative in explaining their absences. Some lost a parent who was killed in the service to the country. Others lost grandparents. One student actually told me he forgot he was taking the course. Others needed lots of sleep or had romances that went bad. During my first few months of teaching, I talked with Dr. Hoffman a lot and received good advice from him. I liked to talk with him about the students who were a pleasure to have in class, as well as a few of the others with problems.

One day towards the end of the semester, Dr. Hoffman invited me to have dinner with him at a local restaurant. This was a little unusual, but I hardly gave it a thought. We met at the Pine Tree Bistro. It was a pleasant place with a bar and ample seating for meals. I got there early and had a beer and listened to Jazz from the juke box. Dr. Hoffman was a little late. He greeted me and we were seated. He ordered a drink.

"Doctor," I asked, "is your wife joining us?"

"No, she wasn't feeling well and decided to stay home. She sends her regards."

We talked of university politics and the war. I thought Dr. Hoffman appeared tired. He was in his early fifties. I wondered if he was happy with his life.

"Mitchell," he said, "my wife was diagnosed with cancer two weeks ago. It has spread to several vital organs."

Shocked, I didn't know what to say.

"I could use your help."

"Anything. I'll do absolutely anything I can to help. You have been like a father to me in the past few years. What can I do for you?"

"The thing is, I need you to cover for me. If I'm needed at home, could you teach my class? Could you give tests for me and grade them?"

"Of course, I can. I sat in on your class, and I took copious notes. It would take a little preparation, but I can do it."

He gave me a weak smile. "I know you can do it. You are

quite capable."

"Thank you, Sir. I know Molly Gilmore would help me. She's a T.A. in Modern U.S. History."

"Yes, I know her. She is first rate."

We ate our meal in silence for a few minutes. Then he continued. "My wife is strong, but some days are very difficult. I never know what to expect."

"I understand, Sir." I gave him a card with my name, phone number and address on it. "Call me anytime day or night, and I will be there."

We finished our meal of chicken, mashed potatoes, and peas. The apple pie a-la-mode topped off our feast. I wanted to split the cost, but Dr. Hoffman insisted that it was his party, and he took care of the bill.

During the next few months, Mrs. Hoffman rallied somewhat. There was little need for me to fill in. Toward the end of the spring semester in April, she had a setback. I gave two lectures on the end of World War I and the Versailles Treaty. Molly monitored one of his final exams, and I covered the other.

It was at this time, in May of 1944, that the Dean of the Faculty sent me a note that he wanted me to drop by his office. It was a large room with shelves lining the walls. He was a tall man, with a balding head and horn rimmed glasses. He smoked quite a bit as affirmed by two ashtrays full of spent cigarettes. We talked about the war briefly, the action in North Africa, Sicily, Italy, the air war and the battle for the Atlantic. He was very knowledgeable, particularly because he had a son overseas. He seemed to know about my involvement at Dunkirk and the

Battle of Britain.

Finally, he got to the point of my visit. The university was expanding the teaching staff in anticipation of the expected rush of new students going into higher education. The G.I. Bill of Rights was in the talking stages, but it appeared that the government was prepared to pay for housing, tuition and books for returning vets.

"My understanding," he said, "is that you will earn your Ph.D. very soon."

I assured him that it was all but done.

"In that case, the university would like to offer you a full-time position in the History Department. The professors are impressed with your work and recommended you highly."

He handed me some papers and asked that I read them over and hopefully sign them. "Talk it over with Dr. Hoffman and your parents, and get back to me as soon as possible."

■ ■ ■

During the summer of 1945 everything fell into place for me. I defended my dissertation and prepared for my first year of full-time teaching. It sounded strange for people to call me Dr. Morgan. It was also a great feeling to have a real salary. Now I could begin to pay off the money that I had borrowed from my parents.

The war news was also promising. The tide of battle had turned in 1943 and by June of 1944 the Allied invasion at Normandy along the French coast was underway. In the Pacific, the island hopping strategy was in progress, as the Allies closed in on Japan. Later in the summer, F.D.R. was dead, and Harry

Truman was President. He inherited the job of deciding on the use of the atomic bomb.

My classes went well, and I absolutely loved teaching. I moved to a bigger apartment, as I had to leave the graduate student dorm. My neighbors, the artists, came to collect the paintings they had loaned me. I decided that I could not part with all of the paintings. I purchased the portrait of the Mexican woman, who had looked down on me from over my desk and also the farm landscape oil. The girls were thrilled to make the sales.

Molly and Kim were still at the university, but they had accepted teaching jobs at women's colleges in Virginia and were leaving in December.

The three of us planned a good-bye dinner and movie before Christmas. I ate at the girls' place, and then I took them to see: "Mrs. Miniver." Kim filled us in on the background of the film.

"It was produced in 1942 and won six Academy Awards, including the best picture award. Greer Garson won an Oscar for her portrayal of an English mother during the difficulties of the bombing on England. Her husband in the film was Walter Pidgeon. Together they demonstrated their British resolve to resist the German aggression against England."

Molly smiled. "How did we ever miss this one?"

"I remember it, also," I said. "It reminded me of where I had been back in 1940. I was trying to forget that part of my life and focus on my studies."

"Well," Kim said sarcastically, "I hope you can deal with it now. If you get too emotional, we can always leave."

"Right," I replied.

As I expected, the film brought back memories of my time in southeastern England. The rescue at Dunkirk, the bombing of England, even the German pilot being shot down over England were all in the movie. It was very similar to my experience, except portrayed from the point of view of the English civilian. The movie put me in a mood, although it was hard to describe. Perhaps nostalgia best expressed it.

Suddenly the house lights came on and a man walked onto the stage and waved for silence. Then he yelled, "the war is over, the war is over! The Japanese have surrendered. The war is over."

A great roar of noise and applause emerged from the audience. We stood and cheered. We hugged everyone that was in our group. Some people were crying including me. The theater was too confining and we made our way outside. We saw a sailor in full uniform walking along the street and girls ran up to him and kissed him. Our gang ended up at the ice cream parlor. It was crowded, and Kim met some of her friends. It was a loud and boisterous group. After a while, Molly and I quietly slipped out and headed to her house.

"After that movie, it might be appropriate to offer you some English hot tea," she said.

"That would be great."

We went into her apartment.

"It seems strange that Kim isn't here," I said.

"She will be back later," Molly said smiling.

We listened to the radio for awhile until the news became

redundant. It was comforting to hear over and over that the war over.

"You know, I can't remember being alone with you. It seemed the T.A.s were always with us."

"You're right," Molly agreed.

"I don't know how to act."

Molly looked thoughtful. "I noticed you got a little teary eyed during the film."

"Yeah. When the small boats and ships were cruising down the river and into the open sea to Dunkirk, I was moved. At that time I was sitting on the European side of the Channel on the end of a make-shift pier, praying somebody would rescue me. A man and his daughter picked me and about ten other guys from the beach. They saved my life. This man took me home. His wife and daughter nursed me back to good health. I fell in love with his daughter. One day I had to go to London to make travel arrangements and got caught in an air raid. I was injured, and my friend at the U.S. Counsel's office put me on a ship. I was quickly transported to the U.S. without any opportunity to talk to Liz or her family. I just disappeared!"

"Liz was the daughter?" Molly asked.

"Yes. When I got home, my memory was damaged. The memory of the time I spent in England was gone. Slowly, they have reappeared in my mind. I've had no contact with that family in about five years."

"That must be difficult," Molly said, looking into my eyes.

"While I'm baring my soul, I might as well tell you that I had an affair with a French girl, while we were biking from the Alps to the coast."

"You were a busy guy, it seems."

"Yes, I guess I was. But now I have met the perfect woman. She's certainly someone with whom I have a lot in common.

"Maybe you aren't ready to get serious," Molly said.

"I don't know. And then I see that movie, and it all comes back to me. I just disappeared from England never to be heard from again!"

Molly was thoughtful. "Maybe you need to go back to Europe to get closure on some of your relationships. Maybe you need to retrace your steps."

I looked at her for a long time. I couldn't think straight.

We heard Kim and her friends coming into the hallway. It was time for me to leave. We stood and walked to the front door. I gave her a quick hug and kiss. We greeted Kim in the hallway, and I was soon on my way home.

"Thanks for the movie," Molly called.

■ ■ ■

The Christmas of 1945 was special. I was halfway through my first year of full-time teaching, and things were going well. I was at home for the holidays, and it was good to see my parents and spend time with them. My father was retired from the university and seemed to be enjoying himself. He had a wood shop in the garage and had learned to make beautiful furniture. My mother also seemed quite happy. She still worked as a music teacher, giving piano lessons almost every afternoon. They had lots of friends and were able to travel now that the war was over. The only thing missing was grandchildren, but they did not pressure me.

Shortly after Christmas, I received a call from the History Department secretary at the university. It was bad news. Dr. Hoffman's wife had died peacefully in her sleep. There was to be a service in two days. I told her I would attend. This meant that I would have to cut my visit with my parents. I had planned to return to the university by the end of the week. Now, I would have to move my time schedule up a few days. I wondered what I could do for Dr. Hoffman. I felt so bad for him, and I knew he would be lonely. He was a church member and would no doubt receive comfort from the parishioners and the priests. But what could I do?

When I returned home from the funeral, a package awaited me. One of my parents must have left it, so that I would see it when I returned. I was puzzled. Who would send me a package? Was it from Molly? No, it was from England. I opened the package. There was a letter and what looked like a book wrapped up. The letter was from Anna, Liz's mother. She explained that she was cleaning my old room and found the enclosed booklet in the back of one of the drawers. Per Mr. Bayley's instructions, they had given my clothes to a church that redistributed second-hand items to the poor. They had missed my journal, when they cleaned out my old room. Later, they found the book. The family thought I might want to have the journal as a memory of my trip to Europe. Everyone was well, and they hoped I had recuperated from my injuries. I opened the package and found the journal, I had kept throughout 1939-1940 on my travels through Europe. I thumbed through the book.

I retreated to my room and began reading. It was a trip down memory lane. Gretchen, Brigit and Liz were all there. So were the Nazis, my biking across France, Dunkirk and Rye. It had been an exciting adventure, but there was no ending. Molly was right. I needed closure. How could I get to Europe? Many of the people were still crawling out from under the rubble of war. I made up my mind to get more information on traveling to Europe.

Back at the university, I saw my friend, Dr. Hoffman. He looked sad and lost. I knew I had to try and cheer him up. I wished Molly were here to help, but she had moved to Virginia. I made a date with Dr. Hoffman for dinner. Later that week, we met and he greeted me with a meek smile. We shook hands, and we were seated immediately at a table with a white tablecloth, cloth napkins and a candle. I was nervous and not sure what to say.

He asked about my classes, and I said they were going well.

"I'm glad to hear that, Dr. Morgan," he said.

"What's with this 'Dr. Morgan?'" I asked.

"Look," he said. "I'm Frank, and you are Mitchell or Mitch. We are colleagues and friends. I know it's hard to call someone by their first name after all this time of calling me Dr. Hoffman. But give it a shot. You make me feel old."

"O.K., Frank," I said. "Let's toast to that. Since we are being up front with each other, Frank, I have to be honest. You don't look so good. I know this is a rough time in your life with losing your wife. Can we talk about that?"

"Sure, we can, but there isn't much to say. She's gone."

"You must be lonely," I said.

"She was a great companion to me. She was someone to share my life. I have my students and fellow teachers, but that goes just so far."

"I kind of feel the same way. When I was a T.A., we graduate students had each other, a built-in support group. Now we're scattered all around. Some are in the army, and two are teaching in Virginia," I continued. "I've been toying with an idea and would like your opinion."

"Yes, go on," Frank said with interest.

"Do you remember that in 1939 and 1940, I was in Europe learning to speak German and French? During that time I met some people, and now I need to know what happened to them. When I got to England, I was in a bomb explosion. The next thing I knew, I was back home in the U.S. I need to know about those people."

"Tell me about them," he said. "Was there romance involved?"

"There was a German man, a vet from World War I, and his granddaughter. There was another German family I stayed with. There was a Luftwaffe pilot who surrendered to me. I have his wrist watch on now with his name and address engraved on the back. I rode a bike across France with a French girl. She had a family in Abbeville. And I met an Englishman and his daughter, who rescued me at Dunkirk. His family nursed me back to health. Then I met an American Consul in London, who helped me return to the U.S. And, yes, romance was involved."

"Hum," Frank said. "It seems simple enough. Go to Europe and look them up."

"There are others," I explained. "The German girl had a soldier boyfriend. One of the T.A.s from here is in Germany. Do you remember Herman Hamilton?"

"Oh, yes," said Frank. " He's in the Army Air Force I believe."

"And one more thing," I said looking Frank squarely in the eyes. I took a deep breath. "I want you to go with me."

"Why me?" he said in a surprised voice.

"Because I need your friendship and support. I need someone to share the trip with me. I would consider it an honor, if you would go."

"That's ridiculous. I'm an old man who would slow you down."

"Look," I said. "You could take notes for a book on the post-war conditions in Europe and include stories about these people and others we might meet."

"Nah," Frank said. "I've got too much going on here to leave for the summer. I need to be here."

I was getting emotional now. "Frank, you stay here and you'll spend all summer feeling sorry for yourself. Get off your ass and do something. It would be good for us both."

I couldn't believe I had said this to Frank.

He looked shocked. Then slowly a smile came to his face. "What are you getting so worked up about?" he asked. "I'll think about it and let you know."

Two months later we sailed on the S.S. President Garfield for Amsterdam.

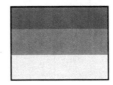

CHAPTER 15
THE SUMMER OF 1946: GRETCHEN

Frank and I stepped off the ship and onto the runway to the pier in Amsterdam. Our voyage had been generally in smooth waters and uneventful. We looked back to the "U.S. President Garfield."

For the first time, I noticed the red, white and blue color schemes of the ship. The smoke stack had stripes of blue, white and red. There were several American flags flying from the stern and the high pole towards the front of the ship. The upper part of the ship was painted white, the lower part navy blue and the water line red. It had been a good trip on a comfortable ship.

Frank had read *The Great Gatsby* on the ship, and now he addressed me as 'old sport,' as in the novel.

"Well, here we are in Amsterdam, old sport. You call the plays and I will just sit back and enjoy the ride."

"We have to find the train station," I said. Then we'll buy tickets for Munich and Bad Aibling."

"That's a plan, old sport," said Frank.

I found myself hoping that he would read another book soon and forget about the 'old sport' routine.

Eventually, we found the train station only to learn that our train would not leave for about two hours. We decided to walk around the city. Maybe Frank could find someone to interview for his book. I expected to see more damage to the city than we found. We observed that cleanliness was not a priority. There was general neglect with dirt and trash cluttering the streets. There were damaged buildings, but I expected many more. I was surprised that so few people were out walking the streets. The one exception was a scantily clad young lady, who smiled at us as we walked by. The woman had on shorts that exposed long thin legs and a T-shirt that was much too small. The smell of cheap perfume hovered over us. She spoke to us in French.

Do you need directions?" she asked. "I could show you around town."

We declined her offer, but she was persistent. "My cousin has a room nearby. We could go there and talk."

"Thanks," I replied. "Some other time, but now I must get my elderly father to his doctor's appointment."

"Too bad, we could have had a good time.

We walked on. Frank smiled at me. "That was a low blow, 'old sport.' I could have interviewed her."

"Sure," I said sarcastically. "You go with her, and you would be too tired to make it back to the train station."

Without further adventures, we returned to the train depot. We boarded our train and found our seats. Eventually, we pulled out of the station. We were on our way to Munich. The train was not crowded. An older couple sat in front of us. They nodded, but did not invite conversation. Two priests sat behind us, and a young woman with two small children was to our right.

The train picked up speed, and I sat glued to the window. I wanted to see as much as I could during the day. I could sleep at night. We rushed pass green fields covered with the bright colors of summer flowers. Farmers worked their crops, and livestock grazed in the verdant fields. We viewed small villages untouched by war and other terrain that was bruised by conflict. Here the earth was gashed, causing deep holes in the ground. Skeletal trees stood with branches bare. It was a savage scene of destruction. We pulled into Brussels and stopped for a short time. After a Coke and croissants, we settled down for the ride to Paris. I read a little, took a short nap, and gazed out the window.

It was a thrill to pull into Paris. There was little destruction. The city had been declared an open city during the war, and the Germans had generally abided by that. Paris was Paris. We did a lot of 'people watching,' took a short walk, and sat in an open air café for a time before we boarded the train again. Geneva was the next big city on our agenda. The lake was gorgeous and the city inspiring. It was a welcome change from dirty and damaged France. We traveled on to the Swiss foothills and then the beautiful Alps. Such natural beauty was a welcome sight.

At daybreak, I learned we were in Germany. In some areas the country seemed unchanged from hundreds of years ago. In other places I could see miles and miles of destruction. I saw burned land, half destroyed towns and many graveyards. Most of the churches had been damaged. There were signs of reconstruction and clean-up efforts were plentiful, however, it would take years before the scars of conflict healed.

Later that day we pulled into Munich. I remembered from my first trip to Munich the hustle and bustle of people that filled the streets and sidewalks. Now the roads were almost empty. Ruble was everywhere. No red, black and white banners or flags were on display. Flowers seemed non-existent. Several American soldiers walked the streets. Many laborers were cleaning up the mess and working on reconstruction of buildings and roads.

At the station, we claimed our traveling bags and checked to see if, indeed, there was still a local train to Bad Aibling. To our relief there was. We had only a short wait, before that train was ready to leave. While we waited, I related to Frank about the time I had visited Munich. I told him about the Wagner Opera I had attended, the mobs in the streets, dancing after the opera and my pushing match with the German soldier. I told him of hiking in the mountains, but I left out the part about Gretchen's family cabin in the valley by the lake.

The trip to Bad Aibling took a while with stops at small villages along the way. As we neared my old home, I began to get excited. Finally, we arrived. The train station was much the same as it had been, when I skipped out of town in 1940. The one big difference was the presence of U.S. Army and Air Force personnel. I wondered if any of my old friends were still here. It was rather late for today, but I would check up on some of them tomorrow.

Frank and I gathered our belongings and looked for a cab. We had no luck. I tried to remember if they even had any taxis here. Frank noticed a luggage accommodation, and we stored our bags there. I decided we should walk to the Café Arnold and get some dinner. Then we would check on hotel vacancies. It was getting late in the afternoon, so we walked briskly to Arnold's. I was relieved to see that it appeared untouched by the war. As we approached, we saw people eating on the upper deck. In addition, tables and chairs were outside on a wooden deck. There was a generous sprinkling of American military personnel at the Café.

Since there were no tables available, we ate at the bar. The bartender was different from the one I had known. Instead of young girls waiting tables, there were older women taking food orders. No one looked familiar. Frank and I sipped our beers. A soldier sat next to Frank, so he tried to make conversation with him. It didn't go very far, as the G.I. was more interested in the young lady sitting on his other side. We listened to American music from a juke box, and most everyone sang the songs in English. The air was filled with cigarette smoke. The airman sitting next to me tried to bum a light from me, but I had no matches. When he realized I was American, he became curious.

"What part of the states are you from?" he asked.

"We are from North Carolina. How about you?"

"Name's Joe. I'm from Maryland. I've got a buddy from Carolina. He went to the university in your state." He took a drag on his cigarette and blew the smoke into the air above him. "What are you guys doing in this corner of the world?"

"My friend, Frank, here, is writing a book about post-war-Europe and I'm just along for the ride."

"Actually," Frank said, "I'm really the one along for the ride. My friend, Mitchell, studied here in 1939, and we came back to see how his old friends are doing."

"Are you guys teachers or what?" Joe asked.

"Yes," I said. "We're history professors at the State University."

"Yeah?" he said. "One of my buddies went to school at the same place, I think."

"I was there in the early 40's," I added.

"Sounds about right for Herman," Joe said thoughtfully.

"Herman who?" I blurted out.

"Herman Hamilton," Joe replied, "but we call him 'Herm the Germ.'"

"Oh, my God," exclaimed Frank. "We know that guy."

"He's a good friend of mine," I said. "And he's here?"

Joe turned to the bartender. "Hey, let me use your phone," he said. "It's an emergency."

The bartender had a phone on a long extension cord. He placed it on the bar in front of Joe. The soldier dialed some numbers.

"Hey, Jimmy, let me talk to Herm."

Joe waited patiently. There was a muffled voice at the other end.

"Hey, Herm, this is Joe. I want you to come to Arnold's immediately. There are some old friends of yours here."

There was another muffled voice.

"Look, Herm, I don't have time to explain. This is not a joke. Just get here as quickly as possible." Joe hung up the phone and thanked the bartender. "He's on his way! You guys finish your meal, and he will be here." He tipped his glass and smiled.

The Café customers were singing: "Gonna Take a Sentimental Journey," when Herm entered the bar. Joe waved to him. Shortly the three of us were shaking hands and pounding each other on the back. Joe bought a round of beers and we settled down to drink and take a sentimental journey back home to North Carolina and graduate school. I filled him in on the activities of the teaching assistants that he knew and my job at the university.

"I could have predicted all of this, except I thought you and Molly might have gotten married," Herm said.

"Nope," I replied flippantly. "She is happily teaching in Virginia."

Herm filled us in on his life since 1942. He had been to officer's candidate school, pilot training and had many experiences. He had been stationed in England, flew bombing runs over Germany and had post-war duty in Bad Aibling.

"What about your love life?" I questioned.

"I was engaged to a girl in Texas," Herm said, "then I moved to England, and the engagement fell apart. In England, I met another girl, but she had to take care of her wounded ex-boyfriend. Now in Germany, I have met the perfect girl, but she doesn't want to move around the world like the Air Force wants me to do. So where does that leave me?"

"Up a creek," Joe offered.

We all drank to Herm being 'up a creek.'

"Very funny, very funny," Herm conceded. "Now, what can I do for you guys? Do you need a car?"

"Thanks, Herm," I said, "but we planned to rent one."

"Nonsense," said Herm. "You can use mine for a few days. I can catch a ride to the air base, where I work."

"We can't argue with that," Frank said.

After several more rounds of beer, we gave Herm a ride home, gathered our bags from the train station and checked into the local hotel he recommended. I hoped the next day would bring me in contact with some of my old friends in Bad Aibling.

■ ■ ■

The next morning, after a generous breakfast of coffee, bread, meat and cheese, we made our way to the Mueller home, where I had stayed for almost a year. Nothing much had changed. The house looked the same, but the bushes and trees looked bigger. Inga answered my knock at the door. She was absolutely shocked to see me. She hugged me, and tears came to her eyes. She called to Fritz, and with some exertion and the use of a cane, he greeted me warmly. I introduced Frank to them, and we had some coffee and bread. I told them about my 'escape' from Germany in 1940 across the lake to Switzerland. I filled them in on my bike ride through France to Dunkirk and the bombing of London. I told them of the good news on the Ph.D. This was the first time Frank had heard in detail about my experiences in Europe. In turn, we asked about them and their family. Their daughter, Greta, still worked in Munich, but now for the American occupying forces. Their son had served on the Eastern Front in the Luftwaffe and sadly, was assumed dead, as he was never heard from again. His plane was shot down somewhere over Russia, and that was all they knew. Frank asked questions about the U.S. occupation. The Germans seemed pleased that they were under U.S. jurisdiction rather than French, British or Russian.

I asked Fritz if German officials had inquired about my whereabouts. He responded that it was several weeks after I left, when they reported my absence. The officials seemed concerned at that time, but when things went badly in Russia, they quickly forgot about me and tried to deal with more pressing concerns. Inga had given my clothes away and could only pray for my safety.

I thanked the Muellers for the generous care they had given me during my stay. We exchanged addresses and phone numbers and promised to keep in touch. We hugged, shook hands and waved good-bye as we returned to our car.

"What's next, fearless leader?" asked Frank.

"A picnic by a stream in the country-side," I replied.

We drove through the hill country and eventually came to my stream. We had picked up groceries and settled down to my private bubbling stream. It was beautiful there. We walked in the woods and sat by the stream. I threw a few rocks into the water, and I told Frank why I loved this sanctuary so much.

"I think the secret police thought I had a radio hidden in the woods, but, of course, I didn't."

"It seems to me that you were much too obvious to be a real spy," said Frank.

"I'm sure you're right," I said. "It was probably a figment of my imagination."

We ate and enjoyed my little paradise. Later we returned to our room to freshen up before we met Joe and 'Herm the Germ' for dinner at the Café Arnold. A plan was beginning to brew in Herm's mind.

"Look guys," he said, "I need to go to Berlin on business for the Air Force. I can get a military vehicle, and the three of us can go to the big city. I also have some leave time due, and I think I can arrange to keep the Air Force car. We could drive on into France. What do you think?"

"That would be perfect," I said.

"Sounds like a plan," chimed in Frank. "We could probably meet all sorts of people to interview."

"I need another day or two here in Bad Aibling," I added.

"It will take a day or so to line up everything," Herm said.

Our waitress arrived with our food. We had ordered hamburgers and fries. She explained that the cooks were trying to learn how to cook American, since so many of their clients were from the States. It looked good, as we were all very hungry from our busy day's activities. The burgers were cooked just right; the potatoes weren't quite there yet; the tomatoes and lettuce were hard to mess up; beers topped off a perfect meal. After apple pie and several more beers, we called it a night. Tomorrow, I would try to locate Helmuth von Schwartz and his granddaughter, Gretchen. If he was still alive, Helmuth would be up there in years. Gretchen was probably married to her Luftwaffe boyfriend, Hans, assuming he made it through the war.

■ ■ ■

The next day was beautiful with sun and blue sky. It was shirt-sleeve weather and a wonderful day to take a walk in the park. After lunch, Frank and I made our way to the lush green land full of grass, trees and walkways lined with benches and flowers. Although many people were in the park, the atmosphere was somber. In the past, I remembered lots of activity with soccer games, people walking and jogging, and groups of young people exercising or singing and, of course, older men playing backgammon. Frank and I walked the paths and noticed people who suffered from injuries. The war had taken a huge toll, as judged by the appearance of the people in the park. Some were in wheel chairs and others used crutches.

We turned a corner, and there they were, the backgammon players. Some things never change. Many elderly men and a few women bent over the game tables playing their hearts out. Some of the banter was still there, but on the whole, it was a solemn gathering. I looked for Helmuth, as Frank and I walked along. I couldn't find him. I asked at one table, if the players knew Helmuth. They didn't. Then I noticed an old man slumped over in his wheelchair. There was something about him. I walked over to him and stood in front of his chair. He was asleep. At a table close by, the game came to a conclusion, and the winner stood and celebrated. "Finally, I beat you!" There was cheering all around. The noise woke the sleeping man. He looked up and around. I stood looking at him and he at me. I wasn't sure if it was Helmuth or not.

He looked at me and his face broke into a smile. "Mitch, is that you, or am I dreaming?"

"It's me, Helmuth, it's me!"

We shook hands warmly and just looked at each other for a long time.

"You made it through the war," I exclaimed.

"And you, also," he said. "I have thought about you many times. I must hear all your news."

"You will," I promised, "you will. But first, let me introduce you to my friend, Dr. Frank Hoffman. He was my advisor for my Ph.D. program, and now we are colleagues at the state university. And Frank, this is my dear friend, Helmuth von Schwartz, a veteran of the Great War."

The two shook hands warmly. Frank looked around and said he wanted some coffee, so that we could sit and talk. Helmuth told him where there was a small coffee house a short distance along the path. Frank said he would get us coffee, and we could all sit and talk. Frank took off, and I leisurely pushed Helmuth's wheelchair at a much slower pace.

"Tell me what you did after you left Bad Aibling," the old man demanded.

I related my train trip to Lindau, the Lake Constance boat crossing, and the train episode across Switzerland to France. I told him of my bike adventure through France to Dunkirk, the rescue, and of my stay in England, including my capture of the German pilot and the bombing of London. I skipped the part about Brigit and Liz and moved on to my university days and my teaching career.

"What, no romance in your life?" he asked.

"Well, maybe a little, but I'm not married, yet," I said.

By now, we had reached Frank and the coffee. We joined him at a table and sipped our drinks.

"Now, it's your turn, Helmuth. Tell us how you survived the war." I added that Frank was writing a book about post-war Europe and might like to use his story of survival. Helmuth nodded and started speaking.

"Well, my story is very simple. When there were bombing raids, my wife and I went to the shelters. When the Americans got here, I was truly glad to see them. It was a forgone conclusion that we were soundly defeated, and I was only glad that the Americans, not the Russians, came into this part of the country. They treated us as well as they could, and provided law, order, and food. Most of them acted in a civilized manner. The only thing I hated Americans for were the deadly bombing runs that killed so many innocent children. But I'm sure they weren't trying to hit the young people."

Frank asked many other questions, and I could tell that Helmuth was getting tired. I tried to change the focus away from the older man to the others.

"How are Gretchen and Hans?"

Helmuth quickly looked at his watch.

"You can see for yourself," he said. "I am supposed to meet them here at the coffee shop about now. As a matter of fact, here they come." He waved a greeting to them, and they came over to our table.

Hans, in a wheelchair, did not recognize me. The two young children with them had no clue who we were. Gretchen looked stunned and not sure if it really was me.

"Mitchell," she said in a meek voice. "Is that really you?"

"Yes, it's me." I shook her hand and introduced her to Frank.

Gretchen, in turn, introduced us to her two sons, Joseph, who was two, and Heinrich, who was five. By now Hans had figured out who I was, and we shook hands. Hans appeared to have lost a leg. He seemed a little put out at our interruption of his day. We pulled additional chairs over to the table and ordered more coffee and juice for the boys.

After a lot of general chatter with Hans and the young lads, Gretchen suggested we walk to a nearby lake that had a fountain. The boys were restless and needed to keep busy. We finished our drinks and prepared for the walk. Frank immediately latched on to Hans and began questioning him about life on the Eastern Front during the war, as he pushed Han's wheelchair.

Helmuth and Heinrich began to toss a ball, and then the boy helped push the older man and his wheelchair along the road way. That left Gretchen, Joseph in a stroller and me to follow along behind in the procession.

Gretchen looked good but tired. I figured she had three people to look after, and the stress was beginning to show. She told me I looked good and healthy. I told her about my various wounds and the rest of my life's happenings.

"Why haven't you gotten married?" she asked. But before I could answer, she apologized for being so forward.

I mumbled something about not finding the right woman.

"At one point I wanted to be that woman, but our situation was too much to overcome. You were an American and about to leave Germany. It made no sense for us to fall in love."

I was surprised at her frankness, but managed to agree that there were too many hurdles to make it work.

She continued. "The time we had alone in the mountains was wonderful. I wanted to ask you to stay, but I realized you had to go. Also, Hans was in the picture. There was just too much pulling me away from you."

"In another time and place it might have worked. But you are right, we had too much going against us."

"Well," she said with a smile, "I still think about you."

"Me, too," I added.

Joseph let out a shrill scream, climbed out of his stroller and staggered over to his mamma to hug her leg.

I was touched. "You sure have two wonderful sons."

Gretchen smiled at me, and we caught up with the rest of the group.

We all admired the beautiful lake and the fountain. There were a few sailboats and row boats for rent, but it seemed time to go our separate ways. We all shook hands. I told Helmuth and Gretchen that they would be in my thoughts often. Frank and I watched as our friends slowly moved away: the two men in wheelchairs, one a veteran of the Great War, and the other a medal winner of World War II. Both men had traumatic experiences in their lives. Gretchen's life was still in front of her, but the future of Germany lay squarely in the hands of the two young boys.

Frank and I turned to walk back through the park. My friend looked thoughtful.

"Helmuth seemed like a cherished friend," he observed.

"Yes, he was," I agreed. "We talked a lot, and he was the epitome of the good German. Hans and Gretchen were a product of the Nazi culture that dominated their generation."

"Gretchen seemed a little bit more than just your good friend's granddaughter," Frank added with a sly grin on his face.

"She was, but it was an impossible situation for affairs of the heart."

"Right," Frank agreed, but with a trace of sarcasm in his voice.

CHAPTER 16
ANTS

Two days later, the Air Force car was packed with food and clothes. Herm had all the papers we needed to travel through Russian occupied territory. It was a long and difficult trip. Many of the cities we passed had been bombed almost flat. There was little traffic on the roads, so we made good time except for the various checkpoints, where we had to show our papers to the authorities. It was clear the Reds were not pleased we were traveling through their sector of Germany where Berlin was located.

Finally, we arrived in the great city, and Herm reported his arrival to U.S. authorities. He secured two rooms for us at the military hotel. After a quick dinner, we went to our rooms, where we read and slept. Frank was busy getting his notes organized for his book. The next day, having recovered from our trip, Herm went to attend to his work. Frank and I toured the city. It was a mess of wreckage, although some buildings were being repaired. We also saw new construction. I learned that being a tourist can be tiring. Eventually, we returned to the military base and met Herm at the officers' club.

The club was full for the cocktail hour. I decided to have a Coke, Frank selected a German beer and Herm had whiskey. We relaxed and related our observations of the day's activity. Herm said he needed a couple more days to complete his work. Then, we could head for France. Frank and I felt we could keep busy during that time. We had our meal and enjoyed the festivities at the club. There were six officers at the table next to us. There was evidently a birthday celebration in the making. Soon a cake and candles appeared, and the singing began. The birthday song did not go well. Someone was off key.

"We will keep singing, until we get it right," one officer announced.

One of them invited our table to join in the singing. We all joined in with the music.

"Whose birthday is it?" I asked.

"It's Colonel Bayley's," someone replied.

We sang it several more times, and others joined in. Before long, everyone was singing "Happy Birthday, Colonel Bayley." The officer looked familiar to me. I wondered if he was a relative of Waldo Bayley, the man at the ambassador's office in London that I had dealt with six years ago. Colonel Bayley was about five-feet ten with graying hair and blue eyes. Waldo was much taller, although they still could be related. Later in the evening, the Colonel came over to our table and thanked us for singing with his group. At this juncture, I asked him about Waldo and explained he had helped me return to the U.S. from England in 1940.

"Waldo is my younger brother," he said.

"How is he doing? Is he still in London?"

"No, he isn't," the Colonel replied. "He resigned from the Foreign Service and volunteered for duty in the U.S. Navy when the U.S. entered the war. He's doing fine and hopes to return to the Diplomatic Service soon."

"I'm glad to hear he is doing well," I said. "He sure helped me out in a time of need," I added.

"So what brings you to Germany at this time?" he asked.

I filled him in on our plans and our background. He seemed particularly interested in the fact that Frank and I spoke German and French. The Colonel seemed lost in thought, and then in a serious tone, he made us promise that we would meet him tomorrow night for dinner at the Officers' Club. We promised, and he bid us farewell.

Frank was the first to speak. "I wonder why he wants to see us?"

"It's a mystery," I said.

Frank and I sat quietly in thought. Two other soldiers joined us at our table. One of them asked: "Do you know who that guy is?"

"Not really," Frank said.

"Well, let me tell you. He's a former college Biology professor. In the army he's a sanitary engineer in charge of Typhus Fever control in the European Theater. That means that he liberates work camps and Jewish extermination prisons."

"You could have fooled me," I said, "although he does look like a scholar."

"He's a tough guy on top of it all," the soldier said. "He landed eight days after D-Day in France. He followed behind an American tank unit in a jeep. I know because I was the driver. We came to a detention camp in western Germany. The S.S. troops who were guarding laborers ran away when we arrived. Colonel Bayley nursed the inmates back to health. He was told that trains would come through the area to take the prisoners back home, but none came. So the Colonel sent his men to a nearby town to knock on doors and ordered that all vehicles be driven to a field outside of town. He threatened to shoot all those who did not deliver their cars. Since there were no trains, the autos would take the people to Poland and France, wherever they came from. Some way the people would get home."

"That's an amazing story," I said, "but it doesn't explain why he wants to see us tomorrow."

"That's not the end of the story," the soldier said. "Later on, he won the Croix de Guerre medal, a highly valued award, for the repatriation of the French. They called him the 'red tape slasher.'"

Frank was thoughtful. "What is his job now?"

The second soldier answered. "He is doing a survey of Museums of Natural History in Europe. He is assigned to survey the status of their collections, specifically the types of insect specimens they have."

"Sounds fascinating," I said, "but I can hardly tell the difference between an ant and a butterfly."

"The Colonel probably wants to hear more about his brother, Waldo, when we meet tomorrow night," Frank said.

■ ■ ■

The next day Frank and I went into the center of Berlin to walk in the parks and survey the damage done by Allied bombing during the war. We noted some bombed out churches and learned that one church, nearly destroyed, would be left in that condition as a remembrance and memorial to the war. What a grim reminder. Some buildings were being repaired. Others were being torn down and replaced with new structures.

We found an outdoor café and sat down for a beer. It was time for lunch. We relaxed in the sun and enjoyed watching the busy people in their daily activities. We ordered our meal and talked with our elderly waiter. When he realized we were Americans, he warned us against walking too close to the construction scaffolding. He explained that if the embittered workers realized we were Americans, we could "accidently" be hit by falling bricks or stones. It had happened before, and he was concerned that we might get hurt. Frank talked to the waiter for a long time and gained another interview for his book. We tipped the waiter generously and made our way for more sightseeing in the battered city.

That evening, we met Herm and Joe for cocktails. We decided to buy several bottles of wine. We talked of the day's activities and were soon joined by Colonel Bayley. He had a Coke and regaled us with stories of his days during the war. While eating dessert, the Colonel got down to business. He needed our help in one of his projects.

"Here's the deal," the Colonel said. "During the winter of 1944-1945, I was in Maastricht, Holland, doing some work with Typhus control. While I was there, I became aware that the Nazis had stolen the famous Wasmann and Schmidt Entomological Collection and Library from the Museum of Natural History at Maastricht and removed it to the University of Berlin. I have decided to take it back to the Dutch."

"How do we fit into this?" I asked.

"I need you and Frank to impersonate Dutch government officials from Maastricht, demanding the return of the collection. You both speak German and French, and I think you could be convincing."

"Wow!" said Frank. "I know zero about ants."

"Doesn't matter," said the Colonel, "just act like public officials."

"Suppose the Germans refuse to give them back?" I asked.

"Leave it to me. They will gladly give them back, when I finish with the curator." He paused. "I'll tell you what. I've got lots of booze I'll give you."

I looked at Frank. He shrugged. "We drink very little whiskey, Colonel," I said.

"Well, I've got cartons of cigarettes for you, also."

"Sorry sir, we don't smoke."

"What the hell is wrong with you guys?" he asked. "How about good old fashioned patriotism? The Dutch would be grateful to Uncle Sam if we got those ants back."

Frank smiled. "You've got a deal, Colonel."

"Good!" he said. "I'll pick you up at 8:00 a.m. tomorrow at your hotel. Meet you in the lobby."

"It's a deal," I said.

■ ■ ■

The next morning Colonel Bayley greeted us. "First stop is U.S. Army Berlin District Headquarters. We need a truck."

We went out to his jeep, and the driver took us to the transportation office. We entered the office. The clerk greeted us and Bayley inquired about the truck he had arranged earlier.

"We need to book passage for Maastricht, Holland," he said.

"For yourself, Colonel?" the clerk asked.

"For some ants," Bayley answered.

"Funny," the clerk said, "but it sounded like you said 'ants.'"

"Precisely," announced the Colonel with a twinkle in his eyes.

"But Colonel, sir, isn't this a trifle irregular?"

"Not at all," responded the officer. "You see, these aren't ordinary insects. They are what is indisputably the world's greatest collection of ants."

"Live ants, Colonel?"

"Hardly," he replied. "Most of them have been dead for a quarter of a century or better."

"And how do they happen to be in Berlin?"

"Stolen."

"Nazis?"

"Who else?"

Bayley obtained a ten-ton truck, a driver and four German laborers. Escorted by the three of us in the jeep, we entered into the Russian sector of Berlin to the University Museum. The Colonel, Frank and I entered the museum. We were met by Professor Hans Bishop, the curator of the Museum. He was a tall, thin, elderly man. Colonel Bayley introduced himself as a professor of entomology and biology from the States. Bishop seemed pleased to meet a kindred soul.

"I'm especially interested in seeing some entomological specimens," Bayley told the curator.

"You've come to the right place. I've got the finest collection in the world."

The Colonel looked surprised. "Why I thought the Wasmann Collection held that distinction."

"That's just the one I mean," said Bishop beaming.

"All right, you old codger," said the Colonel "The jig's up. You stole those ants, and I'm here to return them to the Dutch. If so much as one antenna is broken on one ant," Bayley growled at the German and drew his thumb across his throat in a well understood gesture.

Bishop grew indignant. "This is preposterous," he sputtered,

"I'm not here to argue," said Bayley. "Either I get those ants, 'tout suite' or there will be one more war criminal in the clink before nightfall."

"Let's not be hasty," said Bishop, highly agitated. "When would you like to get the collection?"

"Now!" Bayley said, ending the conversation.

Frank and I stood there translating this extraordinary exchange.

The Colonel turned to me. "Mitchell, would you go outside and bring in the men, and let's get this stuff loaded and out of here."

"Yes, sir," I said.

Most of the collection was in the basement, and there was no electricity. Bayley had bought several flashlights, which we put to good use. There were hundreds of books, boxes of letters, several hundred glass jars containing ant specimens carefully preserved in alcohol, and about 150 glass-topped trays of mounted ants. All of this was loaded onto the truck, while Russian soldiers chained the museum gates closed. They told Bayley we could not take the truck out without written and signed orders releasing the collection.

The Colonel was prepared. He and his cohorts headed for the Russian commander's headquarters with arm loads of candy bars, cigarettes, soft drinks, whiskey and magnums of champagne. They pushed their way through the Russian guards, while handing out generous amounts of their gifts, and into a plush conference room, where about twelve officers were situated. Before the startled Russians could react, they were showered with gifts. The whiskey bottles were opened, and the party began. The officers put packages of cigarettes in their pockets and drank the whiskey and champagne. The candy bars and soft drinks were also popular items. As the party continued, the whiskey bottles emptied. Most of the officers returned to their antique desks and sat in a drunken stupor. By dusk, only one Russian was still on his feet. Bayley pulled from his coat pocket a document written in Russian, authorizing the release of the collection. He thrust a pen in the hand of the swaying officer, who signed it.

The Americans wished their comrades a good day and hastily made their way back to the truck, where the German workers waited. We all jumped into the truck and jeep and drove to the gate. Bayley rolled down his window and handed the guards the signed document. While they were reading the directive, he motioned to hand out more booze and cigarettes. As we drove away, we laughed and waved to the Russians. They cheerily waved back.

"I can't believe we pulled that off!" I shouted.

The Colonel looked surprised. "What would you take, a bunch of dead ants or cigarettes, whiskey and candy bars?"

"You make a good point, Colonel," said Frank.

"Where did all the goodies come from?" I asked.

"The Army gives us this stuff every week. The problem is I don't drink alcohol or smoke cigarettes, and I shouldn't eat candy or drink soft drinks. So I save it for special occasions." Bayley winked and smiled. "This was a piece of cake."

A few weeks later, the Colonel delivered the goods to the Dutch. Frank and I heard later that there was quite a celebration in Maastricht. Colonel Bayley was awarded the Order of Van Orange-Nassau with swords, making him a nobleman and a national hero. General Dwight Eisenhower was one of a few other Americans so honored.

■ ■ ■

That evening, Frank and I met Herm for dinner. He seemed in a good mood. Once we settled around the table, he told us his good news.

"Well, I finished up my work here in Berlin today. Everything went well. I am free to travel for a few days."

"Great," I said. "When can we leave?"

"How about tomorrow noon?" Herm asked.

"That works for me," I said.

"France, here we come!" Frank added.

"What's your plan, Mitch?" Herm asked.

I told them about my bike ride across France, about Brigit and Dunkirk.

"So we follow your trail all the way to the coast?" Herm asked.

"Right, but there will be stops along the way. We might check on Brigit in Abbeville."

"You and your girlfriends." Frank smiled. "You know I pictured you slaving over irregular French verb books. I should have known better than that. You found a much more enjoyable way to learn German and French."

"It worked, and I passed my foreign language exams," I said in my defense.

"It's a good thing you only needed two foreign languages," Frank said.

"To tell you the truth, there was so much German and French, that I found I needed a refresher course in English."

"Right," mumbled Herm. "Somehow, I don't remember graduate school as being so much fun."

There was a pause in the conversation, as we finished our

meal. The waitress replenished our water glasses, and we ordered dessert.

As if to fill the lull in our conversation, Herm asked how our day had gone. "Did you interview more Germans for your book, Frank?"

"More or less, but they were Russians, not Germans."

I joined in the conversation. "We were busy liberating Dutch ants from the Germans in the Russian sector of Berlin."

"Sure, you were," said 'Herm the Germ.'

CHAPTER 17
SUMMER OF 1946: BRIGIT

It seemed like we drove forever. I thought we would never leave Germany. Our maps were outdated and basically, we had no clue where we were going. On the journey we drove south and west and eventually landed in Cologne. The beautiful churches were in ruins. I stood in wonder of the pounding the city had endured. Next, we headed south through Bonn, Remagen, Koblenz, Mannheim and finally Heidelberg. Here we rested and walked the famous bridge, as best we could. There was destruction everywhere.

On the road again, we crossed the German-French border

near Strasbourg and on to Nancy and Reims. We crossed many rivers and witnessed many breathtaking scenes of the French countryside. I insisted that we try a few country roads, so that my friends might have some idea of how a bike ride might have been. I'm sure they appreciated this opportunity. I looked everywhere for familiar farms or children's orphanages. Brigit and I had traveled these roads only six years ago and yet little seemed familiar. Finally, we came to a stream I recognized, and to my delight, there were Gypsies camped there. I asked Herman to pull over to the side of the road, and I rolled down my window. Soon, a man walked over. We talked for a while, but he did not know Francis, the Gypsy, whom I had visited before. He had no objections if we stretched our legs by the stream and had a bite to eat.

"I will send over some drinking water and bread we have just finished baking," he said.

The three of us piled out of the car. I could tell that Frank wanted an opportunity to interview the Gypsies. I wanted to eat, and Herm wanted to eat and drink. We sat on rocks near the stream, and soon several teenaged girls brought over the bread and water. Colonel Bayley had given us the left-over soft drinks, candy bars and cigarettes from our foray into the University of Berlin Museum. There was no whiskey, as the Russians, with their amazing capacity for alcohol, had finished it. Frank gave the Gypsy girls some chocolate bars. Herm shared the Cokes.

Men from the camp built a large fire and invited us to join them. We had lots of tobacco left over from the Berlin episode, and we shared it with them. Some of the women carried over cheese and wine to go with the bread. I hoped there would be music and dancing, and I was not disappointed. A man began playing a guitar, and he was joined by an accordion player. Later a woman violinist joined in. Several of the songs we could sing in English. I noticed Frank had a nice bass voice. On the other hand, Herm did his part by not singing. As it was getting late, some of the people began to drift off to their camp wagons, to rest and sleep. We were given blankets, and we settled down by the fire. I spent a restful night with the Gypsies. The next morning, after coffee and good-byes, we were off to Paris. The time with the Gypsies was a nice change of pace, and of course, Frank interviewed two more subjects for his book.

■ ■ ■

Having four days in Paris was a treat. By day, we went to art museums: the Louvre and the Impressionist collections located in several buildings. We took a boat ride on the Seine River and visited the Notre Dame Cathedral. We climbed the Eiffel Tower and viewed the Arc de Triomphe. I saw a few damaged buildings, and some roads were in disrepair. We spent a day outside of the city at Versailles, the summer home of Louis the XIV. My favorite was the Hall of Mirrors, where the Treaty that ended World War I was signed. One could walk for days around the immense grounds and flower gardens. At night, we went to an orchestra concert, to the Moulin Rouge and the Follies Bergere. Dinner was taken at outdoor cafes, and we enjoyed it all. Frank had an interview with a bartender one afternoon and with a 'gendarme' at another time.

From Paris, we traveled north to the city of Amiens, where I had met Brigit's parents. Here we had parted, she to her home in Abbeville, and I went to Dunkirk.

"What's next?" Herm asked.

"A little west of Amiens is Abbeville," I said. "When the Germans decided to invade France, they sent their tanks out of the Ardennes hills to race across northern France to the coastal city of Abbeville, thus cutting off French and British forces, who had moved into Belgium. I was there when this happened and ended up at Dunkirk, cut off and trapped by the quick moving Germans. I would like to visit Brigit to see how she is doing."

"Here we go," said Herm. "Another trip down memory lane."

"Well, she was a good biker," I said. "She was living with her parents in 1940, but I imagine there have been many changes in her life since I was with her."

"Let's find out how she is doing," Frank said.

"Another possible interview, right, Frank?"

After a brief stay in Amiens, we moved on. The city had suffered a great deal of damage during the war as far as I could tell, and it was still in bad shape. The road to Abbeville took us in a north by northwest direction toward the coast. The country was torn up, and the road was a mess. It was slow going, but finally we arrived. I did not have Brigit's home address, so she could be difficult to find. We followed the Somme River most of the way. There had been horrific battles in this area during both World War I and World War II.

On the outskirts of Abbeville, I had an empty feeling, that

we would have a difficult time finding Brigit Sauveau. "We need a phone book, unless anyone has a better idea."

Frank spoke up. "Let's find a room, get settled, and then look for a phone book."

"Works for me," said Herm.

We did just that. The hotel was small and dirty, but it was in a central location. It even had a bellhop, who also served as doorman. We got a room with two beds and a roll-away bed for me, plus an attached bathroom. What more could I ask for? Besides, there was a café next door. We unloaded our bags, got cleaned up and went downstairs. I asked the man at the check-in desk for a phone book. He said there would be one in the café. At the café, we ordered food, and I borrowed the phone book. Brigit's last name was Sauveau. There were several Sauveaus listed. I remembered that her father had given me a card, when we met in Amiens. The card was lost, but I thought his name was Paul. There was no Paul Sauveau in the book. There was no Brigit Sauveau in the book. I couldn't remember her mother's first name. I was stuck.

"What did her Dad do for a living?" Herm asked.

"That's a good question," I said slowly. "What did he do?"

"You don't remember, do you?" said Frank. "Did he look like a professional, when you met him? You know, coat and tie or did he look more like a worker, a laborer?"

I thought for a minute. "He was a professional."

"Was he a doctor, a lawyer?" Asked Herm.

"I'm thinking, I'm thinking." After a pause, "Oh yes, her mother was Simone."

"That doesn't matter," said Herm.

Frank stood up. "Let's walk around town and look at all the blown-up buildings. Maybe something will come to you. Maybe you will remember his profession. Maybe you will bump into her."

We walked the town. What a mess! At a doctor's office, we looked at the names on the door. Nothing was familiar. There were several law firm offices, but no Paul Sauveau. We passed the police station and a bank. We all stopped. I stared at the bank.

"I think he was a banker, but I'm not sure."

"Let's go inside and ask around," suggested Frank.

The bank tellers were very young looking. Herm advised me to ask for the manager. He was young, too.

"Is the bank president here?" I asked.

After a short wait, we were shown into a spacious office, where we met the head man. After introductions, I got right to the point of our visit.

"I am trying to locate the Sauveau family. I think that he was a banker back in the early 1940's and lived with his wife, Simone, and daughter, Brigit."

"When did you see them last?" the banker asked.

"It was in May, 1940, I think."

He offered us a seat. His expression turned to one of remorse. "I am sorry to tell you Paul and Simone were killed shortly after you saw them last. When the German tanks roared out of the east and drove across northern France, their objective was Abbeville. We were all in the way. There was a great deal of cannon fire and destruction of buildings. Their home took a direct hit. Both were killed instantly."

There was a pause in the conversation while we sat in silence. It took a while for this to sink in.

"What about their daughter?" I said in a soft voice. "Did she survive?"

"Yes, she did, but I know little of her whereabouts," the banker said. "Paul did not work for this bank, but we became friends through the local service club. We had lunch together at the meetings. I really did not know the daughter at all."

I thought for a moment. "Would you give me their old home address and the name of the bank where he worked? Maybe a former neighbor or bank associate could help me find the daughter."

"Yes, of course." The bank president wrote the information on the back of his business card and handed it to me. We all stood and shook hands. He said he was sorry about my loss and walked us to the door.

Once in the street, the fresh air felt good. We took a table at an outdoor café and ordered a beer.

Frank was first to speak. "As you suggested, we can talk with his associates and neighbors and try to locate Brigit."

"This all happened shortly after I was with them in Amiens," I said. "Ah…She was so helpless in the train station in Lyon and for this to happen. She must have had a very bad time of it."

"Yes," agreed Herm. " She sounds like a young, vulnerable girl. I assume the Germans left an occupation force here throughout the War."

"I would like to find her, if at all possible," I said in a determined voice.

Our waiter was very accommodating. Frank had his interview book with him, and the Frenchman wrote out detailed directions and maps to both of our destinations. We tipped the waiter generously and made our way to the bank where Paul had worked.

Inside the bank, I looked for the oldest bank officer I could find. One of the loan officers fit the bill. The sign on his desk read: Mr. Andrew Toulon, Senior Loan Officer. I explained to him the nature of our business. He remembered Paul, but could add nothing to what we already knew. Most of the bankers there were relatively young, and few had worked with him. This turned out to be a wasted visit. We thanked them for their concern and left.

The directions we had for the Sauveau residence were more difficult to follow. We walked to a city park and residential community. There were still shattered trees all around and much destruction of homes. Most of the house numbers were unreadable, but there were several homes that were undamaged or made livable with repair. We began to visit some of these residences. Most of these people were not at home. We deduced that they were probably at their jobs. Finally, we came to an occupied home. I knocked on the door, and an elderly man answered.

"Good afternoon, sir," I said. "How are you today?"

"Fine," he replied in a halting voice. "What do you want?"

"We are trying to locate the Sauveau house, or at least where it was located before the war. You see, I was a good friend of the family before the war, and while I realize Paul and Simone were killed in a bombing raid, I am trying to locate their daughter, Brigit."

"Yes," the man said. "That was a sad time, and we lost some wonderful people." He seemed to be warming up to us. "If you like," he said, "I could show you where the house, or what's left of it, is located." He took a hat off a hook inside and made his way out onto his small front porch. "Follow me."

We walked down the road a bit. Several yards were beautiful with flower gardens and trimmed grass. Most, however, were abandoned and in disarray. We paused in front of one that was about half gone. The living room, dining room and kitchen were gone, but a section where the bedrooms were located still remained. We walked up to the house and viewed the destruction.

The old man continued. "They were sitting down to dinner when the bombs came. This part of town was not normally a target, and they paid no attention to the warnings. It was a scary and freaky thing. One bomber dropped its load, but the other planes flew on. It must have been a mistake, because there was nothing of military value here. Later, the Germans bombed indiscriminately."

I pressed on. "Was the daughter there at the time of the bombings?"

"No, no," he replied. "From what I heard she lived in town and was not injured. She does stop by here from time to time to pick up some of her belongings."

We walked into the rubble and looked around. There were pieces of broken dishes, knives, forks and spoons scattered on the floor. A painting still hung on one of the walls, but by this time it was just rubbish. The painting seemed to be of a young girl playing a flute. I wondered if she was playing Debussy.

"Do you know where the daughter lives now?" I asked.

"Not really," he answered. "One of the neighbors said she saw her down by the railroad station and got the idea she lived near there. You might try that location. There are several cafes and bars around there."

We all walked down the street retracing our steps until we reached his home. We shook hands and wished him well. Following the old man's directions, we soon came to the railroad station. It was in a run-down section with dumpy-looking buildings all around. We tried the train station first, but there were very few people there, and none of them were Brigit.

"Why don't we grab a bite to eat?" offered Herm. "I'm starved."

We picked out a café and sat outside at a table covered in shade.

"Well, we are in France," Frank said. "We should have a French meal."

"Right," said Herm. "I'd like two cheeseburgers and French fries."

"Very funny," I said.

"You guys are embarrassing me," Frank said. "I just hope they can make them. I'll have the same. On second thought, I will have the same with a nice French beer."

A waitress came over to take our order. She looked about thirty, and she was all business. We gave her our order, and she looked a little put out.

"What ever happened to the old saying 'when in France do as the French do?'" she asked.

I smiled and said, "We are homesick," and then looked sad.

She left us, and we looked around the place. It seemed to be a family run business with some friends to help out. One group was having a birthday party for a young, cute, dark-haired kid. Others were at the bar apparently having an after-work drink.

The waitress returned with our beers. I tried to make conversation with her. "Have you been working here long?"

"Seems like forever," she said.

Frank joined in. "I wonder if you could help us. We are trying to locate a girl about twenty-six years old. Her name is Brigit Sauveau. We think she lives around here. You don't happen to know her, do you?"

"We have a girl named Brigit who works here. Sounds about the right age. I don't know her last name. I think she just got off work. I'll see if she is still here."

"Thanks, we would really appreciate it."

A little later the waitress brought out our food. "I told her, but I'm not sure she's coming out. She's busy."

"Thanks," I said, and the waitress left.

"Tell us about her, Mitch," said Herm.

"There are really two Brigits," I confided. "When I first met her, she was weird and distant. She had really long hair, tons of makeup and perfume, bracelets, rings, necklaces and a long skirt and sweaters. All you could see was her hair, jewelry, and clothes. Then she changed into another person. It's a long story, but we ended up riding bicycles from Lyon to Amiens. Gradually, she gave away all four suitcases full of clothes, jewelry and cosmetics to people we stayed with. She got her hair cut short, and she got a suntan. She became an attractive, athletic, nice person. She was fun to be around. She had a natural, healthy beauty."

"I imagine you two had an eventful ride across France," said Herm.

"You better eat your food or it will get cold," I said.

It must have been timely advice, because we all started eating with a certain enthusiasm. We passed the ketchup for the fries, guzzled our beers and devoured our burgers.

"Damn, the French sure can cook," said Herm. "This is better than American fixings."

Frank looked up. "Herm, do you think you are the first person to realize that the French have a certain talent in preparing food?"

"Maybe I'm the second or third to realize this. Who knows?"

Our brilliant conversation was interrupted, when a young lady came to our table.

"Is someone here looking for Brigit?"

I looked up and could not think of anything to say. Everyone looked at me. It took me a full thirty seconds to respond.

"Brigit?"

"That's my name," she said. "What do you want with..?" She stopped in mid-sentence. The hardness left her voice. Then she smiled. "Mitch? Is that you, Mitchell? It's been so long, I didn't recognize you."

I stood and hugged her. Then I stepped back and looked at her.

She said. "You look different than I remembered. You look older."

"I didn't recognize you either. It's been about six years." I was looking into the face of a stranger. She had very short hair, lots of makeup, loads of jewelry and a long skirt and sweater. I was confused about the hair. There was an extra chair at our table, and Herm offered it to her. I made the introductions and signaled to our waitress. Brigit decided on a beer. She asked about our trip. I gave her our condolences on the death of her parents. She filled me in on her life or, at least what she wanted me to know. She shared an apartment with a fellow waitress and seemed to be happy. We talked for a long time, and I thought my friends learned more about our trip through France than they ever wanted to know.

There was a birthday celebration at the next table; the story of my life. So we sang a few songs to celebrate. I remembered that was how we met Colonel Bayley in Berlin. I wondered if I would meet someone else at this party. I did. Two young Frenchmen came up to the table and addressed Brigit.

"It's about time for another haircut, Briggy gal," one said with a big smile.

"Go to hell," she replied.

"We'll see you one of these nights." They walked away.

"What was that all about?" I asked, as I watched the two walk over to another table near the door. One of them was thin and very strange looking. The other was short and overweight. They both looked like out-of-shape punks.

Brigit hesitated to answer. "I guess it's time for the truth. During the war, the Germans occupied this whole area. At first, things were not so bad. I met a wonderful German soldier about my age, and I had a child with him. She's three, and I love her to death. The soldier was transferred to the Eastern front, and I never heard from him again."

"I'm so sorry," I said.

"My parents left me some money, and I have this job, so I get along okay."

I thought for a moment. "What was that about a haircut?"

"When the Germans were forced out of France, some of the local citizens were upset that several local French girls fraternized with the enemy. They showed their concern by shaving our heads and making us unattractive. These two jerks think it's funny and keep threatening to cut my hair again."

Herm turned to me. "Maybe we should have a chat with those two."

"I think you're right," I said, "but let me do the talking as my French is a little better than yours, and they need to understand how we feel."

Brigit joined in the conversation. "Don't cause trouble, please. Those guys are not worth it."

"We're just going over for a little talk," I said.

Frank, Herm and I walked over to the table where the two jerks were seated drinking beer.

I opened the conversation. "I understand you two like to cut girls' hair."

Herm towered over the short heavy guy. "Yeah," he said.

The two boys looked up in surprise. "It's good for some laughs," the skinny kid said.

"Is that right?" I said. " Does Brigit laugh while you do it?"

"No, but we do," the short guy said.

I noticed our waitress giving Brigit three big steak knives and she carried them over to us. "I think you might need these," she said and gave one to each of us.

I handled the knife and got the feel of it. I looked the skinny guy in the eye. "Put your knife on the table."

He hesitated. Herm got real close to the heavy guy and pointed at the table. Frank moved behind the thin guy as if ready for action. The two boys slammed their knives on the table. I saw the bartender give a tray to our waitress and motion to our table. She walked slowly over to the table and picked up the two knives and placed them on her tray. I placed my steak knife on the tray and Frank and Herm followed suit. The waitress smiled and walked away.

I turned back to the punks. "I'm her cousin, and I live in Amiens. If I ever hear that you touched her for any reason, I will come over here with my friends, find you and rip off your fingers."

By now the bartender had reached our table. He had a club in one hand. I had no idea what he had in mind, but he was not short, and he was not skinny. He faced the two punks.

"Get out," he said in a stern voice. "Get out and don't ever come back to this café."

The boys didn't move. He raised the club in the air. Now the punks pushed away from the table and headed for the door. "You are losing two of your best customers," yelled the heavy guy.

"I don't need customers like you! Get out!"

The people in the café started clapping their hands and cheering. He got a standing ovation and nodded his head. "The war is over, dammit. It's over."

We returned to our table, and shortly after the waitress brought over three cold beers. "On the house," she said, " and thanks. Those guys are a real pain. And the bartender said the meal is on the house, also."

That brought a big smile from all of us. Brigit and I talked for a while longer. When we called it a night, we each left a big tip for our thoughtful waitress. I hugged Brigit and wished her good luck.

CHAPTER 18
THE SUMMER OF 1946: LIZ

The next morning, Herm called his commanding officer to see if he could have more time on his vacation. The answer was "no." We made our plans under the shade of a canopy at a nearby café over breakfast. It was an absolutely beautiful morning, and life was good. From my point of view, I had said my good-byes to Brigit. Frank had another chapter for his book called "The Bartender Takes Charge." Herm seemed ready to get back to his army buddies. It was time to move on.

Frank spoke up at this point. "If it's okay with Herm, he could drop us off in Calais, which isn't far from here. Mitch and I could arrange a boat trip across the Channel to merry old England. And Herm could set a world's speed record between Calais and Bad Aibling."

"Works for me!" I said.

"Right on!" Said Herm.

■ ■ ■

Our ferry boat ride across the channel was uneventful. The train ride to Victoria Station in London and on to Rye was likewise. It felt good to walk the cobbled-stone streets of the old medieval town again. We decided to stay at the Mermaid Inn in the historical center of the village. Frank seemed excited to be in England. He looked good and healthy with a charming smile adding to his demeanor. The trip had been good for him. We took tea at the Flushing Inn, and I sounded him out on several matters.

"Frank, I think you know that Liz was the most serious of my girlfriends. We were planning to be married and live happily ever after. We had no specific plans because of the war, but we loved each other. I really don't know how I feel at this point, but that was the plan. I need to see her and talk. I don't know what to do," I confided.

"It's probably better to call," Frank advised.

That afternoon I called, and only Anna was home. She seemed delighted to hear my voice. When I called, Liz was still teaching and not at home. I invited the family to dine with Frank and me in town, but she would not hear of it. Anna invited us for dinner around seven. I told her how much I looked forward to seeing everyone and thanked her for the invitation.

Frank and I picked up several bottles of wine, some cheese blocks and crackers to give to Anna upon our arrival. We walked the town some more, rented a car, which was no easy task, and returned to our room to get cleaned up. I was nervous and didn't know what to expect.

We arrived at Liz's house about seven. She answered the door, and I was immediately struck by her beauty. Her long brown hair, flawless skin and big green eyes caught my attention. We hugged, and I introduced her to Frank. They shook hands, and then Anna appeared. She hugged me and welcomed Frank. She slipped her arm into Frank's arm and led him into the house. Liz held back, took my hand and looked into my eyes.

"I wondered if I would ever see you again," she said. "It's been about six years, since you went to London and disappeared from my life."

"Yes, I know. The war played a nasty trick on me."

"On us," she added sadly. "Before we go in to meet the rest, you need to know that I am married and have two children. I hate to be so blunt, but I didn't want you to walk in there not knowing."

She led me through the house and into the backyard. John, Liz's father, and I greeted each other warmly, although I was still in a mild stage of shock over Liz's news. I met Edward her husband, Colin, her six-year-old son, and Beth, her-one year-old daughter. Edward was tall and thin with sandy hair. He was well-dressed and seemed to be personable and educated. Colin was a solid kid, who loved soccer. He was constantly kicking the ball around, and I joined in the fun. He had dark hair and a cute laugh. Beth cooed and played with a stuffed animal.

Ed was kind enough to get drinks for Frank and me. We sat around a large table outside on the lawn. The flowers were beautiful and abundant. There were blueberry and strawberry plants, and ample shade. It was a perfect day, except for the situation in which I found myself. I was hurt, because Liz had married and had a family. And yet, if she had been single when I arrived, what would I have done? That was the big question in my mind.

At first, I lost myself in the conversation. I told them of my survival in the Battle of Britain, my teaching career, and the fact that I was still single. Frank filled them in on his life and the book he was writing on postwar Europe. John and Anna spoke of their survival during the war and their plans for the future. Edward talked about his life. Liz told us of life after I left for London on that fateful day. She had waited for me, met Ed, married and had two babies. I got the feeling she was holding back, but I let it pass. We drank wine, ate a wonderful dinner, proposed several toasts and enjoyed each other's company. As it was getting late for the children, John took Colin off for a bath and a bed-time story. Anna took Beth for the same purpose. Frank had Ed cornered and proceeded with the inevitable interview for the book. Liz and I were then left with little to do. She proposed a walk to a nearby park. I gladly accepted.

As we walked, I started the conversation. "I want to thank

you so much for sending me my journal. I assumed you got my address from inside the front cover of my diary. It came at a time when I was clarifying my thoughts. I had pretty much regained my memory of the time I had in Europe. Reading and rereading those pages made me realize that I needed to come back and put my mind at ease with the people I had met here. I especially had to see you. I have thought about you so many times. I wondered how you were. I was deeply in love with you, and I could not leave that hanging in the air unresolved. I wondered if you loved me and were waiting for me."

"The answer is that I loved you. I tried to wait for you. I got the message from Waldo Bayley at the U.S. Embassy about the bomb explosion and how he got you on a ship to America. Later, I tried to reach Bayley, but he left the Foreign Service and enlisted in the U.S. Navy. I simply could not reach you. For two years I waited, but I realized that the war made it an impossible situation. Then I met Edward. He had been wounded in North Africa and was sent home to recuperate. We were married later in the year. He is a good person, a wonderful father, and my parents get along well with him and his parents."

"I am confused. Didn't you say Colin was six?"

"That's right," she replied.

"Did you have a boyfriend between me and Ed?"

"No, I didn't," she said.

"Well," I said. "The numbers don't add up unless…"

"No, Mitchell, they don't."

"Colin is…" I couldn't finish.

"Yes, Colin is your son."

I slumped to a park bench. The weight of her statement hit me hard. Tears came to my eyes. Liz sat beside me and put her arms around me. She cried, and so we wept together.

"When I was playing soccer with him, it felt so natural."

"I almost cried, when I saw you two playing," she admitted.

"Does he know that I'm his father?"

"No, I haven't told him. I thought he was too young to understand. He seems happy and well adjusted, and Ed is a good father."

"But sooner or later he should know," I said.

"I agree," Liz said. "When it's time to tell him, I think the three of us should be there."

"Oh, yes, Ed. How does he feel about this?"

Liz paused. "He has been dreading this day, but he knows we have to deal with it sooner or later."

I dried my eyes. "What are your feelings, Liz?"

Liz stood before me. "I'm in turmoil. I messed up royally. I love both of you but in different ways. He is solid, a good provider, a good family man. Mitch, you are probably all of that too, but I remember you as dashing, fun and my first love. I don't know what I want. You probably don't want to live here, and England is my home. My parents are here, and my children belong here."

"I know, I know," I said. "I don't know how I feel either, except we need to do what's right for Colin."

"Let's walk," she said.

The park was quiet. We followed the walkway down the tree-lined path. The moon was bright. We strolled, deep in our own thoughts.

"May I spend tomorrow afternoon with Colin?" I asked.

"Yes, of course. Anna will be with him and Beth. Just tell her when to expect you."

"Thanks. It seems to me that I should leave in the next few days. My being here is awkward, and I need time to think. I never saw this coming."

"It's all happening so fast," she said.

We retraced our steps to the house. The kids were in bed and the other four were playing a game of bridge.

"It looks like I managed to miss out on helping with the dishes," I said to ease the awkwardness of our arrival.

"Ed and I took care of that, old sport," Frank said.

I said my good-byes.

■ ■ ■

That night Frank and I returned to the bar at the Mermaid Inn and settled in for a long night of thinking out loud. We drank beer, and he listened to me telling my story. He was patient and understanding. After exploring the possibilities for dealing with my situation, I realized I should return to America. Through letters and pictures, I could get to know my son, until he was old enough to understand the situation. Perhaps, there could be visits to the U.S. when he was older and, of course, I could visit him in England during the summers. At one point, Frank drifted off to sleep. Later, we trudged up to our room on the second floor.

The next morning after a sleepless night, I told Frank of my plans to see Colin during the afternoon. I asked him if he would eat dinner with me, Ed and Liz. He was ready to do anything to help me through the day.

That afternoon, Colin and I spent time together. I wanted to get to know him better, and I would also take lots of pictures of him. We first went to the park near his home and kicked a soccer ball around. There was a soccer goal there, and he tried to score. I played defense and stopped some of his kicks, but many got through my defense to count as points. Then I kicked a few which he blocked. We also dribbled the ball and in general, had a lot of fun and laughs. It was the best way I could figure for us to bond.

Next, we headed for the ice cream store. He had been there several times and was able to direct me to it. He chose a vanilla ice cream cone, and that was good enough for me, also. We drank a lot of water and relaxed and cooled down. I asked him about his school and his friends. He seemed excited to tell me about his friends and what he learned in school.

"Do you like playing with your little sister?" I asked.

"She's fun to play with, but she sleeps too much."

"Do you play with your mom?" I asked.

"Yes, I do, but we mostly go shopping for food."

"How about your dad? Do you play with him?"

"He likes to play ball, and I help him in the yard." He paused to eat more ice cream. "We pick blueberries and strawberries, and he reads stories to me."

I couldn't help but think of all that I was missing. It made me feel sad, but at the same time, I enjoyed being with my son. I studied him to see what traits he might have picked up from me and those from Liz. He seemed to have my body build, and his facial structure was generally characteristic of mine. He sure had Liz's eyes and her sparkling personality.

After we finished our ice cream, we agreed to go to the small zoo just outside of town. Liz had told me about it but warned not to expect much. Her directions were good, and we found it with no trouble. We saw some snakes, rabbits and then Colin's favorite, the monkeys. We watched them swing around and then stop and look at us from the cage. There was a mirror next to the cage.

"Do you want to see another monkey?" I asked Colin as I held him up to the mirror.

"You look into the mirror," he said and laughed loudly.

Evidently, he already knew that joke. He was a quick kid.

Later, we returned to Colin's house and we went inside. Liz greeted us and offered some lemonade. I sat in the living room with Colin and Beth playing quietly on the floor.

"I think Colin's a little tired," I said. "We had a busy but enjoyable afternoon. He's fun to be with."

Queenie the cat entered the room and climbed into my lap. I took a sip of the drink and rubbed behind the cat's ears.

The children seemed preoccupied with their toys.

I looked at Liz and smiled. "There's so much I want to say and to share with you, but now it seems awkward and out of place. I guess I thought it would be like it was before I left for London. How unrealistic it was for me to think nothing would have changed."

I shook my head in frustration. It seemed to me that Liz's

eyes were a little misty.

"I feel the same way, Mitch. We had so much, and it was snatched away from us. And now here we are," she said helplessly.

The kids were deeply engrossed in their toys and seemed oblivious to our conversation. Liz wiped her eyes. "What can we do?"

"I plan to leave tomorrow and head back to the States," I paused. "It wouldn't be good for me to stay much longer." Now I wiped my eyes. "I would like to take you and Ed out to dinner tonight, so that we can make some final arrangements. Could we meet at that restaurant on the same block as the Merrymaid Inn?"

"About seven o'clock would be good," she answered.

"Great." I stood and thanked Colin for spending the day with me.

"Sure," he said.

We shook hands and then I bent down and kissed the top of my son's head. Beth wanted to shake, too, so everyone shook hands. I went out the front door and they waved good-bye.

That night Frank and I arrived at the restaurant at seven, just as Ed and Liz walked in. Liz was sparkling in a navy blue sweater, pearl necklace and gray skirt. Ed had on a black suit, red and gray stripped tie and light blue, oxford shirt. Frank and I wore more casual clothing. I had arranged for a round table for four in a corner by a window. A number of people were at the bar, and a few others were seated ordering food. It was rather early to eat according to British practice, but we chose our fare and picked out a Merlot to drink before dinner.

I took the lead in the conversation. We talked about the war and its effects on Rye. I asked about Liz's teaching career and her part-time job in tourism. I was not shocked to learn that travel and sight-seeing were not in demand. The state of education seemed to be business as usual. Then I told my story of graduate school and university teaching with Frank's help. Ed talked of the insurance business and we talked about the kids. Dinner arrived and we had an enjoyable meal. Frank excused himself at this point and headed for the bar for an after dinner drink. I took this opportunity to bring the conversation back to my relationship with Liz's family.

"Frank and I will be leaving Rye tomorrow," I said. "Frank has been making travel arrangements. It seems we might have accommodations on a ship leaving Dover for the U.S. in several days. This is a good time to talk about my future relationship with Colin. It is painful to think of leaving him so soon, but I can't stay here in England. I do want to be a part of his life."

Liz and Ed nodded. "We want you to be, also," Liz added.

"When you two decide that he is old enough to understand, I would like to be here, when he is told that I am his father. I will come to England when you tell me the time."

"I agree," said Liz, "the three of us should tell him."

"Good. Also, I'd like to send monthly checks that may be used for his upkeep or put aside for his education."

"I hadn't thought about money, since we are able to take care of his needs," Liz said. "But since you feel it's the right thing to do, we will set up an account for him to be used when it is needed."

"Great." There is one more thing. I would appreciate it if you would send pictures of Colin and keep me posted on his school activities and his life in general."

"No problem," said Ed.

"I want to build some kind of relationship with Colin, and maybe when he is older he could visit me in America. I would like that."

Liz smiled. "I'm sure he will want a relationship with you once he realizes who you are."

"This is so hard," I said. "I wish there were simple answers."

"We can make this work," said Liz. "We all want it to be successful and it will."

I looked at the two of them. "Ed, I'm confident you're a good father and will do what's best for Colin. And Liz, you must be the best mom in the world. This will work!"

■ ■ ■

Frank returned from the bar. "I was talking with a couple of blokes at the bar who were in the war, and I got their stories. They seemed like really nice guys, and they sure enjoy life."

"Right," I said. "But you really were just trying to avoid paying the bill. I know you."

"Did it work?" He asked with a chuckle.

Ed stood and said it was time for them to leave. We all stood and hugged and kissed cheeks and shook hands.

Liz and Ed smiled and walked out of the restaurant into the rain.

It was hard to watch them leave. I felt a sense of finality as the door closed.

■ ■ ■

The next day Frank and I had a leisurely breakfast and packed up the car. We drove up the coast through New Romney, Dymchurch, Hythe and Folkestone to Dover. When we arrived, Frank checked on our travel arrangements. We booked our reservations, and prepared for our departure.

That evening we ate at a place on the beach with a spectacular view of the White Cliffs of Dover. We arrived early enough that the sun shone on the Cliffs. Gradually, the sun moved farther west, and we saw a colorful early sunset. I understood why this scene was so meaningful and symbolic to the English. I was moved, too.

The café was not crowded at this time of the day. We had several drinks, and talked about our trip. We reminisced about our time in Germany with Gretchen, her family and the despair they lived with day after day. Surely, Germany would rise up again and take its place among strong and prosperous nations, but it would take time, and they would have to accomplish this without the greatest ant collection in the world. We laughed and drank our tea.

"And what about France?" I asked. "Do you think that our university students will believe we sang with Gypsies and almost got into a knife fight with French punks? I hope they never find out." I continued, "Also, don't forget sad Brigit and her daughter living without her German lover, who probably froze to death near Stalingrad in the frigid Russian winter of 1942-43."

Frank said, "then there is Herm, probably still driving

through France and Germany trying to find Bad Aibling," We both laughed.

"Finally, there is England with its rain, flowers and wonderful people," I said.

The waiter cleared our dinner dishes and brought us more hot tea.

"We need to leave this wonderful country," I declared, "before we turn into typical Englishmen ourselves."

"Tea is good for you," Frank said. I sipped my beverage in silence.

"Tell me," Frank asked, "what would you have done if Liz was home alone with no husband and no Beth, living with her folks? How would you have dealt with her under those circumstances?"

"We would have to go slow and get to know each other all over again. It's been six years, so we would have needed time. Maybe she'd visit me in the U.S., meet my parents and see how I live. If we became serious again, we'd have to decide where to live. We might have a problem, since I want to live in North Carolina, where my job is. We never talked about this, but maybe she feels strongly about living in Rye. It could be a problem, but if we decided we loved each other, I would hope she would move to America, and we could visit England during the summer."

Frank paused for a bit and then offered another question. "Suppose Liz was married to Ed with no children to cloud the issue? What then?"

"Well again, from my point-of-view, if I found that I loved her and wanted to marry her, I would fight for her. I would try to win her over but only if I was sure I wanted to get married. I wouldn't have much time to make that decision, so I would have to be damn sure. And if she had Beth, I think I would leave quietly and return to the U.S. and feel sorry for myself. But I would have no continuing relationship with her."

Frank persisted. "And so with Colin in the picture as Liz's only child, but married to Ed, you would fight for Liz?"

"Only if I was dead certain I wanted to marry her."

Frank pushed on. "So with our full cast of characters consisting of Liz, Ed, Colin and Beth you've reached a sort of compromise position?"

"Yes, with Colin being the key to the decision. With my son in the picture, I need to be part of the equation. Without him, the happiness of Liz, Beth and to a certain extent Ed, become the main consideration. Does that make sense to you, Frank?"

"Yes, it does," Frank said with a sigh.

I stood and walked around briefly and then returned to my seat. "I'm not trying to be gallant or whatever you would call it. I'm just trying to be realistic. The children are the first consideration."

Frank was thoughtful. "I'm just a self-centered romantic, Mitch, but I would be inclined to dash in like a bull in a China Shop, grab the woman and conclude that love conquers all."

"That approach appealed to me, also," I said. "But I'm too practical to go that route. There are too many unknowns. Does she still love me, do I still love her, what about Beth and her father; where would we live?" These questions kept coming back to me, and I had very few answers.

Frank and I left the café and walked to the dock. We boarded our ship and checked our luggage. We stood on the open deck and leaned against the ship's rail. The sun had set and all that was left of the White Cliffs of Dover was a dark silhouette. There was mist in the air and the image of the cliffs was hazy. The ship eased away from the dock.

"Do you think you will have second thoughts when you get back home?" Frank asked.

"I hope not," I replied. "I could spend the rest of my life thinking about this decision, or maybe now I can get on with my life."

For a few minutes, we admired the afterglow of the sunset as it hung brightly over the White Cliffs of Dover.

"You know, Frank, I've been through a hell of a lot in the last seven or eight years. I've seen the brutality of some Germans and the warmth of others. I've lived a great adventure escaping from Germany, cycling across France and escaping again to Great Britain. I've experienced passion and pain. I experienced two great battles at Dunkirk and the Battle of Britain. I was wounded twice; I captured an enemy pilot; and I never carried or fired a weapon. I also realized the love and support of my parents and the growth of a great friendship with you. I experienced the loss of the chance to be with two people I will miss terribly: Liz and my son. I am certainly a casualty of the war, Frank."

"Yes, you are," Frank nodded, "just like all the other millions of people who suffered their own losses."

"What's more, I could spend the rest of my life regretting and mourning my losses I said. "However, I intend to accept what's happened and find a new purpose for my life, a purpose that will give my English son reason to be proud of his American father."